IRA
SHADES OF SIN

# IRA

COLETTE RHODES

IRA IS A MONSTER ROMANCE BETWEEN A
HUMAN AND HER NOT-QUITE-HUMAN PARTNER,
SUITABLE FOR READERS OVER 18.

CW: SEXUAL CONTENT; ILLUSIONS TO
GROOMING (OFF-PAGE, PRIOR TO EVENTS OF
THE BOOK)

"NEVER GO TO BED MAD.
STAY UP AND FIGHT."

- PHYLLIS DILLER

# MEERA

## PROLOGUE

**D**o you believe me?"

As we stood toe-to-toe in the shabby living room—surrounded by trash bags filled with whatever things my mother had grabbed from my room—an icy feeling made its way from the crown of my head down to the base of my spine.

Because she *did*, in fact, believe me. She was just kicking me out anyway.

"You brought shame to us, Meera. I don't know what you were thinking. I thought you were smart? I thought you were responsible? You've probably ruined your sister's life too, you know. If your father could see you now..." She trailed off, clicking her tongue as she shook her head.

The words were a gut punch, but I lifted my chin, training my gaze stubbornly on the water stain on the ceiling, and refusing to let her see that she'd hit her mark.

I was my mother's daughter, after all. I could wear an armor made of ice and spite just as well as she could.

To think I'd ever felt sorry for her. I knew that she was the way she was because she had to be, because we were on the bottom rung of Hunter society and dependent on the goodwill of our betters to survive. But I still thought that I'd meant more to her than all of that. That when it came down to it, she'd at least have compassion for *me*.

Apparently not.

"Fine. You want me to go? I'll go." My sister made a sound of distress from the doorway where she'd been hovering, despite having been told to go to our room at least four times, but I hardened my heart to it as best I could. How many times had I wished to *not* be responsible for Latika? To not have to get her up and dressed and ready for school each morning, and help her with her homework and make her dinner and get her to bed each night while Mom was working?

It appeared I'd gotten my wish.

With one last look at my mother, I closed the distance between Latika and me. I'd been in the room when she was born. I'd seen her very first moments on this earth. Last summer, she'd had to tip her head back to look at me, but now we were almost eye level.

*You'd been looking after her and yourself for six years when you were this age*, I told myself firmly. *She'll be fine. She doesn't need to be babied by her big sister.*

That it might be the last time I ever saw Latika was too painful to acknowledge. I memorized her features as best I could—so similar to my own, and yet far more like the father she couldn't remember.

Would he have kicked me out if he'd still been alive? A lump formed in my throat, and I swallowed past it painfully. I wouldn't have gotten myself into this mess if he'd been alive. I'd have had someone in my corner.

That would have been nice.

"I love you, Latika," I said firmly, forcing myself to say the words that came so unnaturally to me. To everyone in this household. "I will always love you. Focus on your studies. Be kind. Be smart. And stay away from Randal Jackman."

## EIGHT YEARS LATER

"Meera Jaiswal?"

I clutched the cloth I'd been using to wipe down the bar top a little tighter, scanning over the woman who was speaking to see if I recognized her. Between my doula work and my casual bar work, I *did* meet a lot of people. None of them ever addressed me by my full name though. Most of them didn't remember me at all.

"Can I help you?" I asked, glancing around to see where the other staff were. *They're close. You're not alone. Everything is okay.* Not that I was super close with them or anything, and I doubted they'd come running to my aid, but at least there were witnesses if I got abducted.

"My name is Adela Cooke, I'm a Criminal Investigation Special Agent with the IRS. You're not in trouble, Meera. I was just wondering if we could talk for a moment."

A cold sweat broke out on the back of my neck. A Special Agent? The IRS? That was a human organization. Since I'd been kicked out of the Hunters, I'd lived as normally as I could as a member of the human realm, and I certainly didn't do anything that should bring me to the attention of the authorities.

If there was one thing I was going to do right for the rest of my life, it was pay my taxes.

I'd definitely done stupid and possibly illegal things during my time with the Hunters, confident in the belief that I was doing it for the greater good, but they should have no way of knowing about that.

"You haven't done anything wrong. I just want to talk," Adela repeated placatingly, watching me like I was about to bolt. I was strongly considering it.

"No thank you," I mumbled, not knowing what else to say. Why was I so easily overwhelmed? It was so *frustrating*.

After a long moment, Adela Cooke set a business card down on the bar top and took a step back. "I've been doing this long enough to know that we're not going to get anywhere if I push, so I'll just leave this with you for now. I don't need to tell you what this is about—you already know. And I understand that talking about it isn't a small ask."

It *had* to be what I'd done way back when I was a naive seventeen-year-old. I'd lived like a saint since then. All I wanted was a quiet life. Happiness was too much to ask for, but surely *quiet* wasn't.

The crimes I'd unknowingly committed then did cross over to the human sphere of influence, but it had never occurred to me that anyone would investigate them...

"It sounds like you've got it all figured out. What do you need me for?"

"Evidence. A witness. Something concrete, Meera. What we've got isn't enough. The missing piece is you."

My heart was pounding in my ears. "How did you even find out about me?"

"As is always the case, you weren't the only one, and of course, there was a paper trail. There always is. That's how I know about you, and how I know that what *you* know is valuable. You were there at the beginning."

Ah. So there had been other impressionable young Hunters who'd followed in my wake. Weird that it made me feel less special to know I hadn't been the only one, even though I actively despised him.

Perhaps my self-esteem hadn't recovered as much as I'd thought.

"I don't have anything of value to tell you. It's been years."

That wasn't entirely true. I had literal receipts, though I wasn't sure what my chances were of actually accessing them. There was a lot that I remembered that I could point them to if I was brave enough to open my mouth. If I could just shake off the shame that clung to my skin like oil no matter how hard I scrubbed at it...

I shivered despite the sticky heat inside the bar. No. I couldn't do it. I'd brought this on myself, I'd probably send *myself* to prison if I spoke up. And I couldn't help but think of my mom and sister—despite the fact that it had been eight years since I'd seen them. Hadn't I caused them enough embarrassment? It had probably taken them this long for their reputations to even somewhat recover. To rehash all of that now would be selfish of me.

*Then again, they're still in Denver, and you're in Albuquerque,* a quiet voice in the back of my head said. The voice that had always struggled with the unfairness of it all. Who'd wanted vengeance, even knowing it would never be possible.

"Just take the card," Adela said firmly. "You don't have to do anything with it, but don't throw it away. Maybe one day, you'll be ready."

She was clearly frustrated, and I understood why. I'd be frustrated with me too.

But even with eight years of pretending to be human under my belt, there was still a not-insignificant part of me that felt *some* kind of loyalty to the Hunters. Or at the very least, a strong mistrust of humans instilled in me *by* the Hunters.

Even though the Hunters had betrayed me, just the idea of speaking to

Adela felt like a betrayal to them.

"I'll hold onto it," I rasped, picking up the card and sliding it into my back pocket, fully intending to put it in my box of important documents that sat on the top shelf of my closet and never look at it again. *You've caused enough trouble. Your father would already be ashamed of you. Keep your head down, and don't bother anyone.*

It was a lonely strategy but also a successful one. Or at least it had been up until now, when Adela Cooke had walked through the doors of this sticky, dreary bar and ruined the illusion of solitude I'd carefully constructed for myself. The illusion of being a regular overworked, underpaid, drowning-in-debt, twenty-five-year-old woman. A *human* woman.

Boring. Forgettable. Invisible.

Now, the panic that I was always barely keeping at bay was back in full force, and I had no idea what to do with it. Last time this had happened, I'd channeled it all into running away and building a whole new life for myself.

Suddenly, that didn't seem like the worst idea.

Maybe running away would be the answer to all of my questions.

# VERNER

## CHAPTER 1

**A FEW WEEKS LATER**

I'm going to get myself one, you know."

I glanced at Andrus, positioned on the other side of the archway to where I was standing, at the entry to the royal wing of the palace. We were usually stationed here together, and I assumed it was penance for some terrible thing I'd done in another lifetime because I couldn't imagine much worse company.

"One what?" I asked, suspecting I already knew the answer.

"A Hunter, of course." He scoffed as though it was ludicrous that I'd even had to ask. "There's a few here now. I'm going to get one for myself."

"*Ex*-Hunter," I corrected, since that was the term they seemed to be going by nowadays. Privately, I hoped they'd come up with something that distanced them a little more from their Hunter counterparts in the human realm. "You'll have to clarify what you mean by *get one*. They aren't objects to be collected."

Andrus's shadows flickered in irritation. "Obviously. I will court one. There are plenty to choose from. I'll take my pick."

Hardly. The queen's sister, Astrid, had brought a few through to the shadow realm with her, but some had already left, unable to transition comfortably to life here.

Only four single ex-Hunters remained: Astrid, Tallulah, Verity, and Meera. And of those four, only three of them were considered mate material. They had the pick of the shadow realm available to them—I imagined at least one of them would choose the king's brother, Prince Damen. He was widely considered the most desirable, eligible male in the realm now that King Allerick was taken. Perhaps the chatty one—Verity? They both had cheerful dispositions.

Captain Soren was also a strong prospect. Perhaps Tallulah—confident and social, but not as excitable as Verity—would choose him as a mate.

That only left Meera, with the entire realm at her disposal and seemingly no interest in anyone if her scent was anything to go by. I glanced at Andrus warily. She would have a low opinion of herself indeed if she chose him over every other option in the realm. Andrus was only capable of loving himself, and he did so most assiduously.

"Did you have someone in mind as the object of your affections?" I asked dryly.

"Not Astrid," he replied immediately, recoiling in disgust. "I can't imagine anyone would want her."

"I can't imagine she wants any of us," I pointed out. Astrid had put herself at great risk with her own kind to be here, but she'd done it for her sister. That she had to live among the Shades now was probably the worst part of all of this for her.

I could appreciate that, while still finding her personally repellant. As my parents always pointed out, nothing could undo what was done.

"True. That leaves Verity, Meera, and Tallulah," Andrus mused. "I have no interest in Meera. I've never seen anyone so glum in all my life, of any species."

"It must have been a tremendous adjustment for her to come here. It's unsurprising that she is experiencing some sadness over leaving her previous life behind."

From the moment they'd arrived, Meera had been the former Hunter who I'd paid the most attention to. Perhaps because I recognized something of myself in her. Upon joining the Guard, we'd spent weeks in training and had no contact with the outside world. Even though I'd desperately *wanted* to join the Guard and leave my life in Sunlis behind, actually doing it had been somewhat bittersweet.

Or perhaps I'd misread the situation entirely, and I was seeing what I wanted to see, based on my own experiences.

Andrus snorted. "You are always so quick to jump to someone's defense, Verner. What for? Have you even spoken to this female before? How do you know she's worthy of your compassion?"

"It wouldn't be compassion if it had to be earned."

Andrus fell silent for a long moment, but I suspected it was because he hadn't understood my words rather than because he was mulling them over.

"Did I see your parents at breakfast this morning?" he asked eventually because Andrus wasn't good at silence.

"You did. They arrived last night to stay for a week. Remind the court of their presence, and so forth."

Andrus made a disgruntled sound of agreement, and on that front, we could relate I supposed. His mother often did the same, taking over the family apartments that we usually had to ourselves.

The difference was that Andrus relished the day when the title would become his, and he was free to lord his presence over everyone. I shared no such desire. I didn't want a life of endlessly spinning in circles, accomplishing nothing of value while constantly being praised for my supposed achievements. I wanted to *genuinely* make a difference.

The two of us drew up, standing at full attention at the sound of the royal couple's approach. Once upon a time, these halls had been mostly silent—save for occasional smatterings of conversation between the king and the captain or Prince Damen's laugh. Queen Ophelia had brought this entire wing of the palace to life with her presence.

"…I think they're adapting well. Or as well as can be," the queen said to her husband, walking with her arm tucked into his. "And hopefully, the lifestyle advantages here—or at least the lack of financial pressure—will help make up for the lack of conveniences."

"Some seem to like it here more than others," King Allerick said gruffly.

His wife grimaced, nodding in agreement. Were they worried that more would leave? That was a bleak thought. Travel to the human realm to feed was currently forbidden, which meant we were reliant on the energy stores here to feed. To *survive*. Those stores were currently being fuelled by ex-Hunter lust, and it was a tall ask for the queen to keep the entire realm fed on her own, though her and the king seemed to be doing their valiant best, given how much time they spent in their room.

*I should make more of an effort*, I thought suddenly. I'd mostly kept to myself, observing out of curiosity from a distance. After all, there were many far more desirable males than me for the ex-Hunters to choose from. I would only be making a nuisance of myself by adding to the crowd of Shades that constantly hovered around them.

Perhaps that approach was wrong, though. They would need *friends* if they were going to grow accustomed to life here, and there was no reason why I couldn't be a friend to them and help them with that, if they were open to it.

Andrus and I silently greeted the royal couple as they passed us, and my resolve grew steadier in my mind. I would reach out. I would make more of an effort. I would show the ex-Hunters who lived here that not every Shade was interested in them purely for the purpose of generating power for the stores. We may have needed it to survive, but we could hardly expect them to feel any desire if they weren't comfortable first.

The king and queen were envisioning a whole different kind of future for the realm, and I intended to be part of it.

After years of working at the palace as a guard, it always felt strange to sit at one of the long tables in the dining hall and shred meat with the courtiers who lived at the palace as though I was one of them, even if I technically was. I vastly preferred to simply visit the palace kitchens and help myself to whatever food was left over—Calix seemed to tolerate my company better than he tolerated most.

It was fortunate that my parents, for the most part, preferred to stay at Sunlis, limiting how often I had to endure this.

"Lots of change," Father murmured, surveying the dining hall with a critical eye, his plate of food sitting untouched in front of him. The seasoning was never to his liking here. Perhaps, if I had a death wish one day, I'd pass that on to Calix.

"Lots of change," Mother agreed stiffly. Her gaze was fixed on a section of one table near the front of the hall, where three ex-Hunters sat, surrounded by an adoring crowd of male Shades, all pressing in closer, shamelessly trying to get their attention. Why did they never give them more space? No one would want to be boxed in that way—human or Shade.

Between the three new arrivals, the vibrant ex-Hunter queen sitting on the dais and her brooding sister skulking around one of the side doors, I supposed the dining hall did look a little different from the last time my parents had visited.

"It's nice, no?" I said mildly, impaling a piece of meat from the central platter on my knife and dropping it onto my plate. "The dining hall feels livelier than it has in years. Perhaps in all the time I've been here."

"That will fade," Father countered. "The novelty of them will wear off. And then what happens? Adjustments must be made. Unknowns must be accounted for. It will not be a good thing in the long run, Verner. Mark my words."

Mother hummed in agreement, and I held back my sigh of irritation. As far as parents went—especially considering the social class we belonged to—I supposed I couldn't complain. Levana had it much worse, I'd recognized that even when we were children growing up nearby to each other. But their unwillingness to see even the faintest hint of change as a possibility for something better was exhausting. Whatever direction the winds blew, my parents kept their gaze trained firmly backward.

"Hunters bring nothing but death and destruction wherever they go," Father continued. "I'm sure I don't need to remind you of that."

"Yes, well. Times have changed," I replied uncomfortably. In all honesty, there was nothing I could say in response to that. I wasn't about to argue in the Hunters' favor—there was no defending what they'd done to my kind for generations. To my family. It was indefensible.

I suspected that *we* had plenty to answer for from generations ago, when the Hunters were the Hunted, and the Shades were at their most powerful. The balance had shifted in their favor for centuries, and now we were looking to find some kind of equilibrium.

I hoped in time that my parents would embrace the king's vision, but my expectations were low. Like many Shades, their hatred ran deep.

"You've served the Guard faithfully, Verner," Mother murmured, still staring unabashedly at the table of ex-Hunters and their admirers. "Perhaps it's time to come home? I'm sure the captain wouldn't begrudge it, considering how long and loyally you've served. You were never meant to serve at all—you're a firstborn. Your place is at home."

*Firstborn.* I wanted to contradict that, but now wasn't the time. Not while we were surrounded by courtiers. That Father didn't say anything made me think this conversation had been planned out in advance of dinner.

"Certainly, I plan on coming home at some point," I replied, deflecting. It wasn't a particularly appealing idea, but I couldn't put it off forever. I was the heir, and Sunlis was an archaic estate, governed by archaic rules.

As the only *living* child to the current earl, my future position was secure, even if my father wished to replace me. Unlike more progressive houses, the succession rules at Sunlis were clear and inflexible. The only way out of it was if I chose to give it up.

"I see what you're doing, Verner," Mother said lightly. "You are avoiding giving me a proper response. And I do not approve of it."

"Neither of us approve," Father put in.

I'd forgotten how it was like hearing an echo when the two of them were together. Though I supposed there was something charming about how united they were. I liked to think I would be as devoted to my partner someday, should I be fortunate enough to find one who merely wanted me for myself, and not the wealth I was set to inherit.

"Osric is doing well," Mother said, unprompted.

"Is he?" I had very little interest in hearing about the cousin who'd made himself at home in what had once been my wing of the palace, but I knew my parents would have plenty to say on the matter. While my parents had never explicitly said so, they had undoubtedly allowed it in the hope that it would put pressure on me to come back and stake a claim over my territory, or some other such nonsense.

"He is. He's taken over the renovation of the east wing of the estate—you remember it was always leaking. Very good of him to take on a project of that magnitude, and purely out of kindness, as he stands to gain nothing from it," Father added.

"Perhaps he'll get lucky and I'll give up my position. Then he'll gain the whole estate out of it," I pointed out.

Mother gasped. "Don't say such things, Verner. The very idea of him taking your position has never even come up. Only you would think it—and why is that? Because you never plan on coming home? Because you'd throw everything away—the future the gods have blessed you with—to bow and scrape and take orders? Is that your plan?"

"No, Mother," I sighed, regretting saying anything.

I *didn't* want to spend my days fretting about leaking roofs and the astronomical cost of keeping such an enormous household running. I didn't want to merely pop into court for the purpose of reminding everyone of my illustrious existence. I didn't want the social isolation that came with an elevated position.

Frankly, I couldn't imagine why *anyone* would want those things. But I would be letting my entire family down if I gave up my position, and doing untold damage to my reputation in the process. What would my future in the

Guard even look like if I disinherited myself? The captain likely wouldn't care, but the other guards would.

And if I wasn't an earl, and I wasn't welcome in the Guard... then what? I had no other skills to offer.

"Your vagueness is very tiresome to me, Verner. Why can you not simply do what is expected of you? We ask so very little..." Father muttered, though the rest of what he said floated in one ear and out the other as my gaze drifted back to the trio of ex-Hunters, only occasionally visible through the sea of Shades crowding around them. I presumed they were content enough with it, or their scent would be broadcasting to their admirers that the attention was unwelcome.

But then again, would the others respect that as promptly as they should? Maybe I should go over and check their general scents for myself—

"Verner," Captain Soren said, pausing at our table. "Godwin, Nezetta." He tipped his head respectfully to my parents, and they returned the gesture somewhat stiffly. They would always respect someone in his position, but they had a general mistrust for anyone who resided at court.

"How are you, Captain?" Mother asked.

There went my plan to check on the ex-Hunters and make sure they were comfortable and not in need of assistance. Why had the captain not assigned a guard purely for their benefit at dinner? His mistrust of Astrid—who was a genuine threat—may have blinded him to the others, who seemed less than harmless.

"Well, thank you. Are you enjoying your time at court?"

My parents seemed even more uncomfortable than usual, and I realized they were probably thinking about the scandal with the captain's sister and judging him accordingly. It soothed my ire with him somewhat. The captain should in no way be held responsible for his sister's choices.

"Much has changed from our last visit," Father said disapprovingly.

"How are the ex-Hunters doing tonight?" I asked, hoping both to alleviate my concern and detract from my father's embarrassing response.

Captain Soren blinked at me. "Fine, I suppose."

"It's very crowded over there," I pointed out.

He glanced behind him dismissively. "I just walked past their table, and there were no indications of distress. The one sitting in the middle—I forget their names—is extremely content."

"Verity," I replied, nodding once and ignoring my parents' disapproving stares. That did seem to line up with what I'd learned about the newest residents of the realm so far.

After dinner, Mother and Father immediately made for the apartment while I made my excuses and headed outside instead. Usually, I had the family apartment at court to myself, and their presence there was faintly suffocating. It would have been better if I could stay out until I was ready to sleep, especially if they were going to start suggesting I move home with a heavier hand than they usually did.

The night air was crisp and cool, and I took a moment standing at the top of the steps to appreciate it. Sunlis was sticky and hot year-round, and I'd always found it somewhat unbearable. It was one of the many reasons why I was delaying my return to my family seat. In nearly every way, my life here was an improvement on what it had been in the past.

Unfortunately, I didn't have the luxury of staying.

The breeze picked up, and a faint hint of something unpleasant in the air had me moving down the stairs and along the wide path that separated the circular palace from the extensive front garden.

My shadows flared in irritation as I found a clearly uncomfortable Meera on the path, giving a tight-lipped smile to Wymond. He had kept a respectful distance between them, but he'd still positioned himself between her and the direction of Elverston House in a way that I found unacceptable.

"Wymond," I said loudly, closing the gap between us and clapping him hard enough on the shoulder that he stumbled slightly. "I imagine our newest residents of the realm are tired after so much conversation at dinner each night, and eager to return to Elverston House for some rest."

Wymond straightened, clearly annoyed. "She did not say."

I gave Meera what I hoped was an apologetic smile that we were speaking about her as though she wasn't there. "Were you intending to head back to Elverston House now, Meera?"

She blinked at me in surprise. Had she not expected me to know her name? I was sure most of the realm knew it by now. I almost said as much, but held the words back at the last moment. Meera seemed skittish enough as it was—I doubted reminding her of how famous she was would help at this moment.

"I was, yes." Wymond opened his mouth to speak, but Meera was faster. "Perhaps you'd walk me back?" she asked, looking up at me.

My shadows flickered slightly, pleased that she'd singled me out as a safe choice, and I hoped she didn't recognize what the slight movement meant. It was even more flattering coming from Meera, of all the ex-Hunters. She seemed as though she'd be reticent to consider *anyone* a safe choice.

"Of course. Have a pleasant evening, Wymond," I added dismissively. I knew him well enough, and while *I* assumed he was a harmless nuisance at most, I reminded myself that it wasn't my assessment to make. I'd ended friendships with males in the past who had been perfectly adequate friends to me but had strange attitudes to their romantic relationships that I couldn't abide.

*Another thing to be on heightened awareness of around the ex-Hunters,*

I thought, noting how small and delicate Meera was. No claws, no fangs, no horns... How were they meant to protect themselves? Was the human realm really so safe for them that they had no need for natural weapons?

"Thank you," Meera said quietly as we made our way down the path, leaving Wymond behind us.

"There's no need to thank me—I can't imagine how tiresome it must be to constantly have Shades vying for your attention. Would you like me to walk you the whole way or just until we're out of sight of Wymond?"

Her lips twitched slightly, and I noticed for the first time how soft and full her mouth was. Of course, it hadn't escaped my notice that Meera was beautiful—her skin glowed somehow, her long hair looked impossibly soft, and her dark eyes drew everyone in, though she rarely gave anyone a chance to truly look into them.

To live at the palace was to be well acquainted with the scent of a flirtatious ex-Hunter at this point, and Meera had never carried that scent.

Not for anyone.

For my own sanity, I would do my best *not* to notice how beautiful she was. But I could wonder what her laugh sounded like and how her joy smelled, couldn't I?

Those were friendly thoughts.

"Would you mind walking me the whole way? You don't have to," Meera added hurriedly, as though I was even remotely capable of saying no to her—she looked so lost out here on her own. "I usually make the trip with someone else, but they were busy talking to people—I mean, *Shades*—and I didn't want to bother them."

"I would be most happy to accompany you. My parents are visiting. I was just going for a walk anyway to give us both some space," I said wryly.

"Understandable." Another one of those faint lip twitches. "I'm sorry, I don't remember your name...?"

"Ah, that was poorly done of me, wasn't it? We haven't met before. My name is Verner. I'm a member of the Guard here at the palace."

Her cheeks flushed slightly. It was a most intriguing sight, though I quickly looked away, not wanting to make her uncomfortable by staring.

"Sorry. I've met so many Shades since I've been here. I'm struggling to keep them all straight in my head."

"I assure you, you have nothing to apologize for. I saw how crowded your table was at dinner tonight. It must be overwhelming to meet so many new faces at once."

"It is," she replied instantly before looking contrite. "Though I'm not complaining, of course. I'm very grateful to be here."

"You can be grateful to be here and find the attention overwhelming."

"That's probably the most accurate description of how I'm feeling," Meera said, nodding to herself. "Have you met the other Hunters—*ex*-Hunters—yet?"

"Only the queen. My usual post is outside the royal wing of the palace."

"Oh."

There was a wealth of complexity in that single word, but I wasn't sure where to begin with it. Perhaps she thought I should be making more of an effort to get to know the others?

"Are you close with the queen?" I asked, wondering if that was where the wariness in her voice had come from.

Meera blinked up at me in surprise. "I'm not really close with anyone. No, wait. Pretend I didn't say that—that sounded bad. I'm one of the quieter ones in the group," she corrected hastily.

I suspected both things were true, but the first sounded more honest than she'd intended.

"I, too, am generally considered one of the quieter ones in any given situation," I replied, hoping that finding some common ground would put her at ease. "I suspect this has given others the impression that I'm wiser than I am."

Meera *almost* laughed. I couldn't see it, but I felt as though I could sense it in the air. Or perhaps it was the sudden sweet tinge in her scent.

"I'm not sure I have *that* reputation. But they've definitely made some assumptions about me that aren't entirely true," she added, seeming more baffled than annoyed by that fact.

"Did you all know each other in the human realm?"

The scale of their world was difficult to grasp, though I knew it was far larger than the shadow realm.

Meera shook her head. "I knew *of* Astrid and Tallulah. Astrid's reputation preceded her, and Tallulah's family is well-known. It's possible we met at events as kids, but I don't remember that."

The invisible border between Elverston House and the greater palace complex approached, and I wracked my mind for something to say that would make this interaction an even somewhat lingering memory in Meera's mind.

The discomfort in her scent had lessened, but it hadn't been replaced by the sweetness of a joyful ex-Hunter.

It was important to me that Meera leave here feeling more comfortable than she started.

"How are you finding the shadow realm so far?" I asked lamely. "Overwhelming attention aside."

"It's nice." She sounded as apologetic about her answer as I had about the question. "I guess I'm still finding my footing, you know? It's a lot of change."

"It is," I agreed. "I found it a somewhat difficult transition to come from my home to the palace when I joined the Guard. I can't imagine how much more you've had to adapt to moving to an entirely different realm."

"This was really nice, thank you," Meera said, surprising me as we came to a halt. She looked up at me through thick, dark lashes and it made something in my chest feel odd.

"What was?"

"This walk. The conversation. It's nice to talk to someone that, you know, doesn't *want* anything from me." My shadows curled in closer to my body, ashamed that she'd thought so highly of me when I'd absolutely found myself inappropriately admiring her beauty. Of course, I hadn't *expected* anything from her, but *wanting* was a different matter. If she'd asked me... Well, I'd definitely *wanted*.

"I don't suppose..." Meera trailed off, her face flushing again.

"You don't suppose what?" I prompted. Perhaps she would give me an opportunity to redeem myself—if only in my own mind.

"It's probably silly. I just thought... I don't know. Maybe we could do this again sometime? I really do want to get to know more Shades. To build a proper life here. It's just... I guess there are so many expectations, you know? Even meeting female Shades is difficult. I think they avoid us because they're trying not to intrude, but I really would like to make friends. I'm not very good at it."

*Friends.*

"You and I could be friends," I replied instantly, meaning it. Meera was beautiful. I'd be lying to myself if I tried to convince myself that I wasn't attracted to her. But I would put that attraction aside because it seemed like she really *needed* a friend. I could be that for her. I could help her adjust to life here. Hadn't I been considering the idea earlier today while I was on duty? I'd wanted to make more of an effort to get to know the ex-Hunters, to help them feel comfortable here. To *not* be another male pestering them for their attention, but to help them acclimate to a new realm and a new life.

Meera was entrusting me with that, and I was grateful for it.

"And I could introduce you to more Shades when you're ready for that," I added, suspecting that she, in fact, wasn't quite ready for that just yet.

"That would be amazing, thank you. In the human realm... Well, let's just say it was difficult to make friends. To trust people. And it's not like I'm totally over that, but being here and staying with the others... I guess I realized how much I *want* to be happy here."

I wasn't sure who she was trying to convince with those words, but I was determined to help her, regardless, because I wanted her to be happy too.

"Perhaps I could come by here tomorrow at midday?" I suggested tentatively. "I prefer to have lunch outside. We could sit and talk for a while if you like?"

Meera perked up instantly, the faintest hint of something bright and happy in her scent. "Would you? I'm not sure I'm ready to venture out on my own yet."

"Of course. I'll be here. And if you change your mind and don't come out, that's okay too—I'll take the hint, and I won't feel any kind of bitterness about it. I can't imagine the challenges you've faced since moving here."

Meera's expression gave nothing away, but the hint of sadness in her scent couldn't lie. "They're nothing compared to the challenges I faced *before* moving here. Until tomorrow, Verner."

# MEERA

## CHAPTER 2

Knock, knock!" Verity called, breezing into my room before I had a chance to reply. If it were anyone else, I'd have probably been annoyed, but Verity—although she was older than me—reminded me so much of my little sister that it was impossible to be mad at her. If anything, I felt a little sad whenever I saw her, thinking of the young adult Latika must be now. Though I doubted she'd held onto the carefree tendencies she'd had as a kid, the way Verity seemed to have managed to do well into adulthood.

My mother would have quickly seen to that once I was gone.

"I'm having a crisis. I've run out of lotion, and I'm not leaving this house with ashy knees." Verity gestured at her bare legs in the short pink tutu she was wearing like the severity of the issue was self-evident. "I guess I could change, but I'm emotionally attached to this outfit already."

"I've got lotion."

I climbed off the bed, shaking my head slightly in bemusement as I grabbed a bottle of lotion and handed it to her. I'd briefly contemplated putting more effort into choosing my outfits since Tallulah and Verity were both so interested in fashion, but I'd quickly realized I wouldn't know the first place to start anyway.

Jeans never let me down. Jeans required no thought. Jeans didn't care that my knees were ashy.

Besides, I'd never had any money for clothes back in the human realm—I'd just grabbed whatever was cheap and didn't draw any attention to myself. The clothing budget here seemed to be unlimited—we were encouraged to tell Astrid what we wanted and she just magically made it appear. Even with no cost constraints, I wouldn't know what to ask for other than jeans, shorts, t-shirts, and sweaters.

Some faint hints of glitter in Verity's tutu caught the light as she moved, and I eyed it warily. No. I wouldn't have the first clue what to do with something like that.

"Thank all the stars for you," Verity sighed dramatically, immediately setting to work on her legs. "Astrid said she'd pick up some more for me on her next supply run, but she doesn't seem to think it's an emergency. Like... how? Why? I'm obviously going to befriend her still, but we don't understand each other at all."

"We're all very different personalities," I said diplomatically, sitting on the edge of the bed. I'd been up and dressed for hours, waiting for the others so we could head over to the dining hall together for breakfast. Verity usually overslept, so it was a surprise to have her joining us at all.

I was pretty confident Astrid *wouldn't* join us, and I'd end up bringing her back her favorite selection of sodium-heavy snacks—mostly cured meat—so that she'd at least eat *something*.

I didn't know anything about making friends, but I was trying. Astrid required the most cautious approach. Thus far, food offerings seemed to be the safest choice.

"What kind of level is our friendship at?" Verity asked, finishing up one modelesque leg and switching to the other. No wonder half the shadow realm was in love with her already. "Because I had sex with a Shade last night, and I really want to talk about it."

I choked on my saliva, coughing awkwardly.

"Too much?" she asked, wincing. "Sorry. I'm not good at reading the room on these things, you know? Like, why aren't we besties already? What are the steps that need to be taken here? Would it help if we swapped childhood trauma stories?"

Sometimes, I wondered if Verity's social skills were just as stunted as mine, and it just manifested in a different way.

"It's fine," I said hurriedly. "We don't need to, er, do that. I just didn't expect you to bring *that* topic up. We can talk about it."

"Oh, good. Okay. So does that mean we *are* besties? You can answer that later. Did you know Shade dicks have this, like... *balloon* thing at the base?"

Maybe I wasn't ready to talk about this.

"A balloon?" I repeated, my mind immediately going to balloon-animal-style tubes. Maybe that's what she meant? That what they had was more... *grow* than *show*.

Ophelia had offered us all an in-depth anatomy lesson. Astrid had vanished before she'd even suggested it, and I'd opted out, not knowing how well I'd cope with that conversation.

I was regretting it now, as it sounded like there was a lot to learn.

"It seems to be an optional feature. Like they can wedge it in there and supposedly it feels good, but I passed on that, and the knot—that's what it's called, don't overthink it—stayed on the outside. It was still a great experience. Ten out of ten." Verity paused, her palm still covered in lotion, tilting her head to the side. "Maybe nine out of ten because he was super *quiet,* and I like my dudes vocal in bed. Actually, possibly eight. Eight out of ten is still pretty good, though."

"A very respectable score," I agreed faintly.

"Anyway, I feel like I've ripped the bandaid off, and now Shade sex is on the table for me, which is nice." She shrugged one shoulder before resuming the lotion application.

*Shade sex.*

I'd been avoiding thinking about it, in all honesty. Even in the human realm, sex had been a complicated subject.

Complicated, as in I'd only done it once with another person involved, but I wanted it. But I didn't trust anyone enough to let them touch me, and I couldn't build trust without getting to know someone, and I never did that either.

Briefly, a vision of Verner—the Shade I'd met last night after dinner—flashed through my mind, but I quickly shook it away. He was the one Shade who *hadn't* tried to get in my pants, and I'd really enjoyed how easy his company was last night. I wasn't about to ruin what could be my first real Shade friendship with a ham-fisted attempt at seduction.

I grimaced slightly at the thought. What would that even look like?

*Hey Verner. I like the way your horns curve inwards and nearly touch at the top. And your eyes are such a pretty golden color. Your shoulders are really broad. How tall are you, anyway? 6'8? 6'9?*

I nearly threw up in my mouth at the thought. I'd never spent any time considering it, but I suspected I might have no game. Occasionally, drunk dudes had tried to pick me up at the bar, but I'd always been pretty efficient about rejecting them. It had probably cost me a fortune in lost tips over the years.

Verity clicked the lid closed on the lotion bottle, handing it back to me with the kind of smile that really should have been accompanied by a choir of angels and some stray beams of sunshine. "Ready for breakfast?"

"Sure."

We headed downstairs together, Verity playfully tugging down her tutu while I solemnly pulled down my oversized t-shirt so that the entire top half of my thighs beneath my already-baggy jeans were concealed.

Tallulah was walking ahead of us, already making small talk with a Shade who had been undoubtedly hovering as close to Elverston House as he was allowed to get without provoking the ire of the Guard. Not that we ever saw them, but I knew they were nearby, watching.

Verner was the first guard I'd spoken to, and he'd been surprisingly kind. Or perhaps he was just a regular level of kind, and my view of authority figures was more cynical than it needed to be? They'd never given me any cause for alarm in this realm.

"Have you seen Astrid this morning?" I asked Verity, looking around. Theoretically, she lived here too, though she seemed to vanish into thin air if you didn't keep eyes on her at all times.

Verity shrugged, unbothered. "Of course not. She's like a cat. She pops up when she's hungry and occasionally, if she wants human interaction. If you try to engage with her outside of those bounds, she may or may not hiss at you."

"That analogy ended up being a lot more apt than I thought it would," I admitted, making a note to grab some of the cholesterol she was so fond of at breakfast. Astrid was independent—there was no denying that—but I suspected there was more loneliness there than she'd ever allow anyone to see.

"How did Astrid contact you when she was shadow realm recruiting?" Verity asked curiously. "Did you use social media?"

"Absolutely not," I replied, slightly horrified at the thought.

"Didn't think so," Verity said sagely. "Astrid slid into my DMs. And Tallulah's. How'd she get hold of you?"

"She called me." In the eight years since I'd left the Hunters—since I'd been *kicked out*—I'd never changed my phone number. I supposed I'd naively hoped that my sister might reach out to me one day, and I wanted to make sure she had a way of getting in contact. It seemed rather foolish in hindsight. I'd wiped the device and thrown the phone away before I'd come here, wanting a clean slate.

"Is that something people still do?" Verity asked, sounding so genuinely surprised that I almost laughed. "I can't remember the last time I used my phone to *call* someone. I'm surprised you picked up."

"So am I," I admitted. "Even now, I'm not really sure why I did."

It had been the weirdest conversation of my life, but Astrid had struck gold by calling me on that particular day. I'd been so on edge from my encounter with Adela Cooke that the idea of escaping the human realm had been immediately appealing. In fact, I'd already stuffed a few extra things into my go-bag and was contemplating taking the next bus to literally anywhere when my phone had rung.

I still felt guilty about it all, though. Like I'd let Adela down.

If nothing else, I could have just given her the documents I still had. It wouldn't have been easy to get my hands on them—they were still at my mother's house. But if I could have found a way, if I hadn't been so terrified… Well, maybe it would have made a difference.

It was too late now, of course. My roommates or my co-workers at the bar had probably filed some kind of missing person report by now since I'd vanished with no explanation. There was no going back.

"Aren't you glad, though?" Verity asked, beaming. "What an adventure.

If I was at home, I'd be weeping over my credit card bill, before online shopping to make myself feel better, and then weeping a little more. This is *so* much better."

I gave her what I hoped was a convincing look of agreement, nodding my head. "Of course."

I mean, I certainly couldn't argue with the financial perks. It was like being on a permanent vacation compared to life in the human realm, where I'd been building up my doula business, as well as doing casual bar work to try and claw my way out of a debt I'd never be able to pay off, and was still living with roommates.

But I hadn't *come* here.

I'd *escaped* here.

Walking into the dining hall in the palace always gave me flashbacks to the high school lunch cafeteria, and I hoped Verity didn't notice me holding on a little tighter to her arm. Even though I'd gone to school with other local Hunters, I'd never sat with them at lunch. I'd sat by myself in my thrifted clothes and worn-out shoes, and did my absolute best to be invisible.

Even at the mostly human public schools, the Hunters had always been the popular kids. The Council was very generous to the families they deemed worthy, and those kids had always arrived each morning in their late-model cars and expensive outfits, and acted like they didn't know I existed, even though we'd often be forced into group activities together at evening training.

Sitting with Verity and Tallulah felt a bit like being invited to the cool kids' table for the first time in my life—though Verity's family background was more like mine, so maybe she was just better at faking it. Or maybe even the posh asshole Hunters had accepted her, because she was beautiful and charming and hilarious company.

Tallulah had definitely been one of the cool kids—she was from the

Thibaut family. Even though Verity was the flirtatious one, it was Tallulah that greeted every Shade who came over to our table and made small talk with them, and somehow made all the introductions even though we'd been here the same amount of time and should have theoretically known all the same Shades.

"Ooh look, Astrid's here," Verity said, not bothering to keep her voice down.

Astrid flashed her a slightly impatient look from the side exit she'd stationed herself at, probably resenting the fact that Verity had drawn attention to her. If Verity and Tallulah were the popular girls, then Astrid was the cool alt girl who'd smoked in the parking lot, had an ironic smiley face tattoo behind her ear, and drove a muscle car.

What did that make the Shade guys who were already crowding around our table, angling themselves to show off their horns at the best angle? Jocks?

I hastily took a sip of my tea before I snorted out loud and drew attention to myself.

*Verner wasn't a jock,* I thought idly. He was more like the older, artsy, aloof guys I'd always crushed on in my teenage years. Quiet and kind of mysterious, and seemingly above the petty drama of their peers. Not that I had a crush on him, because I didn't do that kind of thing anymore, but that's just who he reminded me of.

"You look very lovely this morning, Meera," a Shade said, sitting down next to me and angling his body toward me rather than the table full of food. "I trust your night was restful?"

I stared blankly for a moment, translating his formal words into something my pleb brain could process. "Um, yes. I slept well, thanks. You?"

Had we met before? I had to assume so, since he wasn't introducing himself. It really would make my life a lot easier if they wore nametags, but I guess it'd be hard to pin anything to the shadows they wore as clothing.

"Unfortunately, I worked the night shift last night. I'm just stopping by to get some breakfast—and say hello to you, of course—before I head down to the barracks to sleep."

If Shades winked, he would have definitely winked.

"Well, that's very kind," I said awkwardly, busying myself with my tea and the small serving of stewed fruit that had been put specifically at our table.

The mysterious Shade nodded to himself. "My kindness is much noted upon here at court."

I didn't really know what to say to that, so I focused on sipping my tea and making up a small plate of assorted items to take over to Astrid before I left.

"There's been talk of a ball soon."

I startled, realizing the Shade was still speaking. "A ball?"

"Yes. One in the old style, where we ask another to cloak us in shadows for the evening. It's very romantic—a true sign of trust and affection to let someone drape you in their shadows."

*Don't freak out,* I told myself firmly. *If you freak out, you'll start stinking like a skunk.*

"Perhaps you would be open to wearing my shadows to—"

Whoever he was didn't even get the question out before he was wrinkling his nose, rearing back so quickly that he knocked the Shade next to him half off the bench.

Verity leaned around me, a mischievous grin on her face. "Sorry, buddy. I think that might be a no."

# VERNER

## CHAPTER 3

Usually, the afternoon was the part of my shift that dragged on the longest. The mornings usually went by quickly, with far more happening in the royal wing of the palace at that time of day that required my attention.

But not today. Today, each second that passed felt like an hour as I waited for my midday break. Would Meera be there? I didn't want to think about how sorry for myself I would feel if she wasn't.

"You're restless today, Verner," the queen's confidant, Affra, remarked. She paused in the archway, heading out to go and visit her daughters as she usually did. "Is something amiss?"

"Not at all," I assured her, acutely aware of Andrus's interested gaze from the other side of the archway.

Affra hummed, not sounding altogether convinced. "Ah, it's probably nothing, isn't it? You're a good lad, you wouldn't lie to me." She gave Andrus a pointed look, making it very clear that he was *not* a good lad, and he huffed in response. Perhaps if he'd been a little more charming where Affra was concerned, she wouldn't be so ready to malign him. "It's just my daughters getting in my head, that's all."

"About what?" I asked curiously. Usually, Affra only made passing small talk with me at best.

"Lots of change about the place, I suppose."

"I've been hearing that a lot recently," I murmured.

She shrugged, a gesture she'd picked up from the queen. "They worry. Lots of unfamiliar faces at the palace. And they're afraid of Ophelia's sister."

I wished I could argue with that, but I wasn't overly fond of Astrid either. She was the kind of Hunter I despised. The kind who tore families apart.

"Change doesn't have to be a bad thing," I said, searching for words that might offer her some comfort while not being dismissive of her concerns.

"It doesn't," Affra agreed. "And I am very old, don't forget. I've seen much change in my lifetime. Sometimes motivated by a new generation with a different vision for the future, sometimes motivated by circumstance, and often motivated by anger. There's a lot of anger now. Angry Shades who can't travel to the human realm to feed—directing their ire at both the Hunters and the king.

"And that's a bad thing," I hedged, though her tone wasn't entirely conveying that. She sounded thoughtful, if anything.

"Not necessarily." Affra began moving away, her walk even slower than usual. Possibly because her energy was running low and she was reluctant to use the stores to feed when the entire realm was relying on them. "Anger is a powerful tool. Deadly. Efficient. Effective. But only if you wield it right."

On that chilling note, she went on her merry way, humming a cheerful tune under her breath.

Was she right? I'd never given the matter much thought before. Anger was not an emotion that had been encouraged growing up at Sunlis. No emotions had been encouraged there—anything other than a state of perfect calm had been seen as an embarrassing loss of control. I'd never really considered the potential of it as motivation.

"Terrifying old bag," Andrus muttered loudly.

I shot him a chastising look. "This is why she doesn't like you."

"The feeling is entirely mutual."

At least Affra's ominous words had given me plenty to consider, which helped the morning pass with a little more haste.

After stopping by my apartment and then the palace kitchen, I made my way down to Elverston House, my optimism tempered heavily by caution. Perhaps last night, in the moment, suggesting a friendship between us had seemed like a good idea, but there was always the chance Meera had woken up and changed her mind. She was certainly more reticent than the others—with the exception of Astrid—to put herself out there.

Bracing myself for disappointment, I followed the shrub-lined curved path until the full building came into sight and nearly dropped what I was carrying.

There she was. Sitting cross-legged on the ground on the Elverston-side of the invisible line, glowing in a loose pale-yellow top.

*Friends*, I reminded myself. *She wanted a friend.*

Though, surely, noticing how enchanting she looked in yellow was a friendly thing to do?

Meera waved tentatively as I approached, and some of the tension in my shoulders eased. Undoubtedly, there would be some awkwardness, but she *wanted* to see me. She wanted me here. That was the most important thing.

"Hello, Meera. How are you?" I asked, lowering myself to the ground opposite her on my side of the line. It wasn't until I was sitting that I realized how much the overgrown foliage around Elverston House obscured us from view. What had once been manicured garden beds had become almost a jungle after at least a decade of neglect.

Had Meera noticed how private this spot was when she sat down? Surely not, or she wouldn't have chosen it. She struck me as particularly safety conscious.

"I'm good, thank you. How are you?"

"Very well. I brought some things for us for lunch." I handed her two small packages wrapped in paper and tied with twine.

"Oh. You shouldn't have." Meera's smile was tight as she unwrapped the first one, peeking inside it before carefully wrapping it back up again. "I really appreciate it, thank you. But I don't eat meat."

"You don't?"

She shook her head. "I never have. I was raised vegetarian."

For a brief moment, I longed for the shadows of my ancestors to surround me here and now and bring me home. How had I made a blunder so quickly?

"That one doesn't have any meat in it," I said apologetically, nodding at the second package. "It's sweet. A traditional cake from my part of the realm."

"Ooh, I love cake. Did Calix make this?"

I almost laughed at the idea of the mad chef attempting anything so delicate. "No. My parents brought a large stash of it from home for me."

Of course, it was simple enough for me to visit Sunlis and purchase some for myself, but I rarely did. I was too well-known there. I couldn't simply move around the place in peace, getting what I needed. Every trip was a production.

Though, if Meera enjoyed it, I suspected that I would happily schedule more trips home on my days off.

I set aside my own meal as Meera carefully unwrapped it, smiling slightly as the thin gray layers were revealed, stacked in circles that fit into the palm of her hand.

"It's wobbly."

"It's steamed." That was all I really knew about it, but it gave it a sticky, wobbly texture.

I watched, probably too intently, as Meera nibbled on the edge of the cake before shooting me a beaming smile. "This is *so* good. It tastes like... coconut? It's not quite the same, but that's the closest match I can think of. Thank you so much, Verner."

"No problem." I slid the cake I'd brought for myself across to her, already intending to bring her a larger portion the next time I saw her from my stash. "Have both since I'm going to be eating all the meat."

"Oh, are you sure?"

"Very, I have plenty more back at the apartment. And I can always go home and collect more."

"I guess it isn't hard to travel places in the shadow realm, not like where I'm from. Do you visit home often?" Meera asked, taking a bigger bite this time while I unwrapped my lunch.

"Not really. My parents would like it if I visited more often." Meera glanced at me curiously before determinedly looking away as though mentally telling herself not to pry. When first meeting her, it seemed like she was less expressive than the others, but I suspected that she was just expressive in different ways. Ways that required paying a little more attention. "They're very set in their ways. Sometimes, it can be tiring to be around them, constantly hearing about how the old ways were better and how the world is falling apart around us. That kind of thing. Does that happen in the human realm?"

Meera pressed her lips tightly together, eyes briefly sparkling with what I hoped was amusement. "Oh yes. That is definitely a universal experience."

I waited, starting on my first portion of roasted meat and hoping that she'd elaborate a little more. Life in the human realm had always intrigued me—it was probably why I'd stayed in the Guard for so long. We spent more time there than most other Shades, who only stopped in briefly to feed. Well, back in the before times. Who knew when we'd be able to return to the human realm to feed again?

"I don't really know how to do this," Meera said after a long stretch of silence, gesturing between us. "I haven't had friends in a long time."

"That seems impossible," I replied, not necessarily intending to say it out loud, but instantly affronted on her behalf. How could such a sweet, gentle soul not be surrounded by loyal friends at all times?

"It's not a unique story among those of us who have come here." Meera's soothing voice was an instant balm to my irritation. "Only Astrid was actually beloved by the Hunters prior to leaving. The rest of us were outcasts. We've all angered the higher-ups in the Hunters and lost everyone we loved because of it." She shrugged uncomfortably, and my muscles ached with the effort of not reaching for her. "In all honesty, it's taken a little of the righteous wind out of my sails, coming here and realizing just how very *un*-unique my experience was."

"That doesn't make it any less profound."

A glimmer—the faintest *hint*—of a smile played around Meera's mouth before her expression returned to its state of neutrality. "No, I suppose not. Not to *me*. Inconveniently, I never developed humor or charm as coping mechanisms the way the others seem to have done."

"You seem plenty charming to me. And life would be very dull if we were all the same. Though, I can relate in a sense. I always liked the idea of being funny, but the skill hasn't manifested for me, unfortunately."

"Oh good. Then neither of us will be the funny one in this friendship."

"Or perhaps that means we both are?" I teased. There was that glimmer of a smile again, that tempting *hint* of what it could be.

Meera's lips did tip up from time to time, but I couldn't call it a real smile. Having watched the other ex-Hunters and observed life in the human realm, I knew that the eyes were a crucial component. I'd never seen Meera's *eyes* smile.

And while I'd caught faint hints of sweetness in her scent, I'd never smelled the pure *joy* that the queen was usually cloaked in. I was probably more familiar with it than most, since it lingered in the corridors of the royal wing.

Joy, as well as another emotion that Queen Ophelia probably *wouldn't* appreciate the palace guards scenting.

She took another bite of cake, chewing it thoughtfully. "So, you didn't grow up at the palace then?"

I shook my head. The fact that she'd asked gave me a clear idea of the kinds of Shades she'd been talking to during feasts in the dining hall. "My family visited court fairly infrequently. I didn't spend much time here until I joined the Guard."

"Do you like being part of the Guard?"

The question briefly stunned me into silence. Had I ever been asked that before? Freedom had been the deciding factor in joining the Guard, not enjoyment. An escape from the boring predictability of life at Sunlis, and a chance to see the world and meet a variety of Shades.

"I suppose I do. I enjoy being... useful. I like to help."

Meera tilted her head to the side, her long dark hair rippling around her like water. "Do you like fighting?"

"Well, no. Not really," I said slowly. I was physically strong and generally considered to be a calm, reliable presence, which was how I'd been promoted up through the ranks. But I'd never developed the thirst for violence that many other members of the Guard seemed to possess, and I desperately hoped I never did. "Fighting, to me, is always the last and least desirable option. Though I don't have to do much of it, not now. For my current post, temperament was the deciding factor in how I got the role."

I'd never understand how Andrus had been promoted up through the ranks. Perhaps there just wasn't much competition.

"What is it you did in the human realm?" I asked, wanting to shift the subject back to my far more interesting companion.

"My main job was as a doula. I helped with childbirth—with the whole process. Pregnancy, birth, postpartum."

"And did you enjoy it?"

She pursed her lips, and I did my best to memorize the interesting shape. A Shade's mouth was so unexpressive in comparison.

"It was very rewarding, but it wasn't what I wanted to do. The Hunters Council pays for our education, and I'd meant to study nursing. But when everything... happened, they pulled my financial support. I'd already been accepted into college, and maybe if I'd been more levelheaded, I would have figured out how to get a loan in time, but I didn't. Everything fell apart, and I gave up on the idea of college and ran away to start over."

"That must have been painful." Much of the context of her words made no sense to me, but the lingering ache of the wound was obvious.

"It was a long time ago now."

"Then perhaps the pain is less sharp than it once was."

Meera looked at me thoughtfully for a long moment in a way that no one else really had. I was solid. Reliable. And, for the most part, somewhat indistinguishable.

I wasn't one to be looked at closely.

"How was it that you came to be a doula after that? You must have been very determined to make that happen on your own."

It had merely been an observation—how could she not be determined after going through something so difficult?—but Meera's scent sweetened as though I'd given her a great compliment. I silently scolded myself for not coming up with one better.

"I cleaned motels for a couple of years and worked at bars until I could save up enough for the training—fortunately, they had a payment plan because I was... well, let's just say I wasn't in a good place financially. I worked for myself, but I was only just starting out before I came here, so I still worked at a bar to supplement my income." She gave me a wry smile. "Honestly, who knows if it would have even worked out—I wasn't particularly business-savvy, and I struggled with that side of things, even though I loved supporting parents, and helping bring those tiny babies into the world. But if it hadn't worked out, I'd have figured something else out. If I pride myself on anything, it's my resilience."

"Yes, I can certainly tell you're resilient," I agreed, though I was a little saddened by that fact. Meera's strength was admirable, but she'd suffered to gain it.

I wondered if she wanted children of her own? I didn't want to give her the wrong impression by asking. In my experience, children were intimidating little creatures and I didn't feel anywhere near ready for them, though as the heir to Sunlis, I would be expected to produce at least one someday.

"What about—" she began.

"Meera!" Verity yelled, her voice easily distinguishable as the loudest of all of them who lived in Elverston House. "Are you out here?"

Meera started guiltily, scrambling to her feet so fast that her hair caught in the overgrowth.

"I'll be right there!" she called over her shoulder, tugging the strands free so roughly that I winced.

I stood and reached over, taking the now empty wrappers from her hand.

"Would you like me to wait here until you've gone back inside?" I asked, indicating the vines and branches that hid us from view.

"Is that okay?" she asked guiltily. It was clear that Meera wanted to keep this meeting between the two of us, and I felt oddly bereft about it.

*What did you expect, Verner? For her to parade you around the grounds? She doesn't even know you.*

"Yes, of course."

Meera's hands flexed at her sides. "I think you're too nice to be my friend. Or I'm too selfish."

I frowned. "I don't think that at all."

"No, I definitely am. If I was nice, I'd call the others over and introduce you because you're wonderful, and I'm sure you'd all get along." She shifted her weight from one foot to the other. "I will do that. Eventually. But maybe I could keep you to myself a little longer?"

*Keep me to yourself forever.* But I couldn't say that thought out loud.

"I would like that," I assured her. "Perhaps I could return here with lunch another time? I'll bring more ojurac. And something else without meat," I added hastily.

"Just the ojurac would be amazing," Meera replied, that faint smile touching her lips again. "It's surprisingly difficult being a vegetarian here—better if I handle that side of things myself. Same time tomorrow?"

Hopefully, my surprise didn't register on my face. I hadn't expected for her to want to see me again so soon.

"Of course."

I suspected there wasn't a single thing this woman could ask of me that I'd be able to deny her.

45

# MEERA

## CHAPTER 4

I did my best to avoid attachments.

Attachments were dangerous. Attachments made you vulnerable. They'd been the hardest part about walking away when my life had imploded all those years ago. And while I *wanted* friends here, I'd naively thought that I could have them without getting too emotionally invested in the process. Keep things light—like colleagues, but in slightly weirder circumstances together.

But I could see now that I'd been deluding myself.

Verner was doing his level best to work his way past the multilayered metaphorical fortress I'd built around myself, and he was succeeding.

"Some more cake," Verner said, handing me one large package this time. "They really should serve it at the palace, it's the best food in the shadow realm."

"I couldn't agree more."

I gave him my best attempt at a smile—a new thing I'd been trying out recently. It felt weird every time I did it. Did my mouth look right? Why hadn't I gotten my teeth whitened before I moved to the shadow realm? Maybe I should wear lipstick?

As if he knew I was feeling self-conscious, Verner was suddenly very preoccupied with his own lunch, and I happily tucked into my cake, enjoying simply being in his company. Something about his presence felt very easy, in a way I didn't experience with most people—or Shades.

Even with the other ex-Hunters, as much as I *liked* them, I couldn't help but measure myself against them when I was in their company, and I always came up short. They were just such naturals at making conversation in a way that I couldn't grasp at all. Astrid and I were probably the most similar in that respect, but she was even more antisocial than I was, so I was stuck comparing myself to engaging, flirtatious, charming, *and* funny extroverts.

Why couldn't I be just one of those things?

I'd settle for funny.

"What have you been doing this morning?" Verner asked.

*Making notes*, I replied in my head. I didn't say that out loud though, not even as much as I liked Verner. Or perhaps it was *because* I liked him? Detailing all the idiotic—and sometimes terrible—things I'd been involved with felt like a poor reflection on me. I wasn't even sure *why* I was doing it—I had no way of getting it to Adela Cooke now. She probably thought I was dead.

Perhaps it was just for my own peace of mind. A little notebook of regrets that I could use to remind myself how far I'd come. Maybe one day, I'd burn it and set myself free.

"I haven't really done anything," I replied instead. "I had breakfast at the palace and walked around Elverston House a bit. I think the royal couple have intentionally given us as much free time as we could possibly want to incentivize us to stay, but I feel a bit directionless."

I had so much *time* each day. Too much time.

It had given me the uncomfortable realization that I thrived in chaos and struggled in peace.

"What is it you'd like to do? As your *friend*—" Verner paused, looking almost a little smug at that. I almost laughed. "—I feel that I could be of assistance in this. Perhaps something related to your previous career?"

"I'm definitely not qualified to help deliver Shade babies," I said, giving him an incredulous look. Were the babies *born* with claws? My uterus went into full-scale lockdown at the thought.

I shuffled forward a little on my butt to disentangle myself from the hanging vine behind me that seemed to be magnetically attracted to my hair. "I wonder if anyone would mind if I tidied up a little out here? I don't know anything about gardening, but it's so overgrown. I could just hack away at it, so at least the paths were clear."

"Mind? Certainly not. You'd be doing them a great favor. I could source you some tools, though they aren't designed for your dainty hands."

"Dainty?" I examined my hands like I'd never seen them before. I supposed they were rather delicate compared to a Shade's.

"Dainty," he repeated firmly. "Can the queen's sister bring you equipment from the human realm? I believe she does supply runs back with the captain."

I nodded. "Astrid, yes. I could ask."

Was it my imagination, or had Verner grimaced a little when I said Astrid's name? Whatever expression he saw on my face, he looked immediately contrite.

"My apologies, Meera. I know your relationship with her is bound to be different from how the Shades in the realm see her."

The defensiveness I felt for my prickly housemate who was determinedly ignoring all of my attempts at friendship took me by surprise. But Astrid was the bravest person I knew, and I wasn't going to tolerate so much as a hint of disrespect toward her in my presence.

The rest of us had been forced out of the Hunters, and come here out of convenience.

Astrid had walked away willingly, and basically thrown a grenade into the room behind her when she'd left. And nothing about moving here made life easier for her.

"I wouldn't be here if it wasn't for Astrid," I reminded Verner gently. "She searched me out. She brought me here. If, at any time, you're enjoying my company, you have Astrid to thank for that."

"I enjoy every moment of your company. And you're right, I do."

I waited to see if he'd say anything else. To see if he'd make excuses or attempt to justify his actions, but he didn't.

I hated that it immediately made me suspicious. Verner appeared to be nothing but kind. Gentlemanly. My gut instinct was telling me that he was one of the good ones and that I could let my guard down around him, at least a little. I wouldn't have met him alone in this hidden-away spot if I didn't feel that way.

The problem wasn't Verner, I was *almost* sure of it. The problem was me. I didn't trust my judgment anymore.

"Do you like to write?" he asked, startling me.

"Write?" My blood chilled instantly.

"I've seen you out here with a notebook before." The way his shadows moved around him... it was almost sheepish. I'd suspected that the Guard had a better view over Elverston House than we realized, and that basically confirmed it. "I've often wondered what you were writing."

"Oh." *Quick, Meera. Come up with something normal to say.*

"I'm sorry, I didn't mean to pry," Verner said suddenly, his nose wrinkling ever so slightly. Damn it, my stupid scent had broadcast my discomfort before

I'd had a chance to lie about it.

"It's not... I'm not writing. I mean, I am. I'm just rambling about stuff. I'm not... It's not poetry or anything," I managed to get out, tripping over my words.

"I understand," Verner replied kindly, though he absolutely didn't.

And I was grateful for that fact. The less Verner understood about how odd I really was, the better.

"Anyone here?" Ophelia called out from the foyer of Elverston House, her voice echoing around the stones. "I come bearing gray wine and cheese!"

"Oh my god, you shouldn't have," Verity replied, skipping down the stairs. "Gray wine and cheese is my favorite kind of wine and cheese."

"I already have my rollers in," Tallulah sighed, coming down after Verity. She had a blue patterned silk scarf tied elegantly over the barrel rollers, so you couldn't really see them anyway, and her pajamas matched the scarf. Verity—in a fluffy pink unicorn onesie—was slightly less *chic*, but definitely just as cute.

And I was in cotton yoga pants that had a hole in the knee, with a giant sweatshirt that came nearly down to my knees to hide the fact that my leggings were looking pretty transparent around the butt.

"Is Meera here?" Ophelia asked, hugging them each in turn.

"I'm here," I said quietly from the sitting room doorway. I'd been taking notes on the uncomfortable couch, and I discreetly checked the front pocket of my hoodie to make sure my notebook was hidden away.

"There you are! Shall we all sit in there?" Ophelia asked, already heading my way with a wine bottle in one hand and a picnic basket in the other.

"I'll get glasses," Tallulah offered, her fluffy slippers slapping the stone floor with each step.

Verity flopped down on the hard couch, eyeing it with irritation as she wriggled to get comfortable. "What's the occasion, Ophelia?"

"Nothing in particular, I just thought it would be nice for us to spend some time together. It's been a few weeks now, I want to know how you're settling in. You're all so popular at court—I barely get a chance to speak to you in the palace!"

"It's a tough job but someone has to do it," Verity replied solemnly as Tallulah returned with heavy goblets and busied herself with opening the wine.

Astrid slunk into the room while Tallulah was distributing goblets, accepting one with a nod of thanks and perching on the arm of the couch like she was ready to bolt at a moment's notice.

I understood that impulse. Maybe I'd thrown myself a little too far in the deep end with this whole making friends thing. Verner and I had lunch together every day and we had done so for weeks now—that had always felt completely comfortable. Maybe it was the group setting that was making me nervous.

"Cheers, ladies," Ophelia said, holding up her goblet. I wriggled to the edge of the seat so I could reach, clinking the heavy silver cup against the others before taking a sip.

It looked like dirty dishwater, but it tasted like red wine at least.

"What's been going on? What's the gossip? Did you guys enjoy the ball? I want to hear everything." Ophelia beamed while almost every muscle in my body clenched up in terror. I didn't know how to do this. I'd never had girlfriends to gossip with, even before my life had imploded. I'd had a sister five years younger than me, who felt more like a child than a sibling most of the time.

What was I meant to say? What if I said too much and made it weird?

Probably best not to say anything.

"I'll go first," Verity volunteered without hesitation. "The ball was great—ten out of ten, would write a favorable review. Also, I've decided to save my first knot for marriage."

Tallulah choked on her wine, and Verity tilted her head to the side, waiting with a serene smile on her face for Tallulah to finish coughing.

"That's romantic," Ophelia hedged. I was glad that for all of her social skills, even she didn't know how to perfectly respond to that. "Not to be crass and you totally don't have to answer, but have you, uh, been busy? The rate the stores are depleting by has slowed a little lately."

Verity frowned. "I mean, I've been enjoying myself for sure, but I doubt it's enough to make a noticeable difference in the stores. One dude said that without knotting, I wasn't generating nearly as much power as I could be. I feel kinda bad about that—"

"Please don't," Ophelia interjected. "Only do what you're comfortable with. Who said that? I'm going to have words with him."

I didn't hear Verity's answer, because the pink tint in Astrid's cheeks that no one else seemed to have noticed had captured my attention. Was *Astrid* the one generating power for the stores? With who? I looked over to Tallulah to see if she'd spotted it, and maybe I was imagining things, but *she* looked a little flushed too.

Shoot, I was really letting the team down. What was the point of me even being here if I wasn't contributing?

"What about you, Meera?" Verity asked suddenly. There was a knowing look in her eyes that made me nervous. Had she seen Verner outside? The more I cleared the garden, the less hidden our little spot was.

"What about me?"

Verity grinned. "Okay, okay. Keep your secrets. You'll tell us when you're ready."

She totally knew.

"I've been busy gardening. Or just hacking away at the overgrowth, I guess," I said hastily, not wanting to lie but also wanting to provide a plausible reason for why I was spending so much time outside.

Why was I being so weird about Verner anyway? I could have friends. There was nothing wrong with that. I just... didn't want to share that particular friend. Not yet.

Ophelia smiled, but it was definitely a less enthusiastic smile than I would have gotten if I'd been juicing up the stores. "The garden beds are definitely looking much less chaotic outside Elverston House. Is gardening something you enjoy?"

A lightbulb went off in my brain at her question. I wasn't contributing power, but maybe I *could* contribute this way. I could help look after the others, so that they could... do their thing here. And then I'd feel less like a freeloader, and maybe the royal couple would see that I was adding value to the realm and wouldn't kick me out when they got sick of me.

"Sure. Maybe I could try growing some human realm vegetables?" I suggested tentatively. "Since the garden beds aren't being used for anything anyway. And then Astrid wouldn't have to bring back quite so much on her supply runs."

Ophelia blinked at me. "That's a fantastic idea. I mean, we need to find ways to be more self-sufficient anyway—Astrid going back and forth can't be a long-term solution. It's not safe."

"It's fine," Astrid grumbled, crossing her arms to hide her injured hand. Ophelia didn't dignify that with an answer.

"Do you know what you need to get started, Meera?" Tallulah asked brightly.

"I'll make a list," I hedged, not really knowing what I needed. Seeds? A little shovel thing? Astrid had already brought me cutting implements, but I probably needed a few extra things to grow rather than just destroy.

Humans had been growing food for centuries, surely I could figure this out.

"Obviously there will be some trial and error," Ophelia said. "And maybe the climate at the palace isn't right for certain things? I guess we'll find out. But it would be so amazing if you could give it a try, Meera. It'll be a total game changer for us if we can grow our own food."

She smiled, and something settled into place in my chest. In so many ways, I wasn't the right fit for life here, but this was a way I could be genuinely helpful.

*This*, I could do.

# VERNER

## CHAPTER 5

I followed you yesterday," Andrus said as we handed off duties to our replacements to take our midday break. "I know where you've been going for lunch each day."

"I'm aware. Your stealth skills are quite abysmal, you know. I continue to be astounded that you've risen as high in the Guard as you have."

Insults always seemed to roll right off Andrus, it was an enviable talent. His ego was so astoundingly large that mere words had no hope of penetrating it.

"What are you doing, Verner?" he asked, shaking his head and tutting like a disappointed grandmother as we made our way down the hall. "I don't know how to tell you this, but she clearly doesn't like you. She doesn't like anyone."

"Meera likes me," I replied confidently. *As a friend.* And I'd grown to cherish our friendship over the past few weeks, so I had certainly had no complaints on that front.

"She doesn't like anyone," Andrus asserted. "Her scent makes that obvious."

"The emotion you're feeling is bitterness," I told Andrus calmly.

"What? Why would I be bitter?"

"You had hoped that one of the ex-Hunters would choose you, and they never did. It's not acceptable, however, to direct any resentment you may be harboring toward them over that. I recommend you find a way to let it go."

"I hate when you're like this," Andrus huffed, already stomping off. "You don't know everything, Verner."

No, I didn't. And sometimes, I could be too quick to form an opinion and make that opinion known without collecting enough information first. It was a lingering bad habit from my childhood, where I was surrounded by staff who weren't allowed to challenge my words.

This time, I was pretty sure I was right though.

Tallulah had become less open to suitors since the ball, and Verity seemed content not to make a decision. Tensions were running high among all the Shades at court who had been vying for their attention.

I stopped by the kitchen before making my way to the border with Elverston House, feeling the tension ease from my shoulders with each step. It was the highlight of my day—a quiet moment Meera and I had carved out for ourselves where we could just *be*. We could sit in the peace and privacy of the garden, and no one tried to court her, and no one asked anything of me.

For that hour each day, I felt as though I was transported somewhere else completely.

She was in the garden again today, using the odd tools Astrid had sourced for her to cut away at some branches. Today, she was wearing a dark green top, and I liked it on her *almost* as much as I liked her in yellow. The dark colors had a very sultry effect on her brown eyes, that I did my best to ignore. *Friends. Friends, friends, friends.*

I wasn't sure that Meera trusted in our friendship the same way I did yet.

That she trusted that there was stability and longevity in it, but hopefully, time would cure that.

Someday, Meera would see that I was a true and lifelong friend to her. In a different life, perhaps it would have been more. Perhaps she would have been my mate and my wife, and I'd have happily announced to the entire shadow realm that she was mine.

But Meera had given no indication that she wanted those things, and certainly not with me, and so I would appreciate her presence in my life exactly as it was.

"There you are," she said, setting her tools down and peeling off the odd gloves she wore to protect her delicate hands as she made her way over to our usual spot.

"Sorry I'm late. I come bearing proper food for you—some of the colorful things that Calix usually sends up with the queen's midday meal. Sadly, I have run out of cake."

"Oh, Verner, you shouldn't have…" Meera breathed, coming all the way up to meet me. Did she realize that she'd crossed the border in doing so? We'd always kept to our respective sides of the invisible line. I handed her the covered bowl, and she gave me another one of those smiles that almost reached her eyes. "Thank you. I really appreciate this."

"It's my pleasure." The amount of gratitude in her voice was jarring. Did *no one* ever do nice things for this woman? She deserved so much better than the life she'd been given. I should bring her more food offerings. "It looks like you've been busy today."

"I have. I've been putting that garden bed off for a while, thinking it would be really difficult, but actually, the branches are soft and easy to cut. I didn't have anything to worry about. Shall we go eat by the river?"

"I'd like that," I replied, shocked she'd suggested it. The riverbank was only across the path from Elverston House—merely a few feet away. But it was very much on neutral territory, and I was honored that Meera trusted me enough to venture out of the Shade-free zone with me.

We sat on the ground next to each other, leaning back against one of the gnarled old trees that lined the riverbank, the water lazily trickling past, and uncovered our bowls of food.

"Ooh, carrots," Meera said happily, pulling out a violently bright stick from the bowl. "Have you ever tried one?"

I shook my head, eyeing it warily.

"Do you want to?" she asked, holding it out to me.

*Not really*, in all honesty. But I suspected I would struggle to deny this woman anything. "Sure."

I took it carefully from her hand, making sure my claws were well away from her fingers, and took a bite.

"What do you think?" Meera asked, avidly watching my expression. I could get addicted to seeing that expression on her face.

"It's... sweeter than I expected," I replied, hoping my face wasn't giving away my revulsion.

But then Meera laughed, and I felt anything but. I'd eat a thousand of these horrid things a day to hear that sound again. Unfortunately, it was over nearly as quickly as it began, and she looked just as surprised as me that she'd done it.

"Sorry," she mumbled. "I didn't mean to laugh at your discomfort. That was rude of me."

"You worry too much. I would dearly love to hear you laugh more often—I don't mind in the slightest if it's at my expense. In fact, I encourage it.

It's good to know that my presence in your life brings you joy."

"Of course it does," she said quickly, her smile a little more genuine now. It was a little softer around the edges. A littler warmer in the eyes. "I don't suppose you want to try some cucumber? Not for my entertainment! It's not as sweet as carrot."

"On the off chance it makes you laugh again, I will try your strange human vegetables."

Her smile widened as she handed me a green stick this time. The colors of this one were slightly more muted and less intimidating.

"It tastes like water," I told her after chewing on it for a moment. "This one is not so unpleasant."

"Good." She bit into a green stick of her own, staring out over the water. "I sort of volunteered myself last night to try grow these kinds of vegetables so Astrid doesn't have to bring it back for us each time. Ophelia was really keen on the idea."

"I'm sure she was—she would be mad not to be considering how much easier it would make life here for all of you. Do you have what you need to get started? Is there anything I can source for you?"

Meera's scent sweetened ever so slightly, her expression soft and affectionate. It was the prettiest thing I'd ever seen.

"That's okay, thank you. Astrid is going to get me an assortment of things on her next supply run. I can't do anything until I have the garden beds cleared anyway."

It was very unlike me to even consider breaking the rules, but I immediately contemplated occasionally venturing over the invisible border to help Meera remove some of the more difficult shrubs. It was entirely unreasonable to expect her to tackle those on her own.

I glanced at Meera, deciding whether I should suggest it or not. I suspected she wasn't a rule breaker either. Perhaps I could sneak into the garden at night and do some stealth gardening.

"Maybe we used to grow these kinds of food here, back when the Hunted lived here," Meera mused.

I grimaced at the reminder of our kinds' shared history. "I think the fact that we called you 'the Hunted' does not bode well in respect to how we treated you all."

"Possibly not," Meera agreed, tilting her head to the side thoughtfully. "Though I'm sure some of my kind liked being chased around in the dark, if the small sample of ex-Hunters I've talked to are anything to go by," she added wryly.

I coughed awkwardly into my hand. If I'd been given a thousand chances, I never would have guessed *that* was what she was going to say.

"Is that so?"

"Don't get any ideas," Meera added, glancing at me, an almost playful expression on her face. "I have no interest in being hunted, and I'm good with a knife."

I laughed in surprise. "I'm glad to hear it—and I hope you're armed at all times. If you're not, I will procure you some weapons."

I didn't think I could address the first part of her sentence out loud. Though, I wondered if she'd be interested in hunting me...? I certainly wasn't opposed to the idea.

*Behave, Verner. She's looking for a friend, nothing more.*

"All of our weapons were confiscated when we moved here." Meera shrugged, pausing for a long moment to chew on a carrot. "It's fine, though. I feel safe here."

"You barely leave Elverston House," I pointed out gently. "And never alone. If a few silver throwing knives will bolster your confidence in moving around the palace complex, then I will argue with the king on the necessity of such a thing until he sees my point of view."

I watched as discreetly as I could as a fetching color crawled up Meera's face. It was, perhaps, the most enchanting sight I'd ever seen, and I was desperately glad that *she* couldn't smell *my* scent. It might make things uncomfortable if she could.

"You don't need to go to any effort on my behalf, you know. I mean, it's so kind of you. *So* kind. I want you to know that I really appreciate everything you do for me." She held up the bowl of vegetables as though to illustrate her point. "You really don't need to go out of your way for me though. I'll be okay."

I hummed, not disagreeing but not agreeing either. In many ways, Meera reminded me of Levana. Levana often suffered unnecessarily in silence, but I was coming to realize that it was borne of self-preservation rather than stubbornness. If she handled everything on her own, then she never needed to be dependent on someone else, and risk disappointment.

Meera did the same. If she ever asked me for help, I'd know that the situation was truly dire because she wouldn't do it lightly.

"I'll be okay," Meera repeated, possibly aiming for a firmer voice but finding a more wobbly one. "I'm very independent, you know. I'm good at doing things on my own."

"I appreciate that. But you don't always *have* to. You're navigating an entirely new world, Meera. If you ever want help, I'm more than happy to provide it. We're friends, after all."

I was impressed at how convincing I'd made that sound. It hadn't been a lie, after all. We *were* friends. I couldn't switch off the attraction I felt for Meera, but surely it would lessen with time the more diligently I ignored it.

"Thank you, Verner. You're really amazing, you know?"

"No. This is the bare minimum—you don't get to thank me for that."

"I'm going to anyway."

"That's okay, we'll work on it."

Meera almost laughed again, catching herself at the last moment.

"Have you noticed any color in the garden?" I asked, giving her a reprieve by changing the subject. "There's been sightings of pinks and golds and blues around the realm, you know. It's quite the topic of conversation."

Meera tipped her head back against the tree, smiling softly. "I haven't seen any here yet, but that's lovely. Well, it's lovely for me. I'm sure there are some Shades who aren't so fond of such a visible reminder of change," she added wryly, giving me a pointed look.

"My parents are struggling a little, yes," I agreed, certain that was who she was referring to. "They'll adjust in time. It doesn't help that my cousin, Osric, is constantly in their ears, buzzing about how dire everything is," I grumbled.

"You two aren't close, I take it?" Meera teased, bumping me lightly with her shoulder. Something fluttered wildly in my chest, and I did my best to ignore it.

"No. Osric prides himself on being everything I'm not, which means he is the ideal heir. The kind of son my parents want me to be."

Meera frowned. "I don't understand how any parent could not think of you as basically the perfect child, honestly. You're kind, generous, respectful, principled... If I had a son someday and he turned out like you, I'd think I'd done something very right."

I didn't even know how to respond to that. It was the kindest thing anyone had ever said to me.

"That's..." I cleared my throat. "Thank you, Meera. That means more to me than I can say."

She flushed a deep shade of red, but her scent sweetened as though my words had pleased her.

"Um, that's okay. It's just the truth. Will you visit home again any time soon?" she asked, resuming eating. I wasn't sure if it was because she was still hungry or if she just wanted something to do with her hands.

"I hadn't planned on it, but perhaps I will. If only to get more ojurac."

"Not on my account," she said sternly. "But if you're visiting anyway and *happen* to get some…"

"You really liked the ojurac?" I asked, wanting to make sure she hadn't just been claiming to enjoy it out of politeness.

"It's my favorite thing I've eaten since I came to the shadow realm."

Well, that settled it. I would have to return home at the first available opportunity.

"I should probably get back," I sighed eventually, stacking the empty bowls to return them to the palace kitchens on my way past. Undoubtedly, Andrus would be even more unhappy with me than usual, which would make for a long afternoon.

"Oh," Meera said, immediately reaching for them. "I can take those—"

"Absolutely not. We are going to slowly get you accustomed to the idea of not doing everything yourself."

"You already brought me lunch! That's one thing already."

"Then today will be a challenging day for you," I said, gently patting her arm as I stood, keeping the bowls safely tucked against my side.

This time, she didn't catch her laugh in time, and I memorized the sound as she climbed to her feet. "Oh, how I suffer. I'm really glad I met you, Verner."

"I'm glad I met you too. And I'll see you tomorrow, yes?"

"Are you sure you aren't sick of me?" Her tone said she was teasing, but I suspected there was a little more honesty in the question than she wanted to admit.

"I'll never be sick of you, Meera," I replied solemnly. If anyone was going to tire of this arrangement, it would be her, probably when she met a Shade that she *did* want to pursue a romantic connection with.

We said our goodbyes and went our separate ways, and Euphemia fell into step beside me as I made my way back to the palace. She kept to herself mostly, finding the younger members of the Guard tiresome after decades of service, though she seemed to make an exception for me.

"I never pictured you going for one of those Hunter women," Euphemia said quietly, the disapproval in her voice clear.

That was now two members of the Guard that knew I was spending time with Meera. My gut churned uneasily, wondering how Meera would respond to that. I should have mentioned Andrus's words while I was with her, but I'd put them out of my mind.

"I'm not courting Meera if that's what you're suggesting. But I'm curious to know why you'd think that I wouldn't, if I were fortunate to have the opportunity?" I asked calmly, hoping I didn't let my own disapproval show. I respected Euphemia, but her tone had rubbed me the wrong way.

"You should find a respectable female Shade. Someone your own kind. I saw that one you were speaking to interact with the queen's murderous sister at dinner. You are the company you keep, after all," she muttered.

I had no idea how to respond to that. In truth, I had no desire to say anything that might be construed as defending Astrid Bishop. Like every Shade in the realm, I didn't trust her. Where Meera and the others' presence had been easy enough to reconcile due to their mostly nonviolent pasts, there was no overlooking the dangerous nature of the Hunters where Astrid was concerned.

Her hands were blackened with the shadows of the Shades whose lives she'd taken.

"I'm a friend to Meera, nothing more. Adjusting to life in the shadow realm has been challenging for her, and if I can ease that struggle, why would I not?"

"Why *would* you? Perhaps you should spend some time with my niece. She has already had a child—I'm sure she could comfortably bear another. You need an heir, do you not? Your parents must be getting worried about that."

I certainly wasn't dignifying *that* with an answer. My parents' generation were nightmares for setting their children up with whoever they thought would be useful for procreating purposes like we were cattle to be bred at will.

"My cousin, Osric, is next in line after me. The estate is still set to stay within the family."

"Perhaps I should send my niece to him instead, since he's the more promising prospect."

"Perhaps you should," I agreed coolly, though her words had stung a little. I couldn't even entirely say why—I wasn't in competition with Osric, not really. He couldn't take my position unless I chose to give it up. Perhaps it was just weighing on me more than usual that he would uphold tradition far better than I ever would, even if I felt that most of those traditions weren't worth upholding in the first place.

Not when change was bringing so much good with it. If it came down to choosing between my friendship with Meera, or doing things the way they'd always been done at home...

There was no choosing.

The decision had already been made in my mind.

## CHAPTER 6

"H ow do you want me?" Verner asked, standing next to the bed and patiently waiting for my instruction.

"Naked, to start with. Drop your shadows," I ordered breathily, coming to stand in front of him. Despite the fact that I had to tip my head back to meet his gaze, I felt entirely in control of how this would go.

Wordlessly, Verner let his shadows fall away, though the view I had of his body was still hazy somehow. Dark gray skin and defined muscle, a deep V that led down to a vaguely human-shaped cock. It was sexy, but something niggled at me. It didn't seem quite right.

"Lie on the bed." Verner immediately complied, and my clit throbbed in response. He was so much bigger than me. Stronger in every way that it was possible to be stronger.

And he was willingly, desperately, enthusiastically at my mercy.

The power went straight to my head. And my pussy.

"Slide your hands underneath you."

Verner groaned, but did as I asked, sliding his hands under his back, his *cock sticking proudly in the air, beckoning me home. "I want to touch you, Meera."*

*"Later."*

*His cock twitched, and I took my time climbing up on the bed, kneeling next to his thigh to admire him. Why couldn't I see him better? Maybe I needed glasses.*

*"Are you going to let me ride this?" I asked, in a sultry, confident voice I didn't recognize, lightly dragging my fingertips over his thick, hard cock.*

*"I'm going to let you do whatever you want with it. It's yours."*

*"Good answer," I murmured, wrapping my fingers around the base of his shaft and giving it a hard squeeze. Verner bucked into my hand instantly, and I tutted disapprovingly. "Stay still. You'll take what I give you until I tell you otherwise. Understood?"*

I woke up with gasp so violently loud, I was sure that Tallulah could hear it next door through the stone wall.

What *was* that?

That dream had been... I shivered slightly, rolling to my side and pressing my legs together, the movement highlighting how wet my panties were.

Oh my god, I'd had a sex dream about Verner. Not even one that I could plausibly dismiss in my own head as a well-it-could-have-been-anyone dream. It was very explicitly Verner, and I'd very explicitly been bossing him around while he willingly followed orders.

How was I ever going to look him in the eye again?!

He was so attentive too, it wasn't like he wouldn't notice. He'd be all "Meera, what's wrong?" and I couldn't exactly say, "Oh, just remembering how I played with your dick like it was my own personal sex toy in my dreams last night."

Shit. *Shit, shit, shit.*

Should I avoid him? No, I couldn't do that. I didn't think I'd be able to stay away from Verner if I tried, for one. But he also had a sensitive spirit, and I didn't want to hurt his feelings by avoiding him—he hadn't done anything wrong.

It was just a dream. There was no need to get weird about it. My subconscious had probably put Verner in the starring role because I was cursed with an attraction to penises, and he was the only penis-possessor that I'd trusted in… well, since I'd lost trust in everyone.

But that didn't mean it had to make things awkward between us. In fact, I was determined that it wouldn't. Verner's friendship meant everything to me—he was kind, patient, understanding, and seemed to genuinely enjoy my company, though I couldn't imagine why.

Honestly, was it any wonder I'd had a dirty dream about him? Verner was perfect. If I could… no, it didn't bear thinking about. I was in no condition to be anyone's partner.

"Meera?" Tallulah called, tapping softly on the door, making me startle. "Are you awake? I was going to head over for breakfast soon if you wanted to come?"

"Give me five minutes?" I asked, scrambling out of bed and yanking on my robe so I could head down to the baths below the house to wash up.

I was so wet that I spared a few seconds to check between my legs, worried I'd gotten my period over night. Nope. Just hyperaroused.

Cool. Great. Wonderful.

"Of course," Tallulah replied, her voice fading away. "I'll meet you downstairs in a bit."

"It's just a normal day," I muttered to myself sternly, grabbing some clothes to chuck on once I was clean and didn't reek of horny dreams. "You're going to have a normal day and do normal things and act so convincingly like a normal person that everyone is going to believe you."

"So," Verner began, laying on his back with his hands tucked behind his head, staring up at the sky. "Do you want to talk about it?"

I nearly dropped the awkwardly long loppers I was using to hack away at a vine. "Talk about what?"

"Something is bothering you today, Meera," he replied patiently, still staring up at the sky. The food he'd brought us for lunch was sitting in bowls next to him, but he'd insisted he'd wait until I was done mutilating this garden bed rather than eat without me.

"How do you know that? Is it a scent thing?"

It couldn't be an arousal thing. I'd been very intentionally *not* thinking about that dream. And I'd chosen the most obnoxiously difficult garden bed to clear today that was still near enough to the border for Verner to hang out with me.

He hummed thoughtfully. "I only catch vague hints of your scent out in the open like this, surrounded by perfumed flowers. It's the sort of... stomping that gives it away. And the more aggressive breathing. You usually breathe so calmly."

I struggled not to laugh at that. Here I was thinking I'd been playing it cool when I was actually stomping around, heavy breathing all over the place.

Perhaps I wasn't as smooth as I thought I was. Or perhaps Verner was just more attentive than I was accustomed to—definitely no one in my human-realm life ever noticed what mood I was in.

"Why don't you lie down for a bit?" Verner suggested. "It's a very pleasant day for sky watching."

My arms and shoulders were burning slightly from holding up the loppers, which definitely made the idea of staring up at the shadow realm's dark gray sky more tempting. But lying down next to Verner was potentially inadvisable, considering the incredibly inappropriate things I'd done to him in my sleep.

He'd been lying down then, too.

*Stop it, Meera.*

*You're an adult. You can handle this. It doesn't have to be weird.*

I set the loppers down on the low wall of the garden bed and crossed the invisible line to lie down next to Verner on the warm flagstones.

It *was* a pleasant day for sky watching, I thought, observing the swirling motion happening overhead. Not that I had any frame of reference—I couldn't remember the last time I'd just laid back and watched the world go by. Probably not since I was a kid, and even then, memories of relaxing were few and far between.

Verner turned his head, pinning me with the full force of that golden-yellow gaze. Although his expressions didn't give away what he was feeling as clearly as my breathing patterns apparently did, there was still something in it that had me wondering what was going through his head.

"What?"

"I didn't expect you to lie next to me." He watched me for a long moment. "I'm glad you did."

I felt my face heat up as I struggled to come up with a justification he hadn't asked for. It was odd for me to lie down right next to him when there were so many other spots available. Usually, I kept a little more distance between us. Though, whenever we sat by the river, we always leaned against the same tree.

Sometimes our arms even touched.

"I get a little weird about physical closeness," I said eventually. "Not just with you—with everyone. It takes me awhile to warm up to people. Tallulah definitely picked up on it, but I'm not sure Verity noticed. She's a very touchy-feely person. It's more affection than I'm accustomed to, but it's also been kind of nice. She hasn't really given me a chance to overthink it."

"I hope you never feel any pressure with me, Meera. I noticed that you prefer having your own space and I'm very conscious of not encroaching on it, but you're always welcome in mine."

*Deep breaths, deep breaths.* He's just saying it's okay if I want to sit next to him. He's not saying...

*"How do you want me?"*

I wasn't even going to go there.

"Have I upset you?" Verner asked, turning to face me, his nose twitching slightly.

Oh good, my body had opted for panic smells instead of horny ones. That was easier to explain.

"No, not at all. I just didn't realize my hang-ups were so obvious, that's all."

Verner frowned. "Not at all. You're exceedingly mysterious, according to most Shades I've spoken with. If not a little... well, somber."

I snorted, having heard the things Shades said about me. Our hearing wasn't as acute as theirs, but a few of them definitely didn't realize that we could still pick up whispering.

"I don't think *somber* is the word most of them use," I said wryly. They called me things like *glum*, and *sad*, and *dull*. In my human life, I'd have probably appreciated being talked about in those terms—it meant I wasn't drawing attention to myself, and that was exactly what I wanted.

And I didn't *really* want attention here either, yet the descriptors still stung. Maybe I just wanted to be different from the Meera I'd always been in the past, and I was squandering the opportunity.

"Courtiers can be very tactless." Verner's voice was sharper than it had ever been, the disapproval in it clear.

"A little. But they're not necessarily wrong. I haven't given them much to work with—I'm more charming around you than I am around anyone else," I teased, though I wasn't really teasing. Even around the other ex-Hunters, I wasn't quite as open and chatty as I was with Verner.

"Why is that do you think?" he asked, sounding so genuinely curious that I couldn't deflect.

I hummed thoughtfully, wondering how much to say. I'd already told him more than I'd told anyone, but Verner had an aura of calmness about him that I seemed to draw on instinctively. That made the idea of telling him more and more and more about myself, even the parts I usually tried to hide away, to be not a wholly unappealing prospect.

If I wasn't fundamentally broken and incapable of having a relationship, Verner would have been my first choice. My only choice.

But I liked him too much to inflict myself on him.

"I love the other ex-Hunters, you know. All of them. They're so kind, and they understand me to a certain extent, but... well, only to a certain extent." I flailed slightly, trying to think of a way to convey what I meant in terms that would make sense to Verner. "The others... it's not like they grew up in the equivalent of palace life or anything, but they were definitely from a different kind of Hunter family than I'm from. The only one who can really relate on that front is Verity."

We were both from working-class immigrant families, though she'd lost both her parents young while I'd only lost one. We processed our experiences very differently, though.

Verity took nothing seriously, which meant nothing ever mattered enough to hurt her. I took everything *too* seriously, and held it all at arm's length so it never had a chance to.

"I understand that concept," Verner said slowly. "As you may have noticed, the shadow realm is far from perfect in that respect. I regularly see it with our lieutenant, Selene. She doesn't have the highborn background the Shades in her position traditionally require. She didn't grow up the way most of us grew up."

"Right—it's similar to that. We've all been banished for various reasons, but some of those banishments were crueller than others."

"Do you want to talk about it?"

"It's not a very cheerful story."

His shadows flickered, though I wasn't entirely sure what the movement meant. "Yes, I gathered that."

The dryness of his tone had me suppressing another rogue smile. What would it be like to have that gift? To just bring people joy with your presence? Even as a kid, I'd been "quiet" and "serious" and "wise beyond my years." I'd never made people laugh.

"My father died right after my sister was born. I was five. He had a heart attack—one day, he was there, the next, he was gone. My father's family blamed my mother—I don't remember any of this, but she always told us how awful they were. Her brother was living in the US with his family and insisted we move over from Jaipur and join them."

"And you did?"

I nodded, though he wasn't looking at me. "He helped with money and stuff. We lived with him for a while, until my mom finished her training and was working as a dental assistant, though she was always having to give money to her brother to pay him back for helping us get over there. At that point, I was seven years old and fully responsible for my younger sister, Latika."

"That's very young," Verner murmured.

"It was. Too young. I potty trained Latika. Taught her to ride a bike. To tie her shoes. Made her dinner every night. Helped her with her homework. It was a lot."

We were both quiet for a long moment. I suspected that Verner hadn't understood half of what I'd said, but he was politely listening anyway.

"We were inducted into the local Hunters group when we moved," I said guiltily. "They helped with our visas and stuff. They taught us English, taught us how to act, and what clothes to wear. My uncle was already a member, of course. Obviously, I feel a lot of guilt about that part of my life now, but as a kid, that was my main support network. I just wanted to fit in with the kids in my class, I listened to everything they told me without question."

"Of course," Verner agreed readily. "No child is responsible for participating in that organization—that was a choice made for them. Leaving, though, breaking away from all you've known, that is the difficult part. That is what takes bravery."

I grimaced at the sky. "I wish I could tell you that I was brave, but I was kicked out. It was life-ruining at the time—I was shunned by everyone I knew, kicked out of my home, and cut off from my sister. Now, I look at it as a blessing, for the most part. Leaving would have always been the right choice, but would I have been brave enough to make it if it hadn't been decided for me? I'm not so sure."

Verner hummed. "I suspect you're much braver than you're giving yourself credit for. You found a way to survive when the Hunters turned their back on you. And you came here—that was no small feat."

That was true. Those first twelve months after leaving were a blur in my memory—I'd been operating purely in survival mode. That I'd built a life for myself—though it hadn't been a very glamorous one—was my greatest accomplishment.

"There was a man. A Hunter," I began slowly, scarcely believing that I was saying the words out loud. I'd never said them to anyone before. If I had my way, I'd never have to speak them out loud again, but I was willing to move out of my comfort zone for Verner. "He was old enough to be my father. That's how I saw him—a mentor of sorts, an adult that I could talk to. He wasn't on the Council, but he was close to it. He was an authority figure. My mom was always tired from work, and my uncle didn't like to be bothered. We weren't good for my uncle's reputation, I think."

Verner was as still as a statue next to me. I had the odd notion of wanting to move closer, to press our arms together, but I quickly dismissed it.

"The man... The Hunter man"—I couldn't bring myself to say his name—"insisted that I not tell anyone about our friendship. In hindsight, I can obviously see how suspicious that sounds, but I was seventeen." I smiled wryly at my own stupidity. "I think the lie I told myself was that it would upset his kids. That they might feel jealous that their dad cared about me too. We were in the same training group."

"What happened, Meera?"

It was faint, but I picked up the barest hint of a shake in Verner's voice. His shadows rippled again, the movement far sharper and less fluid than usual.

"Are you angry?"

"Not at you," he gritted out. I nodded, though I wasn't sure if he saw it.

"I started dating a guy. A Hunter my own age. I'd never had a boyfriend before. The man... well, he didn't like it. For weeks, he tried to convince me to end it. I thought he was just looking out for me. An overprotective dad, or whatever."

I'd been feeling mostly neutral until that point, retelling events almost as though they'd happened to someone else. But the embarrassment started to creep in now.

"What is that emotion?" Verner asked, inhaling deeply. That wasn't helping matters.

"Shame."

He made a sound of displeasure. "You should never feel shame, Meera. You didn't do anything wrong."

There was an odd, fizzing sensation in my stomach. It wasn't a feeling I recognized. It might have been relief? No one had ever told me it wasn't my fault before. My mother had explicitly said the opposite.

"That's better," Verner sighed, though I didn't know what I'd done. "Though I suspect it's short-lived, based on how this story is going."

"Probably," I agreed, rushing the next part because it was humiliating. "I suppose the crux of the issue is that this man was jealous that I, um, slept with my boyfriend."

Why was that so hard to say out loud? If only I was a little more like Verity. She wouldn't blush the color of beetroot just because she'd alluded to having sex one time.

"The man kept pushing and pushing until I admitted to it—I didn't want to tell him, obviously. He was like my *dad*. When I finally *did* tell him, he flew into a rage. Said I'd had no right. That I'd ruined myself by giving away something that I could never get back." I swallowed thickly. "Something I should have been saving for him."

I'd *never* talked about this. It was the kind of thing I'd intended to bring up in therapy if I ever got a job where my insurance covered it.

"Anyway, he yelled, and then he grabbed my blouse when I tried to leave, tearing it half off me. It was at Council Headquarters, and at that point, one of the staff walked in on us. He immediately lied and said I'd been coming on to him, that I'd been trying to seduce him for months, that I wanted nothing more than to destroy his marriage... I can't remember all the details, but there was a lot. I was reported to the Council for misconduct and kicked out without anyone ever speaking to me directly or asking for my version of events. My mother was mortified and promptly kicked me out of the house. She told everyone she only had one daughter after that if the rumors are accurate. I'm sure they are."

"That is *awful*," Verner said, his low voice shaking with rage. "Please tell me that anyone involved ever faced some kind of justice."

"No. He's still close to the Council, as far as I know. My mother was promoted for disowning me so promptly. My then-boyfriend ended things, afraid of reprisal. He believed me, at least. He gave me his last two hundred dollars to help me get out of town."

"Coward," Verner muttered.

I laughed silently. "Yes, well, we can't all have your integrity, though both of our worlds would be better if we did."

There was far more to the story than that—the financial implications had been far-reaching, and I'd still been paying for my mistakes in a very literal sense right up until I'd come to the shadow realm. But I wasn't sure I had it in me to delve into all of that right now, and I wasn't sure Verner would really get it even if I did. They didn't have social security numbers in the shadow realm.

We were both quiet for a long while, staring up at the sky. I could smell the food that Verner had brought us for lunch, but I doubted I'd be able to eat anything now after that conversation.

"Got any traumatic stories you want to share?" I teased, nudging his arm with my elbow and giving him what I hoped was a bright smile.

He frowned slightly. "Not really, and now I'm a little disappointed about it. I want to be vulnerable with you too."

My heart melted into a puddle. "I'm glad you don't, Verner. Very glad. You're kind and wonderful, and not jaded like me."

"You're not jaded, Meera. You're wary. Cautious. Those instincts probably served you well when you were left to fend for yourself at such a young age."

I nodded, my throat tight. He was probably right about that, but I wasn't sure they were serving me well now. I *wanted* to build real and meaningful connections with people, and I couldn't do that if my initial instinct was always to turn inward and bury every hint of feeling I had in an ironclad cage.

"Thank you for sharing all of that with me, Meera. I imagine it wasn't easy for you to talk about. And, of course, that conversation stays between us."

"Thank you," I rasped. I'd already been debating how to ask him not to tell anyone else what I'd said, and he'd already thought of it.

Truly, if I could pick anyone and give them the kind of love that they deserved, it would be Verner. He was perfect in every single way.

And I had nothing to offer.

# VERNER

## CHAPTER 7

It was a good thing that I was due for a training session that afternoon, because I had a lot of built-up anger to work out and standing at the entrance to the royal wing wasn't going to cut it.

"Verner?" Captain Soren said, doing a double take. Probably because my shadows were exploding out everywhere.

"Captain."

"Is everything alright?"

"Yes. I'm looking forward to training today."

"Apparently so," he murmured. "But only Astrid is free."

I hesitated at that. I didn't want to interact with Astrid, despite repeatedly reminding myself that she was Meera's friend. Or at the very least, she was the reason Meera was here. But I couldn't let go of my own bitterness where Astrid was concerned, not entirely.

And even if I could, I had no desire to spar with anyone who wasn't a Shade. For all I disliked about Astrid, she was physically much smaller and weaker than I was, and she had been even before one of her hands had been rendered all but useless.

"Scared, big guy?" Astrid asked sarcastically, twirling the baton the captain must have formed for her between her fingers. "I'll go easy on you."

"Don't antagonize him," Captain Soren grumbled. "Batons only—no contact. Deal?"

"Sure, Cap."

I waited for the captain to reprimand her, but he merely huffed in annoyance and took a step back, giving us space to get into position.

It seemed a little absurd to even consider, but was he... interested in her? Why would he let her speak to him that way?

I mostly stayed on the defensive, uncomfortable with the idea of even trying to land a hit on Astrid. I'd been all fired up when I came to the training ground, but interacting with her had thrown me off-balance enough that my ire had cooled.

"It's no fun when you don't fight back," Astrid said flatly, moving with impressive speed and grace for a human.

"I don't want to fight you."

"You sure about that? Everyone wants to fight me."

She was like a wounded animal, I realized. Lashing out to protect herself. It didn't erase what she'd done or how I felt about it, but I immediately understood her better.

"Did you train like this with the Hunters?"

Astrid stopped, her hands dropping to her sides and she took a step back, staring at me with that unsettlingly probing stare. The captain was distracted with another sparring set, though she didn't look to him for backup.

"Why do you ask?"

"Shades can't join the Guard until they reach their age of majority. As I understand it, Hunters are inducted as children. I wondered how rigorous the training regime was—surely, they can't expect that much of you when you're young?"

The question had come out unbidden, and I was surprised that Astrid appeared to be giving it consideration. Meera's childhood was hardly the only thing I was reflecting on after that conversation, but it was one of them. What kind of organization were the Hunters, really? How did they form her core support network as a child, yet seemingly provide her with no support at all?

"We don't start knife throwing until around age twelve," Astrid said with a small shrug. "Prior to that, it's a lot of running drills. Obstacle courses. Being left outside in the dark a lot to get us used to it."

"That's... horrifying."

She shrugged again, a little less confidently. "I mean, yeah. It's shit. On the plus side—sort of—there's a hierarchy even among the youth. Less based on who your family is, like it is for the adults, and more based on skill. The more promise you show, the more training you do."

"How is that a plus side?"

"It means that the *less* promise you show, the *less* training you do. I spent far more time in training than Ophelia did when we were kids because even then, it was clear she wasn't cut out for it."

That was unexpectedly nurturing of her, considering the kinds of things she had done. Then again, the whole reason Astrid had left the Hunters in the first place and thoroughly torched her future with them was for her sister, so maybe I shouldn't have been surprised.

If only I hadn't lost *my* sister at the hands of a Hunter just as deadly as Astrid. It made it difficult to reconcile the different sides of the person in front of me. Bitterness wasn't a feeling I was accustomed to experiencing, I liked to think I was above it. Clearly not.

"Are you wondering what kind of regime Meera would have been subjected to?"

I startled, staring blankly at Astrid.

"Meera hasn't said anything, I've just noticed you hanging around her a lot," Astrid added.

"I've never noticed you in the gardens."

"I'm told that I can move quietly for a Hunter."

Yes, that much was certainly true. "I suppose I am wondering about Meera's childhood, yes. But it would be intrusive of me to ask you about her."

"I can't tell you much anyway. We didn't know each other as kids. But I can tell you that of all of us, Meera is second only to me on the daggers, so she was probably a busy kid too."

I'd suspected as much, in all honesty. That was probably how that *man* had gotten access to her in the first place.

"Does it bother you to know she's good with knives?" Astrid asked, shooting the captain an irritated look as the baton vanished into smoke in her hand. Apparently, he'd decided that our training session was over.

"No. I'm glad to hear it."

Astrid looked at me strangely. "I guess I see why she enjoys spending time with you then."

And with those confusing parting words, she was gone.

I'd forgotten how oppressive the heat at Sunlis was. It descended over me like a heavy blanket, immediately sapping my energy. Had I really spent my whole childhood here? It felt like a different life.

The market was loud and busy, and the smell of various meats prepared in a multitude of ways permeated the entire square. From almost the moment I arrived, I felt the attention of all the Shades present on me. This was a local market, and my family was well-known here—equal only to Levana's family, though her father was a recluse and mine made a point of being involved in the community.

I hoped Meera really enjoyed the ojurac, because the number of stares I was receiving in order to get it was stifling.

"Cousin," Osric said, walking directly through the middle of a small group of Shades, a skewer of meat in his hand. "How unusual to see you in the region."

I hummed in agreement, staring Osric down until he inclined his head in respect.

"You are well, I see. Spending a relaxing day at the market. How lovely." I gestured vaguely at him, and his shadows rippled in annoyance. It was hardly *my* fault that he was lazy and unambitious.

"What can our small, humble market have to offer you? Surely, you're used to the luxuries of court life by now," he said loudly, drawing attention to our conversation.

"The finest ojurac in the realm, of course," I replied, projecting my voice so that our audience would hear it. "One of the ex-Hunters pronounced it to be her favorite food in the shadow realm."

"They eat ojurac?" someone whispered. "Did you know that?"

"I though they would only eat their own foods."

"It's probably some kind of trick," another said. "But what can we do?

They're the only reason the stores aren't completely empty."

Interesting. I didn't know what reactions I'd expected the general population to have, but I supposed it made sense that they were suspicious since they never spent any time with the ex-Hunters. No one could be suspicious of Meera if they had an opportunity to speak to her—she was quiet and reserved, but also kind and honest. Anyone would be able to see that.

"I have plenty of ojurac here, Master Verner!" one of the stall owners called out. "Freshly made this morning."

"Perfect—I will take the lot."

"Ever the beloved son," Osric said coolly, his shadows flickering. "At least out here, among the community."

But not at home.

I smiled at him. "Indeed. Thus far, their affections have proven to be much less fickle than the ones you're courting. I wish you all the very best with that."

With a slightly harder than necessary clap on the shoulder, I left him standing there with his meat skewer while I went and got as much cake as I could carry for Meera. Let Osric play his games here. I wanted no part of them.

#  MEERA

## CHAPTER 8

"Just let me carry it," Verner all but pleaded, sitting on the other side of the border, looking helpless. "You've done it all yourself so far, Meera. Let me do this one thing."

I looked around at the rows upon rows of empty garden beds that I'd cleared over the past few weeks, and felt proud of myself in a way that I never had before. Of course, I'd accomplished things in my human-realm life—like my doula training, and the first baby I'd helped bring into the world, and so on—but this was a slightly different feeling.

This had cost me blood, sweat, and tears and now it was done. Nothing was growing yet, but I'd gotten everything ready with my own two hands and some serious determination.

And Verner, secretly sneaking in whenever I wasn't looking to pull out the bigger, heavier plants and making them magically disappear.

If Astrid still lived here, he'd have never gotten away with it, but she was long gone now.

"I've got this," I insisted, dragging the heavy shrub thing by its roots along the path. Whatever I left just outside the border always magically disappeared too—I wasn't sure whether that was Verner's doing or if the palace had assigned some helpful Shades to dispose of it for us.

"I'll just dart across and do it. No one is around."

I shot Verner a scandalized look. "And here I was, thinking you were an upstanding citizen."

"I am," he replied, pained. "But watching you struggle is an acute kind of torture, Meera. Just leave it there—perhaps it will grow lighter overnight and you can move it tomorrow."

I snorted. "It won't be here if I leave it overnight. Anything even moderately heavy that I might have to lift seems to vanish into thin air as soon as night falls."

He looked me dead in the eye, bold as brass. "Well, that's very convenient, isn't it? Thank the gods for that."

I tossed a stick at him before resuming my huffing and puffing, moving the shrub—maybe it was a small tree?—a few more inches before giving up and heading over to sit with him.

"What does Hunter sweat smell like?" I asked, lying back on the ground. Fortunately, I was already gross and covered with dirt, so what was a little more seasoning at this point?

"You've smelled better," Verner replied diplomatically, lying down next to me, and mock wincing as I nudged his leg with my foot. "Though you've also smelled much, *much* worse. Sweaty and happy is a vast improvement over clean and sad."

I let out a proper cackle laugh at that—the kind that only the true inner circle, which had only ever consisted of my sister in the past—got to hear.

"Noted. I'll bathe less."

"Very considerate of you." Verner turned his head toward me and grinned, showing off a row of sharp fangs. The very first time I'd seen that smile, I'd found it a little alarming. Now it was one of my favorite sights each day. He inhaled deeply, really taking in the reek. "You're very happy today, Meera."

"I am," I agreed, feeling my face heat. "Why wouldn't I be? I'm done clearing the garden beds. I checked in with Selene this morning, and her pregnancy is going well. Verity seems really happy with the duke. And it's my favorite time of day—when we have lunch together."

Verner hummed happily. "It's my favorite time of day too. Though, I've run out of ojurac for you again, I'll make another trip home on my day off."

"You really don't have to, you know," I insisted. "Especially if you don't enjoy the visits."

"It's not that I don't like them... I suppose it's complicated." Verner was quiet for a long moment, the mood shifting in an instant. "There's something I've been wanting to talk about, but there isn't really anyone I can speak about it with. And I didn't want to burden you with my problems when you're already going through so much—"

"Verner," I gasped, outraged. Or perhaps guilty—had I not made him feel safe enough to share things with me? I hadn't meant for our friendship to be so one-sided. "It's not a *burden*. We're friends! You can always talk to me."

He briefly touched my hand, and I felt oddly disappointed when he pulled away again.

"You're right. I think I knew that deep down." Verner sighed heavily, sounding more world-weary than I'd ever heard him sound. "It's a forbidden subject—both at home and in the realm at large, given my father's authority and his ability to dictate how his family is perceived."

I waited silently for him to say more, not having the first clue about where he was going with this.

"I had a sister."

"Ah," I breathed, unease settling heavily in my gut. For the most part, Shades were pretty hardy. They didn't perish of disease or in accidents the way humans did—so long as they had access to power, they could heal from most anything.

But they could be killed by a silver blade, and they were especially susceptible to that when they were in their vulnerable human-realm forms. If a Shade died young, that was usually the reason why.

"She was killed on a trip to the human realm to feed." I nodded, wanting to reach for Verner's hand but unsure if he'd welcome it. "We weren't close. She was twenty years older than me. The true firstborn. The true heir to Sunlis. In truth, she wasn't the most pleasant company. Aside from our difference in age, we just never particularly liked each other."

He grimaced, shooting me a wary look as though worried I'd judge him for saying those words out loud.

"I think that's a perfectly natural way to feel, Verner. Grief complicates things and sometimes it's hard to reconcile those conflicting emotions."

"Did you ever have that with your father?" he asked, catching me off guard.

"Well... yes," I admitted. "I think I've probably idealized him a lot in my head since he died, especially since Mom was so absent. But if I'm honest with myself, I doubted he'd have been any more sympathetic than she was when I got kicked out of the Hunters. They were both very image conscious."

"You understand then," Verner said with a wistful sigh. "It was already complicated, but then my father wiped her entirely from the records, and claims that I am his firstborn. That it's always been this way. My parents act like she never existed."

"*Why?*" I asked, failing to hide the horror in my voice.

"At the time, he claimed he was humiliated by how she'd died. Ashamed that a Hunter had been the one to do it. Perhaps it was just a cover-up for his own grief."

I understood that a little. Mom hadn't gone *quite* that far, but there had never been any pictures of Dad in the house either. The few occasions she'd brought him up seemed more like a slip of the tongue, and she'd always gotten immediately snippy afterward.

"Regardless of his reasons, it makes my already difficult relationship with my parents even more strained. And I know when the staff at Sunlis look at me, they see her. The heir they adored and expected to serve someday."

"Will you tell me her name?" I asked softly.

Verner smiled, his golden-yellow eyes warming my face like sunshine. "Elisaria. Her name was Elisaria. I haven't spoken it aloud in years. Thank you for letting me talk about this with you, Meera."

"You can always talk to me, Verner. You do so much for me—including plenty of things that I'm sure I don't even see. I want to be there for you too."

"You already are. I'd be quite lost without your company, you know. I feel a sense of... *peace* around you that I'm not accustomed to feeling."

There was a little flutter of warmth in my chest at his words, followed by a wave of abject terror at what that little flutter might mean.

Because what if I *liked* him?

The dream still haunted me. And I craved Verner's company like I'd never craved the company of anyone else. I felt comfortable physically touching him. He made me laugh, he listened when I confided in him, and he was opening up to me in return.

Where was the line between friendship and something more? I didn't have enough experience of either to know.

On top of that, there was nothing more viscerally upsetting to me than the concept of catching feelings for a guy—man or monster. Verner was incredible, but I still didn't trust my own judgment.

Verner's nose twitched. "I'm sorry, was that too much?"

I cursed internally at my stupid scent giving any hint of negative emotion away.

"No, not at all. I feel super at peace around you too. " He didn't seem convinced by that, and I hurried to explain myself. "Sorry, I'm just overthinking things I guess. I'm not used to having friends."

"What part are you overthinking exactly?"

Damn it, I hadn't really expected him to ask a follow-up question. But I should have, shouldn't I? Verner paid attention. He listened, like every word out of my mouth was valuable and worth hearing.

There was a sort of gooey, affectionate feeling in my chest and I scrunched my eyes shut, bracing myself for scent impact. Why did he have to be so wonderful? So comforting and safe and easy to be around? It made me... want things.

Things I hadn't let myself want for nearly a decade.

"Meera," Verner rasped, inhaling deeply. The movement brought his face closer to mine, so close that he could probably feel my breath on his jaw. "What is going through that beautiful mind of yours?"

I was a goner.

The one time I should have been overthinking it, I didn't. I leaned, half rolling so that the entire front of my body brushed against the side of Verner's, and touched his lips softly with my own.

It was immediately clear that it was nothing like kissing a human, even though it had been eight years since I'd done that. Verner's lips were hard and inflexible—or maybe he just didn't know how to use them?

Was he kissing me back?

Oh my god.

He wasn't.

I'd totally misread this situation.

"I'm so sorry," I gasped, scrambling upright so fast that I scraped my hands in the process. "I'm so sorry, Verner."

"Meera, wait—" he began, climbing to his feet and reaching for me, but I was already gone, sprinting through the empty garden beds back toward the safety and privacy of Elverston House where I could wallow in my humiliation in peace.

What had I been thinking? Why had I done that?

*Way to go, Meera. You've ruined everything.*

# VERNER

## CHAPTER 9

I knew before I even left the palace the next day that Meera wouldn't be waiting for me at lunchtime. It was my day off at least, so I didn't have to hear Andrus's complaints as I stopped by the kitchen to pick up food for Meera and made my way toward Elverston House.

The garden was empty, of course. I'd come back at night and disposed of the heavy shrub Meera had been wrestling with, and she'd clearly been out at some point to sweep the paths free of dirt, but she wasn't here now.

Tallulah made a quiet sound of surprise as she appeared on the pathway, reeking of sex as she often did, though I only knew that because I was regularly in this part of the grounds. I doubted the other Shades at court had noticed.

"Could you give this to Meera please?" I asked, handing her a bowl. Calix had been trying some new meat-free recipes with ingredients Astrid had sourced from the human realm, and I was eager to ensure Meera could have some.

"Sure," she squeaked, her cheeks blooming an impressive crimson color. "Thank you."

I inclined my head respectfully before heading back in the direction of the palace, hoping the worry I was feeling on the inside wasn't showing on the outside.

How were we going to talk about what had happened yesterday if Meera kept avoiding me? I didn't even *know* what had happened. Everything had been fine. We'd been talking. She was in a good mood. Her scent had been magnificent.

She'd pressed her lips to mine, and I didn't know what it meant or what she was trying to achieve—it was almost certainly some kind of human action that I didn't understand. Perhaps some kind of... gesture of friendship? Though it was a very intimate one if that was the case.

I adored Meera, but I also knew that she hadn't handled that well. There was nothing the two of us couldn't get through if we talked it out—that was one of the things I treasured most about our friendship. If she hadn't run off, we could have discussed it. I could have asked her for an explanation of what the gesture meant, and how I should reciprocate accordingly.

But I couldn't be angry at her, even knowing she'd put our friendship in a difficult position. I knew Meera well enough to know that she was probably panicking right now, and almost certainly blaming herself. I just wanted to be there for her. When she was ready.

Instead of returning to the palace, I made for the portal instead. Perhaps more cake would help? If nothing else, it might help Meera feel certain that I wasn't angry or upset, and she could come to me whenever she felt comfortable talking.

Rather than going straight to the market like last time, I found myself heading in the direction of Sunlis instead, stepping out of the entry room near my family's home and immediately being weighed down by the thick humidity in the air.

No good was going to come of this visit, I already knew that. This was undoubtedly some form of self-flagellation for not reacting better yesterday, even though I didn't know what I was meant to be reacting to.

"Oh," Morcant, the steward, said as I arrived at the doorway. "I didn't realize we were expecting you, Master Verner."

"You weren't. I thought I might visit with my parents awhile."

Morcant fussed unnecessarily, his shadows flickering in irritation. He was clearly struggling to come up with a suitable response, but he was saved by Mother, who rounded the corner at that moment.

"Verner!" Mother said, freezing when she saw me. "Were we expecting you?"

My smile grew tighter at hearing the question again. "No. I thought I would stop by. It's my day off."

"Oh, I see." Mother's shadows flickered restlessly.

"Is that okay?"

"Morcant has only set out tea for your father and me," she fretted. "And if we don't drink it now, it will go cold."

"I'll sit with you while you take your tea. There's no need to make any accommodations for me," I assured her.

"Perhaps you could stand next to us so we don't have to ruin the table arrangement with an additional chair."

Gods forbid.

"Of course, Mother."

She made a sound of discontent, but gestured for me to follow her. This was an even more terrible idea than I'd initially suspected. I should have known that when my parents had encouraged me to spend more time at home, what they actually meant was send a message several days beforehand with the exact timings of my visit. Or just move home, and be here all the time, at their disposal.

"Is Osric not joining you today?" I asked as we walked down one of the curved open walkways to the covered sitting area where they took their midday tea. The thick, lustrous foliage grew along the sides of every walkway, and I always felt like I was outdoors even when I was inside at my parents' place.

Was that a hint of green in the leaves? I wanted to stop and take a closer look, but I suspected that acknowledging that particularly visible sign of change in the realm might push my mother over the edge.

"He has decided to court a very respectable female from Skulen. He is with her today."

"Is he?" I asked dubiously. I'd never seen Osric show a romantic interest in anyone, but perhaps he'd decided he wanted a child. I hoped she was aware of his intentions and felt the same way.

"Yes," Mother sniffed. "Osric takes his responsibilities seriously."

"I wasn't aware he had any."

"Continuing the family line is a responsibility we all share," she snipped, shooting me an impatient look.

This was a new development. Usually, I was only pressured to quit the Guard and move home.

"Verner has decided to join us," Mother announced as we walked down the few steps to the seating area where two chairs had been set up around a small circular table. "He will stand so as not to ruin Morcant's lovely arrangement."

The lovely arrangement in question was a teapot and two cups, but I kept silent. No good would come of pointing that out.

"Have you left the Guard yet?" Father grunted as I stood next to the table, clasping my hands behind my back.

"Not yet."

Father harrumphed as he poured his tea. He set the teapot down, and Mother reached across the table for it to pour her own. They were very unaffectionate with each other, I realized. It was strange to see their relationship through the eyes of an adult. Then again, that they were still together at all was an oddity among Shades, whose relationships tended to be more short-lived. Quietly, I suspected that no one else would tolerate either of them, so they'd wisely stuck together.

"I was just telling Verner about Osric, and the female from Skulen he is courting," Mother said, her tone conversational. "Won't it be nice if a child results from their union?"

I must not have hidden my expression fast enough, given the look Mother gave me.

"It will be nice," Father agreed pointedly. "Finally, a new generation of Shades at Sunlis. As it should be."

Well, that was probably enough suffering for one day.

"I certainly hope he is successful in his endeavors," I said dryly. "I'll be on my way now—I'm sorry for interrupting your tea."

"Just give us warning next time, Verner," Mother huffed. "It really isn't that difficult."

*Neither was bringing out a third chair and cup,* I thought silently, inclining my head respectfully before making my way back to the walkway. Instead of heading for the door, I went to the western wing of the estate, confidently greeting the staff I encountered as though I was meant to be there. My own rooms had been taken over by Osric—the prick—but that wasn't where my feet were taking me anyway.

Instead, I went to my sister's rooms.

They were the second largest in the estate after my parents' suite, and remained untouched to this day. For all of my father's talk about forgetting Elisaria had ever existed, my parents certainly weren't rushing to erase her presence here.

I closed the door behind me and made for the window seat, throwing open the shutters to let light and fresh air in. She'd requested that heavily perfumed flowers be planted right outside her window, and the sudden rush of scent through the open window gave me an unexpected pang in my chest. No, we'd never been close, but she still should have been here. She'd wanted this life. She knew the estate back to front, and seemingly enjoyed the responsibilities that inheriting placed on her.

My parents wanted me to fit into a Elisaria-shaped mold, and I never would. I never wanted to.

The insects buzzed outside, and the breeze through the window made the heat of Sunlis slightly more bearable, so I didn't rush to leave. What was Meera doing right now? I hoped she'd eaten her lunch and enjoyed it. It worried me how few food options she had here since she didn't eat meat.

Would she go out in the garden this afternoon? Perhaps she'd stay inside and write more in that mysterious notebook of hers.

I sighed heavily, tipping my head back against the wood paneling behind me, careful not to catch my horns.

We would work through this eventually. Friends didn't give up on each other, and I would show Meera that I had no intention of giving up on her.

But until then, I had to pull myself together. I had to decide how to proceed with my family, with my future. I couldn't put it off forever.

# MEERA

## CHAPTER 10

I hate it here," Rainy complained, decimating a piece of meat with her claws. "I want to go home."

"Well, you know why you can't," Damen said cheerfully, clapping her shoulder on his way up to the high table. "Try not to look so miserable about it."

While I understood that Theon's sister had to be exiled here for a while—both for her idiotic actions, and to give Verity some time to recover in peace after her chaotic journey to the human realm—I didn't quite understand why she was sitting right next to me at dinner.

Rainy didn't like the ex-Hunters as far as I knew. Then again, she might have some misplaced guilt since Verity had only gotten hurt because of Rainy's dumb impulsiveness. Maybe complaining next to me throughout each meal was her version of extending the olive branch.

"Is your mom here today?" I asked, making one valiant attempt at small talk while Tallulah charmed all the male Shades who were sitting at our table with her polite but distant flirting.

"No. I was mean to her yesterday, and she said she would give me a day to myself to think about my actions."

If Shades could roll their eyes, Rainy would have.

"And did you think about them?"

"Yes. And I think Mother should be more understanding as I'm obviously going through a very difficult time. Everyone is *very* mad at me, and I can't help that it makes me angry."

"Right..." I said slowly, not having the first clue how to respond to that. I definitely wasn't ready for motherhood. Teenagers—Shade, Hunter, or human—were absolutely terrifying.

*Verner would know what to say to her*, I thought suddenly. Immediately, I felt as glum as Rainy looked. I'd seen him multiple times from a distance now, but the idea of approaching him made me freeze up in terror. Why was I like this? I was sure other people didn't have this problem. They probably screwed up and then went and addressed those screwups head on, and everyone moved past them and got on with their lives.

I wanted to be like that. Why couldn't I be like that?

"I wish I'd never gone to the human realm," Rainy sighed, pushing her plate away and slumping down with her forearms resting on the table.

"Why did you?"

She cut me an annoyed look. "Because everyone else got to. Obviously. Why should this stupid Hunter-Shade war get in the way of my generation getting to experience the things that *all* other Shades got to experience? That's so unfair."

Huh. Looking at Rainy, hearing her speak... Suddenly, the idiotic girl I'd been at seventeen seemed a lot more reasonable. Maybe I hadn't been particularly naïve, or particularly desperate, or particularly shortsighted.

Maybe I'd just been a regular teenager. I'd only been able to conceptualize the world as far as I could see it, never thinking beyond that, always confident that I knew best. And ever since, I'd punished myself for it, thinking that anyone else would have known better. I could let a little of that anger at myself go now.

That kid had been doing her best.

The one next to me probably was too. One day, she'd look back on this moment and shake her head at how worried she'd been about having perfect experiences in the middle of a cold war.

"Why doesn't Austin ever eat at the palace?" Rainy asked suddenly, giving me an accusatory look. "He's much more interesting company than you."

Maybe Rainy was a few years off that epiphany, though.

"Meera!" Ophelia said cheerfully, stopping me in the hallway. "Where are you off to?"

"I thought I might visit Iris."

I felt nervous at the idea of dropping in on someone I didn't know unannounced, but I figured Iris had to be more nervous than me. She needed friends, and I was going to do my best to be that person for her.

She'd only arrived from the human realm yesterday, escorted by Soren and Astrid, and accompanied by her guide dog, Tilly. Coming to the shadow realm had been terrifying for me, and I'd been able to physically see what I was walking into. Iris might be the bravest person I'd ever met.

"Oh, good." Ophelia exhaled. "I was actually going to stop by there later myself, but the Elders have convened a meeting that I can't miss. I'm glad she's not going to be sitting by herself all morning."

"I don't have anything on. I can stay with her all day," I assured Ophelia, awkwardly returning the hug she gave me before heading down the corridor to Iris's room.

It was still intimidating to go places by myself, but I was pretty sure that I was getting the hang of it. As always, I'd been panicked over nothing—most of the time, I got a quick "hi" or a wave, and everyone continued on with their day. I dreaded to think how many opportunities I'd missed in life because I was too busy worrying about the hypotheticals to go out there and just *do* it. I'd probably miss a few more too, though.

As much as I wanted to banish those demons, they insisted on hanging around in my head.

"Come in," Iris called when I knocked on the door, sounding far calmer than I would have under the same circumstances.

"Hi," I said awkwardly, letting myself in and closing the door behind me. "I'm Meera. We met yesterday."

"I remember. Please come sit. I'm still figuring out where everything is," she added with a laugh. She'd taken a seat by the double doors that led out into a private courtyard—a room Prince Damen had chosen for Tilly's benefit. I pulled over one of the dining seats so I could sit by her without shouting across the room.

It was a very nice room. Much nicer than the rooms at Elverston House. We'd all been given the opportunity to move into the palace, but I wasn't ready to give up the space and privacy of the crumbling old manor just yet.

"How was your first night?" I asked, doing a double take when I realized that Iris didn't look quite the same as she did yesterday. When she'd arrived, I'd thought she had light brown hair, but I was guessing that was temporary dye, since patches of pale blonde were catching in the light.

"Strange," Iris admitted. "I didn't sleep much. Honestly, I might have been dozing when you knocked on the door."

"Oh, I'm sorry—"

"Please, don't be! I'm very glad you came, and I can nap later. I spent almost every night of my life in the house I grew up in. It just feels odd to be somewhere else."

"Do you have everything you need? Is Tilly okay?" I asked. The dog in question opened one eye lazily before resuming her snooze on the floor. I wasn't entirely sure how guide dogs worked, but it seemed that she was off duty right now.

"Oh, yes." She shot me a guilty smile. "I feel bad not cleaning up after Tilly, but Prince Damen assured me it would all be taken care of. And they brought a tray of food right to my room for me this morning—how kind."

"There are definite perks to living in a palace," I said with a quiet laugh. "If you ever want to come and eat dinner in the dining hall with the rest of us, I could come and get you?"

"Oh, would you? I would love that. Gosh, everyone has been so very kind and welcoming."

My protective instincts were in overdrive where Iris was concerned, and I'd only just met her. She was just so... *sweet*.

"Do you like living here, Meera? My parents told me the most terrible things about Shades and I don't think they're true at all."

"Everyone has been amazing," I assured her, swallowing past the lump in my throat that arose every time I thought of Verner. If I could do half as good a job of making Iris feel welcome here as he'd done for me, I'd be doing pretty well. "The human realm was a pretty tough place for me. Life here has been a lot easier. The Shades have been really accommodating, and all the other ex-Hunters are wonderful."

Iris nodded thoughtfully. "It can't all have been smooth sailing, though. Adapting to a new culture must have its challenges. I don't want to do something wrong and offend everyone."

She was so thoughtful. Definitely more thoughtful than I'd been when I'd arrived.

"I don't think you need to worry about that," I said slowly, wondering if I just hadn't found that part intimidating because I'd already done the big cultural adaption before when I'd moved from India to the US. "Especially not here at the palace. The Shades who live here come from all over the realm. It's a melting pot, I guess."

Iris hummed. "Okay. But will you help me at dinner to make sure I don't make any faux pas? My nana was very strict on manners. I want to live up to her expectations of me."

"Sure, yeah. I can help with that." I looked around her room. "Do you need help to unpack?"

"I didn't really bring anything," Iris admitted. "Just food for Tilly."

"Well, we need to get you set up then," I said, standing up and surveying the space, grateful that I had a concrete task I could help with. Keeping busy kept my mind off my own failures, and if I could channel that need to keep busy into something helpful, so much the better. "Let's start with clothes—you look to be about the same size as Verity, and she's somehow accumulated so many clothes that she left a bunch behind when she moved out. We can start there until Astrid has a chance to get you some of your own." I grimaced. "I don't know how comfortable they'll be. I don't think Verity has dressed for comfort in her life."

Iris laughed, clasping her hands together. "Oh, what an adventure this is already! I'm so glad I came here."

# MEERA

## CHAPTER 11

I exhaled heavily as I sat down opposite Tallulah in my new bedroom in the palace. The past few days—weeks, even—had moved at a relentless pace. After the loneliness of just Tallulah and I in Elverston House, suddenly the realm seemed to be filled with fresh faces from the human realm.

I'd wanted to keep busy, but I definitely wouldn't mind if things slowed down a little now so I could wrap my head around all the changes.

"So," I began. "What should I do about the garden?"

Ten new Hunters had arrived from the human realm—none of whom were particularly happy or healthy—and we'd all agreed that they should get Elverston House to themselves to acclimate to life here. Moving out had also been for my own protection though, since the last new additions to Elverston House had harbored a traitor in their midst.

But my *garden* was at Elverston House, and it was actually starting to produce some food now. I couldn't just abandon it and start over. Both for practical reasons, and because it felt like the garden was all I had left. I'd put everything I had into it, and I didn't want to let it fall by the wayside now.

Tallulah frowned. "I think you should just go and talk to the new residents, let them know that you won't go in the house but you still need access to the garden. Everyone needs to eat, Meera. I'm sure they'll be reasonable about it. Do you want me to come with you?"

It was tempting, but I shook my head. Tallulah was busy enough as it was—she was taking over the negotiations with the Hunters Council, working alongside a small delegation to come to a new and fair agreement.

All I had to do each day was grow my little vegetables. And I was spending time with Iris, wanting her to get accustomed to life here too, but that was definitely more for my benefit than hers. Without Verner for company, I was maybe lonelier now than I had been in all my time in the human realm.

"Is everything okay?" Tallulah asked softly.

"Of course." I swallowed past the sudden tightness in my throat. Tallulah looked more content than I'd ever seen her. She was in love, and perfectly secure in that love.

And I was...

Jealous.

Yes, I was pretty sure that's what that emotion was.

I could never have what Tallulah had. But I wanted it.

Or *did* I want it? Did I just want what everyone else had? I didn't even know how to make sense of my own thoughts anymore.

"Okay..." Tallulah said slowly. "You've been kind of tense recently—I was wondering if you were struggling with living in the palace now? It's a lot more crowded."

I exhaled slightly in relief. "Yes, it is. Um, it's fine. I'll get used to it. Or maybe I can move back to Elverston House later once the new Hunters are more settled?"

Tallulah pursed her lips. "Well, yes. But if the negotiations go well, then there might be even more new Hunters coming through eventually, right? We need to come up with a solution that's sustainable for you."

"For me?" I repeated, surprised. "You don't have to worry about me, Tallulah."

"We all worry about you," she replied with a wry smile. "We've never really talked about what happened in the human realm," she added uncomfortably.

It was very clear to me that Tallulah didn't *want* to talk about it, either. That had been a terrifying moment for her, and she was only trying to revisit it now because she thought I needed to.

"We don't have to," I said firmly. "You really don't need to worry about me, Tallulah. I'm fine. I'm doing great."

She hummed, not looking particularly convinced. "Are you sure you don't want me to come and talk to the new ex-Hunters with you? Honestly, I'd usually just invite myself along and put my best HR face on, but I kind of get the feeling that they don't like me."

"I don't think that's true," I assured her. Though, I did wonder if they perhaps didn't *trust* her. It was Tallulah's psycho grandfather who had sent them over here as sacrificial lambs in the first place. I imagined that they might feel a little less confident around her and Austin than me, for example.

"I'm still worried. I'm just going to keep being worried, you've offered me no reassurance whatsoever. Do you want to come and have lunch with me and Evrin?" Tallulah asked, yawning as she stood.

"No, I'll go down to Elverston House. And you need a nap," I said firmly. "Make sure you're not doing too much, okay? Growing a baby is hard work."

Frankly, we had no idea what kind of work went into growing a human-Shade baby, or even how long gestation would take. At least Tallulah had a wonderful mate, who'd do anything for her and the baby. If he'd seen her yawn, he'd have probably carried her out of here already.

"Okay, okay. We're going to come back for dinner tonight—Ophelia wanted to chat about some things, so I said I'd be there. You can tell me about how it goes at Elverston House then?"

I nodded, letting us both out of the room. "I'll keep you updated."

My new bedroom was on the ground floor, right next to Iris's. It was nice that I could visit her easily, but the moment we were in the corridor, we were bumping into courtiers and palace staff going about their day. I hadn't appreciated the peacefulness of Elverston House enough when I'd had it.

We parted ways outside the dining hall, and I headed outside, taking a moment to myself once I was free from the crowd. The manicured gardens outside the palace were bright with splashes of color throughout, and it took my breath away every time I saw it.

We'd done that. Well, maybe not me. I wasn't sure I was contributing much, except radishes—I was contributing plenty of those. But the others had. They'd made their mark on the realm in such a profound way that we could all see it.

"Meera."

I sucked in a breath at the sound of Verner's gentle voice, my fight-or-flight instincts going into overdrive. He smoothly moved around until he was on the steps in front of me, a couple below, putting me at a height advantage over him and giving me plenty of space.

The urge to run dissipated like it had never been there.

"Hi, Verner."

His mouth crooked up into a slightly ironic smile. Admittedly, I probably could have said something a little more enthusiastic than "hi."

"Hi, Meera. Are you well?"

I opened my mouth to reply before closing it again. Oh god, what was that feeling? Was I about to cry? That would be so humiliating.

Verner stepped down another step, his smile sad. "I've upset you."

"No," I said quickly, moving forward. "No, you haven't. I've upset me."

"Were you walking to Elverston House?" he asked after a long pause. "Perhaps I could escort you there."

"Just like the first time we met?" I replied hesitantly.

His smile grew a little less shaky. "Yes, exactly."

"That would be nice."

We fell into step beside each other, and while the ruined-everything-with-a-kiss awkwardness was still there, it was *so* nice to be in Verner's company again.

"We should probably talk about it, right?" I said eventually.

Verner hummed in agreement. "Unless you'd prefer to keep avoiding me."

"No, I wouldn't prefer that." We hadn't avoided each other entirely—we'd found ourselves in the same place a few times and exchanged words. He'd been there after Verity came back, and there was no one I trusted with my friend more.

But it hadn't been like it was, because I'd destroyed that. Not with the kiss—though that had been a terrible idea—but by running away. I'd fallen back on terrible habits, and avoided the things that scared me. In this case, it was simply owning up to my own idiotic mistakes.

"I'm sorry—about everything. That whole afternoon..." I shuddered. "I wish I could take it all back. I wish we could go back to how things were. I've missed you like crazy, and I just feel so *stupid* about the whole thing—"

"Don't, Meera. Please." He lightly rested his hand on my forearm, pausing for a moment to see if I'd pull away. "I've missed you too. We can forget all about it and go back to how things were. Of course we can."

"Is that what you want?" I asked, looking up at him, relief and disappointment warring for dominance in my head.

"I want our midday meals together back," Verner said firmly.

I nodded, my throat tight. "Me too."

"I'm going to hug you now," he warned, gently pulling me in, giving me time to move away. "I know you're not fond of physical affection—"

"It's okay when it's you."

I wrapped my arms around his back, startling at the faint tickling feeling of his shadows moving against my skin and trying not to contemplate whether they were actually acting as a barrier or whether I was essentially hugging a naked dude.

*Definitely don't think about that.*

"You know I don't actually live here anymore?" I said with a shaky laugh as we pulled away, resuming our slow walk down to Elverston House. "We might have to meet by the river for lunch instead."

"Yes, you're in the palace now. How are you finding it?"

"It's... fine."

Verner laughed, and it was the best sound in the world. "You hate it."

"I don't hate it! I'm glad that I have a place to live, that's for sure. I don't know. I guess it's a little more crowded than I generally like. I'm heading to Elverston House now to ask if they'd mind me still tending to the garden."

Verner frowned. "I certainly hope they wouldn't have a problem with that, considering what a valuable resource it is. One that they benefit from directly."

"I know, I know, but they're skittish." I dropped my voice as we approached the border, both coming to a halt. "I suspect that, like me, these were Hunters who really didn't have an easy time of it. Except, unlike me, they didn't do anything to warrant getting kicked out, so they just lived with the horrible treatment."

"If anyone can get them to feel more at ease here, it's you." Verner's expression softened, and he gave my arm a quick squeeze before stepping back. "I'll meet you by the river tomorrow?"

"Yes please." I smiled, finding myself biting my lower lip and quickly releasing it. I didn't want to look like I was flirting with him now when we'd agreed to go back to the way things had been before.

"Until tomorrow." He inclined his head, which did something incredible to his half smile that I tried to view in a platonic light.

*Friends,* I told myself sternly, heading up the path to Elverston House. *Friends, friends, friends.*

I winced at all the weeds I could see popping up in the garden beds, desperately hoping no one would have a problem with me doing at least a little maintenance. Fortunately, we'd had a rainy couple of days so at least the plants hadn't died of thirst.

Before I could even get to the front door, someone was opening it to let me in.

*Jade,* I recalled from our brief introduction. She couldn't have been older than twenty, yet she seemed to have taken on the role of spokesperson for the group. Which I guessed wasn't surprising—she was a big, firey personality, and many of the other Hunters who'd been sent over with her were... well, definitely not that. I suspected the older ones may have been once upon a time, but they'd had their spirits thoroughly broken over the years.

It was why I had to approach this so carefully. The last thing I wanted was for these people who had already suffered so much to feel any kind of pressure.

"Hi, Meera." Jade tipped her chin up, her arms crossed over her chest. Her words were cordial, but her body language very much wasn't.

"Hello, Jade. How are you this morning? Have you guys had breakfast?"

The new Hunters didn't come to the dining hall for meals yet, and even though food and raw ingredients were delivered to them here, I worried. The kitchen facilities at Elverston House were pretty medieval.

She blinked at me. "Um, yeah. I mean, we all just kind of forage for ourselves throughout the day, then cook together in the evenings."

I made a note to check in with the palace chef that they were being sent forage-type food. Bread. Sandwich fillings. That kind of thing.

"I came here to ask a food-related question actually. I was wondering if you would all be comfortable with me coming here to maintain the garden." I gestured at the beds behind me. "It's all planted with fruit and vegetables from the human realm so we don't have to rely on supply trips for them."

Jade frowned. "I mean, we don't want to starve, so yes. Obviously."

This one could give Astrid a run for her money when it came to being painfully blunt. Probably best if I kept the two of them away from each other. Tallulah wouldn't do well here either—she did her best not to show it, but Astrid's sharp words often rubbed her the wrong way.

"Patrick used to be a gardener," she added begrudgingly, almost as though she realized she'd been a little snippy and was making an effort at politeness. "He mentioned the garden too. Something about helping out. I don't know. I can't remember."

"Perhaps he could speak to me about it?" I suggested gently. Patrick was in his forties and walked with a pronounced limp. He wasn't skittish like the others necessarily—or I didn't *think* he was. I'd never heard him speak. He seemed more gruff than frightened, though.

Jade watched me silently for a moment, unabashedly sizing me up. She was deeply mistrusting and quick to protect herself regardless of the circumstances, and I had the slightly terrifying realization that I was looking into a mirror. Though, it was more a reflection of who I was when I'd first arrived in the shadow realm than who I was now, I liked to think.

"I saw you. Through the window. Hugging that Shade." She tipped her chin up, daring me to argue.

"Yes. That's my friend, Verner."

If my voice wobbled a little on the word 'friend', Jade didn't seem to notice.

"Are you sleeping with him?"

I choked on my own saliva, coughing loudly for a moment. "No. That's a really personal question, you know."

To her credit, she didn't argue with me. "Does he not want to sleep with you?"

"That's an even more personal question."

Jade shrugged. "Just trying to work out if they all want to have sex with us all the time. I don't want to do that."

"You don't have to," I replied sharply. "I haven't slept with anyone since I've moved here and no one has suggested that I should."

"What's the point of you being here then?"

I felt my eye twitch. "I grow the vegetables."

Jade nodded, apparently satisfied by that answer. "I guess that's helpful. I'll make sure the others are fine with you working in the garden. I'm sure it'll be fine. And Patrick will probably want to help you—he's bored and restless."

"He's more than welcome to."

Jade gave me one last lingering look. "The queen keeps visiting us, trying to make friends."

"Ophelia is very friendly."

"Tell her we'd rather you come instead."

And with that, she closed the door in my face.

"Hey," Ophelia said, touching my arm gently to catch my attention in the dining hall after dinner. "We haven't had a wine-and-cheese night in a while—we could round up the others and commandeer a sitting room for a bit if you're free? Tallulah, Verity, and Austin are all here tonight, and that never happens."

"Sure, I'm free."

"Perfect! Do you want to grab Iris and Verity and I'll find the others?"

I agreed, following Ophelia's instructions and leading the other two— with Tilly accompanying Iris, of course—to one of the sitting rooms on the first floor. By the time we arrived, there were bottles of wine and goblets set out for all of us, as well as a spread of cheese, crackers, and cakes along the center of the coffee table. The perks of being queen, I guess—if you wanted to throw a spontaneous party, you could just make it happen.

"Come in, come in," Ophelia said, fluttering around the room like a butterfly, shooing her sister out of the way so Iris could have the seat with room at her legs for Tilly. "Oh my gosh, it's so nice to see you all."

"We didn't invite Cora?" Tallulah asked tentatively as she sat down next to me, adjusting her position a few times to accommodate her swelling belly.

While Cora had opted to stay in the shadow realm after her brother's betrayal, she'd withdrawn from public life here almost completely. She was pretty similar in age to Jade, and I wondered if they'd bonded at all since they were both living in Elverston House.

"I tried," Astrid replied with a shrug. "She didn't want to come."

Ophelia narrowed her eyes at her sister. "How did you ask, though? Was it nice?"

"I'm always nice," Astrid deadpanned, somewhat gently shoving Austin's leg out of the way so she could sit down.

"You're in a cheery mood," he snorted, already a couple of pastries deep.

"I'm cheerier now that you're not manspreading all over the couch."

Ophelia massaged her temples, and I poured her a goblet of wine.

"I imagine Cora is struggling a little," I volunteered, handing Ophelia her drink. "With everything that happened with her brother... Well, that must have been challenging. And the new residents of Elverston House are suspicious as it is, I'm not sure she'd have made any friends there. Cora is also from quite a respectable Hunter family, and they've not had good experiences with those..." I trailed off, realizing everyone was staring.

"You know," Austin began conversationally. "That's the most words I've heard you say in a row ever."

"It's hard to get any in edgewise when you're around," I replied mildly, slightly miffed that he'd called me out.

Austin laughed, unoffended as always. It took a lot to ruffle him.

"I'd like Cora to move into the palace, but I guess there are some security concerns about that," Ophelia mused.

"Very reasonable ones," Astrid added under her breath.

Jade's words from earlier floated into my mind and I cleared my throat awkwardly. "I went to Elverston House earlier to ask if they were okay with me still working in the garden out front."

Astrid narrowed her eyes. "They better be."

"They are," I said hastily, not wanting her to get any ideas and march down there. That would not be good for our tentative truce. "Though, they did request that perhaps I could take over visits for the time being."

I shot Ophelia an apologetic look as her jaw went slack.

"Do they not like me? Everyone likes me!"

Astrid smirked at her sister's outrage, and it might have been the most cheerful I'd ever seen her.

"I'm sure they like you," Tallulah soothed. "Maybe it's the whole royalty thing throwing them off. It might be a little intimidating, that's all."

"Or maybe it's your personality," Astrid suggested. Ophelia threw a balled-up napkin at her, and I suddenly missed my own sister fiercely. Not that our relationship had ever been like that—we'd never been peers the way Astrid and Ophelia were. But it was nice to imagine a life where we were.

"How's all your important negotiating-shit going?" Austin asked Tallulah, taking a break from demolishing all the pastries. "Are you like a foreign dignitary now? Do you get diplomatic immunity?"

She rolled her eyes at him. "It's going good, I think. Though, I do think it would be helpful for you guys to come along—not all the time, but perhaps taking turns accompanying me if you're open to it. I know I'm not thinking of everything, and Sebastian is... well, very Hunter Council-focused in his approach."

I grimaced. Sebastian was the Hunter Council's errand boy, his job was to negotiate on their behalf to formulate a new peace treaty. Verity gagged dramatically at the mention of her ex-boyfriend before taking a sip of her wine. She'd been awfully quiet so far—either she was bored of the somewhat administrative conversations, or she was plotting something. It was difficult to tell where she was concerned.

"I'll come to the next one," I volunteered.

"I'll come to the one after that," Iris added. "I want to be more involved. You guys don't have to hide me away anymore. The Hunters know I'm here, and I'm not going anywhere. No matter what they say."

# VERNER

## CHAPTER 12

I wasn't taking any chances today. I'd gathered a whole selection of meat-free meal options from the kitchen, and a fresh batch of ojurac that I'd gone home yesterday to get. I'd even filled a clay pot with a lid with boiling water, so I could make us fresh tea.

Everything had to be perfect. I'd missed Meera's company dearly, and I wanted it back. Whatever I had to do for things to go back to the way they were, I would do it.

Since Meera had cleared the overgrowth, the river was visible from the upper windows of Elverston House. While I'd laid down a blanket next to one of the large trees so we weren't entirely on display, I was very much aware that there were eyes on me from the house.

It was a little unsettling, in all honesty, but I did my best to ignore it. It was important that the new Hunters grew comfortable around Shades, and I felt the weight of responsibility with each set of eyes on me, wanting to model impeccable behavior for them.

"Hi!" Meera said, slightly out of breath as she flopped onto the blanket next to me. "Did you plan a picnic? Verner, this is so nice."

"It's a special occasion."

"Is it?"

"Yes. We're having lunch together again. That's special to me."

I could have sworn Meera's scent turned to liquid so syrupy sweet that I could taste it. It wasn't desire, of course. I knew what that smelled like—I worked for the queen.

It was something nearly as potent though. Rich and bright and addictive. As I uncapped the jar of hot water, tea seemed like a poor substitute for whatever that emotion was.

"Ooh, ojurac!" Meera said, peeking inside the basket. "Verner, you went all out. Thank you so much."

"Of course," I murmured, watching her. "Help yourself to anything you'd like—Calix has been trialing lots of meat-free options."

Something about Meera seemed different. *Felt* different. It was a little disconcerting to realize that she seemed *happier*. Had her life been more pleasant without me in it? Or was this joy related to seeing me again? It seemed delusional to hope for the latter.

"How did your conversation at Elverston House go yesterday?" I asked as Meera helped remove the lids from all the bowls, setting them out in front of us and handing me the one filled with roasted meat.

"Good, I think? I went back this morning and everyone had agreed that they were fine with me working in the garden." She paused, her face going a little pink. "They asked that I be the one to go and visit them going forward, rather than Ophelia. I don't know why."

I tilted my head to the side. "I do. You have a very soothing presence, Meera. They may feel that they have to live up to the queen's enthusiasm and that might be difficult for them."

She nibbled on the edge of one of the hard flat breads Calix was so fond of making these days. "Maybe you're right. I used to find it a little overwhelming."

"But you don't anymore?"

Meera frowned thoughtfully. "No, not really. I wonder when that happened."

"Perhaps the time we spent apart was good for you?" I suggested, trying and failing to keep my voice light.

"Absolutely not." Meera gave me a sharp look that sent an odd shiver down my spine. "It wasn't that. Well... Okay, it wasn't *because* we spent time apart, but rather that I've spent time apart from everyone recently. The others are all getting married off, and they're busy. I've been spending time with Iris, but she's in pretty high demand—she's basically the nicest person you'll ever meet in your life, so of course everyone wants to befriend her."

"Have you been lonely?" I asked, hating the thought.

"I think I knew I didn't *have* to be lonely, and that was the difference between what I felt here and what I would have experienced in the human realm. At any point, if I'd reached out and said I was struggling, someone would have been there."

"I would have," I said firmly.

Meera nodded. "I know. I'm really sorry I ran. That was cowardly of me."

"I knew you well enough not to take it personally," I said wryly, nudging her leg with my foot. "But I'd appreciate it if you didn't do it again."

She nodded firmly, her expression solemn but her scent still soft and sweet. "Never again."

We ate in silence for a long while and I was desperate to ask about her brief trip to the human realm. From what Evrin had said, she'd saved Tallulah and Austin with her bravery, but he'd also mentioned that she hadn't wanted to talk about it all afterward—even when Tallulah had asked. It was probably the most interaction Meera had had with the Hunters in years, and perhaps the impact it had on her was further reaching than she'd expected it to be.

"Did you visit your parents?" Meera asked, holding up the ojurac.

"Not on that particular trip back, but I did stop by and see them on a different day."

"How was it?" The calm understanding in her voice was everything. No wonder the Hunters still staring at us from the windows of Elverston House felt more comfortable speaking to her than anyone else.

"It was as expected. Though it was illuminating too, I suppose. Speaking of illuminating..."

I pulled a small velvet bag out of the basket, loosening the strings and letting the contents spill out onto the grass.

"Are these... mini orbs?" Meera asked, picking one up and holding it between her fingers. The small orb glowed with a pale silvery light, though it was difficult to see during the day.

"They are," I agreed, clearing a space on the ground for us before drawing a circle with my finger, leaving the faintest hint of a shadow behind. "Do you want to play a game?"

"With the orbs?"

"Sure." I divided them in two groups, pushing one toward Meera. "It's a battle of sorts. We each have one orb in the circle at a time, and we are trying to knock the other's out of the ring."

I demonstrated the motion, flicking the orb with my thumb to shoot it across the circle. "If you knock mine out, you keep that orb. The winner is the one who has most of their opponents orbs at the end."

Meera smiled softly, surveying the game. "Like marbles, I get it. Is this a popular game?"

"Not among adults," I admitted, setting two orbs in the circle so we could begin. "But it is among children. This type of set is probably more popular among children of the nobility," I added, slightly embarrassed of the fact.

Shades from families who weren't like mine probably played with balls made of clay.

"Have you had this set since you were a kid?" Meera asked, angling her hand when I gestured for her to go first.

"Yes, actually. I didn't take much with me when I left Sunlis, but for some reason, I didn't want to leave this behind."

"Maybe it had some fond memories for you."

I watched curiously, expecting Meera's lack of claws to make the movement more challenging, but if anything, it was easier. She got a surprising amount of power behind the movement, and her orb clinked against mine immediately, though it didn't push it far enough to knock it out.

"You get another turn as you hit it," I told her.

Meera glanced up at me with a mischievous smile so bright and beautiful, it could have brought any grown Shade to their knees. "Don't sound so surprised about that. I have good aim, remember? I was great at throwing daggers."

"I remember," I assured her.

Was I broken? The reminder should have cooled my ardor like anything else, but it seemed to have the opposite effect. Time apart hadn't eased my affection for Meera even a little. She was still so...

So everything. So *everything.*

# MEERA

## CHAPTER 13

Are you sure you don't mind coming along?" Tallulah asked quietly as I took a seat next to her at the circular table. "I know you don't like these things."

"No, it's fine. Honestly."

I mean, it wouldn't be my first choice on how to spend my afternoon, but I wanted Tallulah to feel supported in this massive undertaking. Sitting in with her and offering whatever feedback I could come up with that might even be marginally helpful seemed like the least I could do.

"Hello, hello, everyone. Sorry I'm late," Sebastian announced, swanning into the room with his most charming smile, shoving his sandy-blond hair back out of his face. Verity truly didn't have a type because I couldn't see a single similarity between Sebastian and the duke.

Actually, maybe the arrogance. Possibly that was something they had in common.

Duke Theon wasn't in attendance today, though he did sometimes like to make an appearance—mostly to make Sebastian nervous.

Today, the Shades in attendance were Captain Soren—sans Astrid because she was too confrontational, and Sebastian was scared of her—and Evrin, Tallulah's mate.

To give Sebastian his credit, the two Shades made a formidable duo to face on his own, and he was doing his level best not to show that he was intimidated.

Soren and Evrin could probably smell it though.

"Meera," Sebastian said politely. "Nice to see you."

"Meera is going to be joining us today," Tallulah put in with her best HR smile. "I've asked the others to sit in where possible—it's good to get a balance of opinions from everyone."

"Absolutely," Sebastian agreed. Hearing the two of them talk made me feel like I was about to get a performance appraisal. "I'd like to pick up where we left off last time with the discussion on portal usage. I'm running late because I was just meeting with one of the Councilors, Randal Jackman, to get his thoughts on the matter..."

I didn't hear the rest because my brain was immediately... loud. Fuzzy and loud. Like I'd submerged myself underwater while everyone talked around me.

*Randal Jackman.*

I hadn't heard that name in years. Was it warm in here? It felt really warm.

"Meera," Tallulah whispered, resting her hand on my forearm and startling me back into reality. "Are you okay?"

"Of course," I croaked.

*You're being ridiculous,* I told myself firmly. While I hadn't seen Randal Jackman in years, it wasn't exactly a shock that he was still alive and an active member of the Hunters. He was only the same age as my mother. Last I heard, she was still healthy and active and nowhere near retirement.

"Everything alright over there?" Sebastian asked from the other side of the table. He had a smile on his face, but he was clearly irritated by the interruption. I would never understand how vibrant, fun, *kind* Verity had ever seen anything in this tactless asshole.

"I haven't heard that name in a few years," I said weakly before clearing my throat, hoping to sound more calm and collected. "*That's* your point of contact on this? I didn't realize he was on the Council."

"He's not the only one, but yes, of course Randal is involved," Sebastian replied, instantly affronted. "Who else? He officially joined the Council five years ago, and he's mentored me since. There's no one better for the job."

Tallulah was watching me closely. Too closely. She'd see everything. "It doesn't look like Meera agrees."

"Respectfully, Meera hasn't been part of the Hunters for years," Sebastian countered.

Tallulah narrowed her eyes at Sebastian, and he shrunk down in his seat slightly.

"I have some concerns about the suitability for Randal Jackman as our point of contact," I began, aiming roughly in the direction of professionalism.

"Based on what?" Sebastian snapped.

"My personal dealings with him."

"Which consist of?" he pressed.

Damn it. I could hardly say *none of your business*. I was making it his business by objecting to it. And yet I *really* didn't want to disclose the nature of my history with Randal Jackman.

"Perhaps you and I could take this conversation offline?" Tallulah suggested, seamlessly slipping back into human resources mode.

"This isn't a decision I can be left out of," Sebastian huffed.

"I'm not suggesting it is," Tallulah replied firmly. "Merely that we table the topic for now. Moving on. Let's discuss the feeding schedule—as you know, we'd like to still have the option for Shades who prefer to feed in the human realm to do so directly. As multiple people have pointed out, the sudden withdrawal of Shades from the realm has had a noticeable effect on the human population."

She'd given me a much-needed reprieve, and yet it still felt like there wasn't enough air in the room for my burning lungs.

"Will you excuse me for a moment?" I said, vaguely in the direction of the rest of the room. I gave Tallulah's hand a light squeeze before standing, making my way for the door without really seeing it.

The walls felt like they were closing in around me, and the moment I was in the corridor, I all but threw myself toward the other side of the hallway, which had an open-air balcony overlooking the circular garden below. The fresh air helped some, but not entirely—not enough.

I'd handled that *so* badly. What was wrong with me? Briefly, I contemplated marching back in there with my head held high and telling them everything I knew about Randal Jackman, but my legs wouldn't cooperate. I didn't want to lay my idiocy out on a platter for everyone in the room to pick at.

If only Sebastian were actually one of us. Then he wouldn't *need* an explanation. Then he'd understand what it was like to be on the losing side of a power struggle with a Councilor.

The door creaked behind me, and I took a deep, steadying breath, attempting to pull myself together. Tallulah was sweet, and I'd already been more open and honest with her than I had with the others—something about her made it difficult to hide anything. But I still did my valiant best to act like I was a normal, functioning human in her presence, and I wasn't sure I could pull it off right now.

To my surprise, it wasn't Tallulah who emerged but Astrid.

She came over to the half wall where I was standing, leaning her hip against it and crossing her arms.

"Where did you come from?" I rasped.

"Good fucking luck keeping me out of those meetings. I don't trust Sebastian as far as I could throw him. I just stay hidden now."

That shouldn't have surprised me in all honesty.

"Oh good. Are you here to give me a pep talk?" I asked somewhat dubiously. We were probably as close to friends as Astrid was capable of, but she was not pep talk material.

Astrid shuddered. "Absolutely not. But I got the feeling that you weren't in the right space to be treated with kid gloves, so I told Tallulah I'd come out instead. Also I wanted Sebastian to know that I had eyes on him."

Maybe I didn't give Astrid enough credit for her observational skills. "Thanks. You might be right about the kid gloves."

And the idea of her scaring the crap out of Sebastian by popping out of the shadows was pretty funny.

"So?" she prompted. "What's the deal with Randal Jackman?"

I grimaced at hearing his name again. "Do you know him?"

Astrid shrugged. "Sure. I know everyone. He's a prick, of course. But they all are, so I'm trying to understand why this guy stood out for you."

"This one was a prick to me personally."

"Well that'll do it."

"We can't work with him, Astrid."

She straightened slightly, frowning. "We kind of have to, Meera. I know you don't like the guy, but he's the Council's representative. There's no guarantee we'd get someone better even if they agreed to replace him—and the chances of that are slim at the moment. They're already very cagey with us since we haven't allowed them to assign Sebastian a new buddy."

"We can't," I replied stubbornly, shaking my head. "We can't work with him. It'll ruin everything."

"What exactly did he do?"

I chewed on my lower lip, trying to force out the words I wanted to say, but it felt like I'd be sick if I did. In the end, I gave up with a small sound of frustration. Logically, I knew I hadn't done anything wrong. And while I was frustrated with myself for the choices I'd made, I'd been seventeen at the time and known very little about the world. *He* knew better.

"Do you want me to get Tallulah? Or Ophelia?" Astrid asked, frowning harder now.

"No."

"Look, I'm not good at this whole being understanding thing," Astrid said, frustration etched all over her face. "If it were anyone else, I probably wouldn't bother trying."

That wasn't true, but Astrid was still in denial about being a nice person.

"I want to help, Meera, but I need a little more to go on. And suddenly replacing Jackman isn't feasible."

*I could replace him myself.*

"What?"

I startled, looking at Astrid.

"What did you say?" she said, a little more insistently. "You could replace him yourself?"

Had I said that out loud?

"Yes. I could." Astrid snorted, and I immediately took it personally.

"You don't think I could do it?"

"I'm not even sure what you're suggesting—it could be anything ranging from writing a strongly worded letter to actual murder—but, well, no. You're not a fighter, Meera. You don't rock the boat—and that's awesome. We all love that about you," she added hastily. "You don't like Jackman. I get it. And maybe, when things have settled down a bit more after the whole Lochan thing, we can table that for discussion and talk about finding a replacement—"

"There *is* no negotiating with someone that dishonest, Astrid. All of these conversations are pointless if he's the one we're dealing with."

She shrugged uncomfortably. "They're all dishonest, Meera. It's not like there's a *good* option there."

An oddly helpless feeling washed over me, mixed with a hefty dose of regret. I'd been in a position to do something about Jackman and I'd run away.

That was something I was trying to do less of these days. And yet I still couldn't force the words out. I wasn't sure it would make a difference if I could.

"I'm going to go for a walk," I said stiffly.

"Okay. Yeah, that sounds good. I'll see you later?"

"Sure," I replied, already backing away. If Astrid could smell my emotions, I'd be in trouble. As it was, I was keen to get out of the confines of the palace before any Shades scented me and started enquiring after my well-being.

I walked as fast as my legs would carry me without drawing attention to myself, quickly swinging by my new room that I felt so wildly uncomfortable in. I didn't even know what I was doing, I was operating on autopilot. There was a small purse that I hadn't used since I'd moved here, and I grabbed it now before pulling my notebook out from under the bed and shoving it inside. I pulled the crossbody strap over my head before tugging my oversized hoodie on top of it, smoothing down the bulkiness as best I could. Out of habit, my feet carried me back toward Elverston House, though I veered left rather than right at the last minute, heading for the solitude of the riverbank.

My room in the palace just made me feel so accessible. Anyone and everyone could just walk right up to my door and say hello. Sometimes, they'd even ask if I was free and wanted to hang out. It was my worst nightmare.

Maybe I could move back into Elverston House? Jade sort of seemed to like me. I suspected the ex-Hunters there might understand me better than my own cohort in some ways. Some things were difficult to relate to if you hadn't lived through them.

*You're not a fighter, Meera. You don't rock the boat.*

What a damning indictment of my character. I didn't think she'd meant it that way—Astrid generally wasn't offensive on purpose—but her honesty had exposed a part of me that I hated.

A part of me that knew I justified my spinelessness as calmness. Peacefulness. Friendliness.

Most of the time, it was just cowardice.

"Meera?" I froze for a moment, recognizing Verner's voice anywhere. "What's going on? Are you okay?"

"What are you doing here?" I asked, confused. We'd already met for lunch today.

"It's my day off," he replied, looking almost a little bashful. "I was just going for a walk and I guess my feet brought me here. Talk to me. What's going on?"

Everything about myself today had me wanting to crawl out of my own skin. Why couldn't I be... *better*? More normal? More capable?

In my head, I said *of course I'm fine. I'm just getting some fresh air. Isn't it pretty out here? What a lovely day.*

I soothed, and I deflected, and Verner went about his day, his mind totally at ease.

But that wasn't what I said out loud.

"I want to go back to the human realm."

"You want to... what?" he repeated, reeling back. "Meera, what's happened? Did someone hurt you? Give me their name. I'll see that justice is done myself. There's no need to leave—I can keep you safe here."

Oh, I believed him. If I asked Verner to, he'd probably give up his entire career to become my personal bodyguard. Not because I meant that much to him—that was a crazy thought—but because he was so honorable, he'd never walk away from someone in need. He'd never ignore a request for help, even if that request was patently absurd.

And I was about to exploit that generosity.

"No one. It's not about that. There's just something I need to do in the human realm. I can find someone else to take me—"

"Meera, I will take you," Verner said firmly. "I wouldn't entrust the task to anyone else. But tell me why you need to do this, *please*. It's dangerous. It's... well, it's not technically banned any longer. Not for me. But visiting the human realm is still considered an extraordinary risk."

Guilt squirmed uncomfortably in my gut. "You're right, it is. You shouldn't take me. It's not worth it. I shouldn't have said anything."

He watched me expectantly for a long moment before sighing. "You didn't say you're not going to go."

*Should I lie?* I didn't think I could. Not to Verner. Something about him had me spilling all my truths.

"I'm definitely still going to go."

Verner sighed, but it wasn't in irritation—more like resigned acceptance.

And yet I still didn't feel like a burden in his presence like I did with most people. More like a minor, and hopefully still endearing, inconvenience. "Then I am definitely taking you there. Just help me understand why you need to do this."

How was I meant to answer that? How could I explain that I'd spent the last decade of my life being torn in two as shame and anger warred for dominance in my head? Shame had kept me away all these years. Anger was taking me back.

And, perhaps, not a small amount of stubbornness.

*You're not a fighter, Meera. You don't rock the boat.*

We'll see about that.

"Unfinished business," I said eventually. "I thought I could let it go. That I could come here and move on, start a new life for myself. But I can't, Verner. I can't. I heard his name and..." My voice cracked and I cleared my throat, hating that I showed any sign of weakness. But hating it less than I would if it was anyone else, because Verner would never hold it against me. "He's just living his life like he didn't ruin mine. He's still in a position of power in the Hunters. He has *more* power now. He's the lead on these new negotiations. And I *know* him and I *know* his character. I know how he accumulated the wealth that he has. There's no one I would trust less at the negotiating table, and the outcome of these discussions matters so much. I was too young and too helpless to fight back then. I can fight back now."

Was I making sense? Probably not. The words were spilling out of my mouth faster than my brain could arrange them into a logical structure.

Verner gave up trying to keep his distance, closing the gap between us. "Meera, are you talking about that man from your past? If you want to see him punished for what he did to you, then that's what we'll do."

"Not we," I said firmly, reining in my mental spiral instantly. "It's too dangerous for you in the human realm. Just get me there and back before anyone knows you're gone, and don't tell them it was you who took me."

"You know we can't do that. They'll panic if you disappear."

Unfortunately, I could see the logic in that. I knew exactly how terrifying it was when one of my friends vanished from the realm—it wasn't a new experience at this point.

"I'll leave a note. They'll all try to talk me out of it, and I have to do this. I *have* to."

"Did you try speaking to the others first?"

"They don't get it," I deflected. I *did* try to speak to Astrid, and she hadn't gotten it. But I also hadn't done a good job explaining myself because talking to her wasn't as easy as it was talking to Verner.

"I can't say no to you, Meera," Verner said, sounding slightly pained.

"I know." I swallowed thickly, reaching out to tangle my fingers with his, careful to avoid his claws. "And I know I'm exploiting it. I'll never ask you for anything else."

"Don't say that," he replied sharply. "I want you to feel comfortable asking me for anything, whatever and whenever you need."

I hoped I'd never make him regret those words, though I wouldn't blame him if he did.

"I'll just write them a quick note in Elverston House," I said, giving his hands a squeeze, not wanting to go back to the palace. "Meet you back here in ten minutes? Or are you meant to be somewhere right now?"

"No. I have today and tomorrow off. I'll wait right here."

Impulsively, I went up on my tip toes, wrapping my arms around his shoulders and pulling him in for a hug. My lips brushed his jaw in another entirely inappropriate kiss—if he was any shorter I probably would have gone for his lips again without even thinking about it. What was wrong with me? *He*

Verner looked slightly shell-shocked when I let him go, his arms raised like he was going to embrace me again for a beat too long, but I was already jogging up toward Elverston House.

There were writing supplies in one of the upstairs storage closets, and I almost headed right for it before remembering that I was technically a guest here, and knocking on the front door after I'd already opened it.

"Meera," Jade said, appearing at the bottom of the stairs and watching me warily. "Everything okay?"

"I, um, need to write a note for the palace. Is it okay if I go grab the writing supplies upstairs?"

Jade watched me closely for a long moment. "You're leaving."

"Not... not forever. There's something I need to do."

Shoot, our conversation had attracted a crowd. So much for getting out of here unseen.

"Can we help?" Patrick asked gruffly, leaning against the door jamb to take the weight off his leg.

"I was sort of hoping to get away without the others noticing. I don't want to worry them, but I don't know that they'd necessarily... get it."

Jade nodded immediately, her expression fierce. "They're different from us. Except Verity. They don't know what it's like."

Part of me thought that I should object. That I should try to convince her that *yes*, they were like us deep down. That we'd all suffered at the hands of the Hunters Council, though the degrees did vary. But I wasn't sure I had it in me right now.

"How long do you need?" Patrick asked. "Maybe you don't need to leave them a note. We could cover for you. Say you decided you wanted to stay here for a bit."

That wasn't implausible. After that conversation with Astrid, she may well believe that I wanted some space. It didn't feel *great* to exploit that, but they'd barely know I was gone. I'd be there and back before Astrid even realized I'd left.

I couldn't leave her with nothing, though. After finalizing arrangements with the others, I grabbed a pencil and paper from the storage closet and scribbled a quick note for Astrid.

*I love you. I need some space.*
*I'm sorry I couldn't explain it all properly.*
*I'll do better next time.*
*- Meera*

# VERNER

## CHAPTER 14

The wait for Meera to come out of Elverston House was excruciating. I stood, half concealed by a tree, my claws tracing the spot where her lips had touched my jaw.

It was similar to that gesture that had made her panic last time, though not quite as intimate. Perhaps that meant she was less fond of me now than she was then? No, that didn't seem right. I suspected I had no idea what that gesture meant at all.

Maybe I should have asked someone. Shades I knew were now mated to Hunters—I supposed I could have asked them. But it felt too intimate to share, even if it was with someone I trusted.

With each rustle of a leaf or quiet whoosh of breeze, I was startling, looking around for a member of the Guard to appear and demand that I explain myself. I hadn't actually *done* anything yet, and I felt as though I was going to be dragged away by Captain Soren at any moment and be thrown into the Pit.

It went entirely against my nature to rebel. But not helping Meera was a greater affront to my instincts.

If anyone else had asked me for such a favor, I'd have said no without question. I'd have reported them to the captain. I'd have followed procedure to the letter. But Meera needed me, and I wouldn't disappoint her. Even if I didn't entirely understand what we were setting out to do.

Vengeance, I understood. Why now and how she intended to accomplish it, I was a little less clear on, but I trusted that Meera knew what she was doing.

Her eyes were a little too wide, a little too bright, when she came back outside, trailing her fingers over the leafy green plants she'd so diligently planted as though she was saying farewell to them. That wasn't going to happen. This was not goodbye.

"Ready," she breathed, straightening her spine and pushing her shoulders back. I wasn't sure who she was trying to convince, but I had to admit that her scent didn't indicate any hesitation. "They're going to cover for me."

I glanced up at Elverston House, finding eyes peering down at us from the upper windows again.

"Okay. Follow me—this way. They must be very fond of you if they're willing to do that."

"Yes," Meera said hesitantly. "I guess they are. I don't intend on abusing that. I'm very grateful for what they're doing."

"Do they know what *you're* doing?"

"They know the basics."

I hummed, ushering Meera along, staying close to her side. "Then presumably they believe in your cause, or they wouldn't be willing to lie for it."

It bolstered my faith in this endeavor a little. From what I'd seen of the new ex-Hunters who'd moved here, and what I knew of Meera's own history, I understood that not all experiences within the Hunters were equal. And I knew enough about my own privilege and what it had afforded me to know that I would never be able to wholly comprehend what that meant.

"This way, Meera."

"This isn't the way to the portal?" she whispered, clasping my hand and lightly squeezing my fingers. The small movement made something swoop alarmingly in my chest.

"No." Because I could be so reliably trusted not to break the rules, I was entrusted with information that not everyone had, and I used it to my advantage now as I guided Meera to a quiet, densely grown area to the east of the palace gardens. "There's a passageway. Only the highest level of the Guard have access to it."

I would be relieved of my post immediately if anyone knew I'd taken Meera there, but I suspected I would be relieved of my post either way after all of this was said and done, if anyone found it.

What would happen to me then? I supposed I would have to return to Sunlis, and live with my parents while they bemoaned the shame I'd brought to the family name.

I reluctantly released Meera's hand to clear some brush out of the way before finding the edge of the loose stone cover with my claws and prying it up. A network of passages ran beneath the gardens—fully illuminated so no one could shadow walk to or from them.

"Wait here, I'll help you down," I instructed, lowering myself into the hole. I could stand up straight while the cover was off, but I'd need to crouch or risk getting my horns stuck on the ceiling once we started moving.

"Here," I said, holding my arms up. "Let me lift you down."

Meera sat gingerly at the edge, her legs dangling into the hole. "I'm pretty heavy, Verner—"

I planted my hands firmly on her waist and lifted her down before she could argue. It wasn't something I'd usually do, but I suspected that Meera would work herself up into more of a state if I let her, and I was very eager for us to be ensconced in the privacy of the passageway.

She grabbed my shoulders with a faint squeak of alarm, and I held her tightly so she felt secure in my embrace, releasing her slowly so she wouldn't be startled.

Somehow, I hadn't predicted the way it would make her body slide down the length of mine, the softness of her curves pressed against the hardness of my muscles. A shiver of desire ran down my spine, and I desperately hoped she hadn't noticed as I set her down.

"Sorry—" I began, inhaling for any sign of concern in Meera's scent and finding none.

"No, don't be. That was probably the best way of handling that," she mumbled, still pressed tightly against me, though standing on her own two feet as I reached up to slide the cover back into place.

I frantically thought of everything other than how her body felt against mine.

"Is it far to walk?" Meera asked quietly, her soft voice echoing in the tunnel.

"Just a few minutes," I assured her, taking her hand again as the light wasn't as good in here with the cover back on the entry hole. Meera tangled our fingers together, sticking close to my back as I hunched down and began the winding journey through the tunnels. There was no signage, and the passages could be mazelike. Even those who were familiar with them usually opted not to use them, but I'd made it a point to memorize the routes. I wasn't even sure why, in hindsight. Perhaps to prove to the captain that I had value. That I was worthy of the position he was entrusting to me, even when my future as heir of Sunlis made me feel as though I didn't deserve it.

"Are there bugs in here?" Meera whispered, huddling a little closer to my back. There was enough orb light in here that no one could shadow walk, but it was still dim, and probably even more so to Meera's eyes than it was for a Shade.

"Maybe," I prevaricated, wondering if she could hear the scuttling sounds as critters cleared out at our presence. They were far more afraid of us than we needed to be of them, but I suspected it wouldn't ease Meera's mind at all if I pointed that out.

Her fingers squeezed me a little tighter. "There are absolutely bugs in here, Verner."

"Well, yes, but they're leaving if it helps."

Meera made a noise of discontent, her scent souring slightly, and I picked up the pace despite how difficult it was to move quickly while hunched over to protect my horns.

Eventually, I found the spot we wanted and released Meera's hand so I could slip open the cover above us. This one was harder to move, and I suspected the overgrowth had matted over it. There was a glimmer of fear in Meera's scent—perhaps at how long it was taking to get us out of here—and that was the boost of energy I needed to rip through the tight vines overhead and push the heavy stone slab out of the way.

Unfortunately, my claws caught on the foliage almost instantly as I tried to clear it enough for Meera to get through without getting stuck in it. I pulled my hands back down with a grunt of frustration, annoyed at myself that I wasn't carrying a knife to slice through it.

"If I'm not too heavy, maybe you could boost me up?" Meera suggested, rising up on her tiptoes and still coming up short. "I think that's a job for clawless hands."

I gripped her around the waist, holding her up in the air so she could efficiently push the vines out of the way with dexterous fingers.

"You're so strong," Meera breathed once we were both above ground, crouching next to the hole while I shifted the heavy cover.

"Yes," I agreed because that was true. I'd been a small child—the healers suspected it was because my mother had been so old when she'd had me—and I'd trained hard to grow in strength and ability as I'd moved toward adulthood. "Though that was hardly a demonstration of it," I added, slightly concerned she would think that the heaviest thing I could lift was her. That was outrageous. I could comfortably carry *two* of her if I wished.

We both fell still and silent as the stone scraped loudly, settling back into place. This exit had taken us out near the barracks, which shouldn't be busy at this time of day. Shift changeover wasn't for several more hours.

"Wait here," I instructed, leaving Meera obscured by the overgrowth while I circled around the building, checking that we were alone. The captain never came this far—he usually went directly to the training grounds. Selene was the greater concern. This entry room was her preferred route to return to her home in Cartava.

Fortunately for us, Selene was working less now that she was expecting her first child and our way was clear. I quickly collected Meera, ushering her into the entry room and shutting the door behind us, ensconcing us in darkness. While I could still see her perfectly, Meera fumbled slightly as she reached for my arm, and I swallowed thickly at the faint brush of her hand just south of my hips.

"Where exactly am I taking you?" I asked quietly, tucking her hand securely into the crook of my arm and away from my cock as we set off into the in-between.

"You've accompanied Astrid to Harlow Miles's apartment before, right?"

I frowned, remembering the odd Hunter with the black and green hair and the room full of square orbs. "Yes. That's where you want to go? I thought you didn't want Astrid to know your whereabouts."

Meera winced, and I wondered if perhaps I shouldn't have stated it so plainly. She *didn't* want Astrid to know where she was, but she also didn't want to feel like she was deceiving her friend.

"I don't. But Harlow's apartment is a safe harbor for us, isn't it? She's set it up as a permanent entry point. And she won't be surprised by your presence. It's safer for you."

"It's your safety I'm worried about, Meera."

"Well, I'm worried about *your* safety," she shot back stubbornly. "The human realm is far more dangerous for you than it is for me—even if you're only going to be there for a few seconds."

Should I mention that I had absolutely no intention of leaving her alone there? Probably best not to. I would simply beg for her forgiveness after the fact.

I could hear movement not far from us, and my jaw ached with how hard I was clenching it.

"Can I carry you, Meera? We need to move faster. Climb on my back."

"Oh. Um, if you're sure—"

I didn't give her a moment to hesitate, crouching in front of her and gently guiding her wrists to my shoulders so she could jump on. She clung on tightly and I expended power that I didn't really have to spare to cover her in shadows. Anyone who got close enough would still pick up her scent, but they at least might not notice her vibrant, colorful presence from a distance.

It wasn't a comfortable journey for her—I suspected I was jostling her terribly—but I moved as quickly as I could through the in-between without attracting attention to myself. The moment we moved through the veil to the human realm, Meera landed on her feet with a surprised gasp in Harlow's closet while my body turned ephemeral beneath her.

And then Meera was effectively on her own. I was here, but I was useless.

Helpless.

And incredibly fucking restless, hoping that Meera knew what she was doing.

## CHAPTER 15

The reality of what I'd done only really set in once my feet hit the ground in Harlow Miles's closet.

It smelled like popcorn.

Buttery, microwaveable popcorn.

In a matter of minutes and just a few steps, we'd gone from one realm to a very different one, and my skin itched a little with the panicky need to go back. The faint whirring of electrical equipment and the quiet *thud, thud, thud* of the heavy bass from whatever Harlow was listening to felt immediately more foreign to me than anything in my life in the shadow realm.

And then there was Verner. Ghostly, incorporeal Verner.

In this form, he was basically a giant floating cloak with hands.

"Go back," I whispered, reaching out to touch the edges of his form. I'd never touched a Shade in this form, and I was surprised to find that I could feel *something*, though it was as light as a feather beneath my fingertips.

Without giving myself another second to chicken out, I knocked on the closet door to announce my presence before turning the handle, finding it unlocked.

I'd only briefly met Harlow Miles in the shadow realm, and I'd never been to her apartment—Harlow had originally come to the shadow realm with the first group of us, but hadn't been able to handle the medieval way of life. She was some kind of tech expert, and Astrid had been working alongside her to wage a subtle kind of war against the Hunters from afar. Though that had probably gone on hold, now that negotiations were open again.

"Oh," Harlow said, blinking owlishly as I stepped out of the dark closet and directly into her computer room. Despite my instructions, Verner floated into the room behind me, keeping away from the small pool of light around Harlow's desk that was generated by neon light strips. "I wasn't expecting guests."

"I'm sorry for dropping in without any warning." I glanced around. "It does seem very trusting of you to put your makeshift entry to the in-between directly next to your workspace."

She shrugged. "It was here or my bedroom. Anyway, come in, take a seat." She pulled out a rolling stool from beneath her desk, lounging back in an enormous office chair that dwarfed her slight frame. "Meera, right? We met in the shadow realm. I remember you—you were the quiet one. How can I help?"

*The quiet one.*

The quiet one who didn't rock the boat and didn't do confrontation. The dull one. The *sad* one.

Not anymore.

"Are you willing to lie to Astrid about seeing me here?" I asked, tipping my chin up to meet Harlow's gaze.

She snorted. "Fuck no. Astrid is the scariest person I've ever met."

That was probably fair, though she could be bribed with jerky and pickles. Or frightened away by the merest hint of an emotional conversation.

"Okay, then I don't need help. Just directions out of your building."

Her eyebrow rose up to her short black hair, which was dyed green at the ends. "I don't know how to tell you this, but you have a Shade hovering right next to you who is going to implode if you go outside right now—it's the middle of the day."

"Yes, well, he's not staying."

Harlow looked over my shoulder, and I felt an odd, proprietary urge to stand in front of Verner, blocking him from her view. "Does he know that? He's sticking pretty close to you."

I turned, giving Verner what I hoped was an encouraging smile. It was so unsettling seeing him in this form, and not being able to communicate with him. Honestly, it hadn't really occurred to me—the others who'd been back to the human realm had all been able to communicate via their mating bond. Apparently, the bite worked as some kind of antenna, and I didn't have one.

Verner's form rippled, and I realized with a start that I was rubbing my neck and quickly dropped my hand.

"You need to head back now, remember? Just like we talked about," I said encouragingly, my face hot.

Verner was still for a moment before slowly—and deliberately—shaking his hooded head.

I narrowed my eyes at him. "Don't be difficult. You said you would."

He shook his head again. Actually... had he said that? On reflection, I couldn't remember him agreeing to leave. Then again, it didn't really matter. I could just walk out into sunlight and he'd be forced to concede defeat and go home.

I didn't feel great about that option, but it *was* there.

"Look," Harlow began placatingly, holding her hands up. "I'm not going to lie to Astrid because I value my life, but I don't necessarily have to tell her everything either. Why don't you chill here until nighttime? We can hang in the kitchen. I'll make it dark enough for your friend. You can eat whatever human realm snacks you've been craving—don't bullshit me, you've got to be missing processed sugar, right? Ooh, or we could order in. Do you like wings?"

I blinked at her as my brain tried to catch up to how we'd landed on that question. "I'm a vegetarian."

"Oh." She pursed her lips. "Fries then?"

"I'm not hungry. And I really have to go—I haven't got long." The more time I spent here, the more difficult it was for the ex-Hunters in Elverston House to cover for me.

"Look, I'm not like a... make-good-calls-in-a-crisis kind of person. Like, that's not really an area of expertise for me. But I'm going to go out on a limb and say that you need to think whatever you're doing through, and wait until it's dark so your friend here doesn't get fried by the sun."

It was hard to tell in this form, but I could have sworn Verner nodded, the absolute traitor. He was meant to go home! I had a rampage to go on. My bag felt heavy, weighed down with the throwing knives Verner had sourced for me, as well as my thick notebook of memories.

I hadn't entirely ruled out using the knives, but I was a fight-back rather than a fight-first kind of person.

Besides, physical violence seemed so... temporary.

I wanted to destroy him. I wanted to destroy his *legacy*.

"Do you want a ramen bowl?" Harlow asked, heading into the room off her office. Immediately, the light that filtered through the door when she'd opened it shut off, and I could hear her closing all the blinds. "I have vegetarian ones."

Honestly, that did sound pretty amazing.

Verner continued to hover nearby as I followed her into the room and hopped onto a barstool at the kitchen bench. Harlow's apartment was tiny but sleek and modern—though with a lot of anime-inspired touches. I wondered if the Hunters Council funded it, since as far as I knew, she was still on their books. The reason Astrid worked so closely with her was because Harlow was a double agent.

"So," Harlow began. "I assume the plan involves eventually returning to the shadow realm if your friend here is willing to wait—does your friend have a name by the way?"

"I'm not sure I should tell you that," I replied hesitantly. "I don't want to implicate him."

Harlow glanced over at me from the bench where she was preparing two bowls of instant ramen. "Girl, what are you planning? Are you going to get arrested?"

"I'll be back in the shadow realm before that," I replied absently. Shoot, I didn't have a phone. How was I going to call Adela Cooke without a phone? I couldn't sneakily borrow Harlow's without her knowing—she probably had some super tech-savvy security stuff on there, she'd know instantly.

It seemed foolish in hindsight that I'd left mine behind when I'd moved to the shadow realm.

Harlow spluttered. "What do you mean?"

"I'm kidding," I said hastily. "I'm not going to do anything crazy."

"Really? Because it sounds like you're going to do *premeditated crimes*," Harlow replied with an accusatory look.

"Don't you do premeditated crimes all the time?" I asked, genuinely curious. Whether it was for Astrid or for the Hunters, I doubted Harlow's job description was entirely above board.

"Well, yeah. But on the internet, so it doesn't count."

"That's a convenient loophole."

"It is. Have you thought of one for yourself yet? It's best to plan these things out in advance. Meditate on it. *Pre*meditate on it, if you will."

She handed me the bowl and some chopsticks, and I stirred the noodles around slowly, watching her. "I can't decide if you're encouraging me or not."

"I can't decide either," Harlow said serenely before starting on her own noodles. Maybe Harlow was just one of those who liked to watch the world burn. A Verity, so to speak.

I'd never been one of those, not in the past. While I'd definitely concocted a few revenge fantasies over the years, I'd never had the means nor the courage to even consider pulling one off. No, that wasn't quite right. Adela Cooke had offered me the means, and I'd walked away.

I'd never had the *rage* to pull it off. But knowing that Randal Jackman was still out there, living his best life, unaffected by what he'd done when he'd ruined mine?

I couldn't let that slide.

"I'm assuming this criminal activity of yours is directed against the Hunters, right?" Harlow asked, not sounding particularly bothered if it was. "You've picked a good time—they're kind of in an uproar right now with everything that went down with Cal Thibaut and Lochan. I think the higher-ups are starting to realize how much control they've lost over the community—people are fractured and doing their own thing. Austin's conspiracy theory-seeds have flowered nicely, and a lot of the middle-class band of Hunters have been distancing themselves from the group to avoid unwanted attention. For a while there, people were filming their neighbors' driveways and posting online about if they went out frequently at night and stuff. It was wild."

"All that from what Austin said?" I asked, surprised.

"Don't underestimate the allure of a conspiracy theory. Or the willingness many people have to attribute Why Life Sucks to something nebulous and nonspecific." She shrugged. "Sometimes that's easier than, like, dismantling oppressive power structures and systems designed to keep us in little boxes and whatever. You know?"

"I do know," I replied, though we were probably thinking about different things. I wasn't exactly sure what it was that Jackman had involved me in, but there was a very real chance that it involved other Councilors. There was a chance that *I'd* dismantle an oppressive power structure—or at least a small portion of one.

"Does that mean the Shades are in a good position right now, as far as negotiations go?" I asked, feeling a slight glimmer of unease. I didn't want to ruin all of Tallulah's hard work. Then again, Randal Jackman wouldn't honor a goddamn thing he promised anyway, so what did it matter?

"I guess so. I don't really understand that side of things. It's not lost on the Hunters, though, that the Shades are bargaining for access to a source of power that they'll literally die without—either Hunter desire or human fear. However weak the Hunters Council's position gets, they've always got that advantage."

Verner's shadowy form rippled next to me, a clear sign of his agitation. It was pretty bleak, hearing it laid bare like that.

"There are a lot more ex-Hunters in the shadow realm now," I pointed out, hoping to ease his discomfort.

Harlow hummed in agreement, though her eyes said plenty. None of the group that Cal Thibaut had sent over were in a position where they wanted to contribute to the energy stores—they never even left Elverston House. Perhaps he thought they'd be a burden and that the king would resent them. Or maybe that it would sow discord between him and Ophelia. Fortunately, no one seemed to have a problem with them being there, or at least they hadn't said as much within earshot of myself or any of the others.

"What else has changed since I was last there?" Harlow asked curiously as we finished up our meals and she cleaned up.

Hm, what had changed since the very beginning when we'd all first arrived in the shadow realm?

Everything. Everything had changed.

The very land itself had changed, filled with vibrant bursts of color that hadn't existed before we'd moved there. The attitudes toward us had changed—some growing more open to our presence there and seeing us more as a fixture of the realm than interlopers. For others, they'd been *very* keen to have us there, but in a way that felt pretty objectifying at first. That had changed for the most part too. Obviously, it wasn't perfect, but the more we'd found our own footing in the shadow realm, the more we seemed to be recognized as individuals with the ability to do more than just generate power.

"I'm not sure you'd recognize the place," I replied eventually. "The colorful flowers. The vegetable garden outside Elverston House. The new faces around the palace and beyond—Austin performs all over the realm." I watched Verner for a moment, absorbed in the floating, rippling movement of his shadows. "It's not perfect, but I think we're building something pretty great."

It bothered me that I'd never acknowledged that in the past. That I'd been so focused inward that I'd never taken the time to look around and realize how much things had changed, and how much we'd all been a part of that. How much *I'd* been part of that. In the human realm, I'd just floated through life barely touching the sides.

In the shadow realm, I was part of something. I'd made a difference—even if it was just growing vegetables, though I hoped I could eventually do more.

*This* would make a difference. Hopefully, one for the better.

"Harlow, I don't suppose you have a phone I could use?" I cleared my throat. "Ideally, one that, you know, can't be traced."

Harlow sighed dramatically, though her lips twitched like she was trying not to smile. "I don't mean this to be offensive, but you're a lot more interesting than I first gave you credit for."

"I'm confident you won't be the only one saying that after all this is said and done," I mumbled, face heating with embarrassment. Being boring and unmemorable had been a feature, not a bug. It had kept me out of trouble, and beneath anyone's notice.

It was a protective instinct, and it had served me well. But I'd outgrown it now. Now was the time for change.

Harlow hummed, watching me for a long moment. "Hold on, I'll get you a phone."

Harlow ended up lending me her van and some money as well, and once it was dark out, Verner and I loaded up—him in the back, which she usually used for transporting equipment, safely ensconced in the dark—while I drove.

The burner phone felt heavy in my pocket, but I hadn't used it yet. Before I called Adela, I wanted to make sure that I'd collected as much evidence as possible, which meant I had a pit stop to make first. If I was going to do this,

I was going to commit to it wholeheartedly.

Would I see Latika tonight? I couldn't decide if I wanted to or if I didn't. If it didn't go well, there would be something very final in it. She wouldn't be a confused kid this time, begging for me to stay. She was twenty years old, and as far as I knew, had been entrenched in Hunter ideology the entire time.

Who knew what she'd think of me now.

"I hope you're okay back there," I said, speaking to Verner through the cab wall. "I really hate that we can't speak to each other."

Silence. Because of course that's all there was. I contemplated turning on the radio so I had some noise to keep me company, but I'd never been a super confident driver, and I felt even less sure of it now after taking a long hiatus from being behind the wheel.

The roads weren't exactly busy this late, but they still felt much louder and scarier than anything in the shadow realm.

"Maybe I should just keep talking?" I suggested. "I feel like this must be really boring for you—the least I can do is keep you company as best I can."

After some hesitation, I said the words that had been weighing on my mind since I'd stupidly kissed Verner all those weeks ago. The words he'd generously let me off the hook from saying by not bringing it up and letting me pretend that nothing had changed.

It wasn't a facade we could maintain forever. I'd thought it was going to crumble when he was manhandling me into that tunnel thing and I'd slid down his body. Just the memory of it sent a shiver down my spine—if the circumstances had been less stressful, my scent would have been broadcasting just how much I enjoyed that loud and clear.

"It was really lovely of you not to bring up the kiss. You're so kind, you know. So careful not to push a subject if you think it might upset me, and in the beginning of our friendship, I really needed that. It was probably the only reason our friendship was able to get to the point where it is now. You made me feel so... safe. But I think we're beyond that now. We have to be. You've got to feel comfortable speaking openly and honestly to me, and I need to put on my big girl pants and deal with that. No more freezing. No more running."

I blew out a long breath, my hands tightening on the steering wheel. It was still cowardly of me to be having this conversation while Verner couldn't talk back, but in my mind, it was progress.

"I'm sorry for kissing you. Or, at least, I'm sorry for kissing you like that. For not talking about it with you first. I'm not sure I'd have even known how to bring it up, but it was wrong of me to just go in without us discussing it—honestly, I don't even know what I was thinking. Maybe I just read the situation wrong or something. Whatever feelings I have for you... I mean, our friendship comes first. That's the most important thing to me," I finished clumsily. Was it hot in here? It felt hot in here.

It had seemed so easy to say whatever I needed to say in the dark silence of the van, not having to look into Verner's eyes as I apologized. But I regretted it now. The lack of response was unnerving.

"Um. So, yeah. That's all I wanted to say," I mumbled lamely. "You're the best, and I'm really sorry that I am the way I am. I'll be quiet now."

# VERNER

## CHAPTER 16

I'd never felt so helpless in all my life.

Meera sat in the front of the moving contraption that was conveying us to wherever it was she wanted to go, while I hovered in the blackness of the room at the back, constantly moving to keep up with it since nothing could actually hold my form. It was blessedly dark back here at least. If it weren't traveling so quickly, if I had a mate bond to track Meera through, I might have let my body slip back into the in-between like it was begging me to do. I'd never spent so long in this form, and it was wearing on me.

But if I lost sight of Meera for even a second, there was a very good chance I'd never find her again.

The farther we went, the more acutely aware I became of my weariness.

I needed to feed.

Eventually, there were no coherent thoughts going through my head. My only focus was keeping up with Meera's conveyance—every drop of energy I had was devoted to not losing her.

*"Whatever feelings I have for you... I mean, our friendship comes first."*

I heard the words as though I was underwater and someone was speaking above me. Honestly, I wasn't entirely sure that I'd heard them at all. Perhaps my mind was merely playing tricks on me. Perhaps I was dying, and it had conjured up some pleasant thoughts for me to pass from this world with.

*"Whatever feelings I have for you..."*

That couldn't be true. But I desperately wished it was.

The vehicle slowed, and I slowed with it. My shadows flickered dangerously as we came to a stop, and I clung to the sound of Meera's footsteps to keep me in place.

"Verner?" Meera whispered, opening the door as little as possible and slipping inside before closing it behind her, blanketing us in darkness once more. "Are you here?"

I reached out, my claws ghosting over her skin.

The in-between was calling to me, dragging me back to its dark embrace. It was more effort to hold on to this ephemeral form than it was to shift back into my solid one.

Saying a quiet prayer to the gods that Meera would forgive me, I wrapped her in my embrace, and hoped she understood.

After a second's hesitation, she crouched low in the conveyance, which was just long enough for her to take a few steps. That was all I needed to shadow walk us back into the in-between, and I collapsed onto the ground the moment my form solidified.

"Verner!" Meera dropped to her knees beside me, pulling my arm over her shoulders, visibly struggling under my bulk. "Oh my god. What is it? What happened?"

"I need to feed," I rasped, struggling with just the effort of speaking. "I'm low on power. I need to get to the stores—"

"There's no time for that. You can't walk and I can't carry you." She helped me lie back on the cool ground before kneeling beside me, eyes worried. "I'm really regretting not having that conversation with you earlier. Can I... can I touch you?"

Touch me?

Was she offering to feed me?

"Meera, I can't ask you to do that."

"You're not asking, I am. And honestly, I'm struggling with it a little because I very much want to make an executive decision here to save your life."

"You always have my permission. You can touch me whenever you want. However you want."

Perhaps I wouldn't have been so honest if I hadn't been half delirious, but in the moment it seemed essential that Meera know that I was hers. That she was everything to me.

"Just... let me take the lead, okay?" she asked softly, her scent sweetening.

"Of course." Not that I could move anyway.

The moment Meera's hands landed on my stomach, what little energy remained in my body immediately went to my cock. If I wasn't able to feed from her soon, this erection might actually be the death of me. It was using up everything that I had left. The shadows I normally wore as easily as a second skin vanished, baring me to Meera's gaze. Could she see me? I didn't think so—she didn't react to my sudden nakedness.

As though she could feel my desperation, Meera's hand slid down my body, her fingers wrapping around my shaft.

"You're already hard," she said, surprised.

"Of course. It's you."

Meera's grip seemed to grow a little more sure at that, sending a shudder down my spine. "I don't really know what I'm doing," she whispered.

"You can do whatever you want with me, Meera."

Suddenly, her perfume was so thick in the air that I could have choked on it. Had that been what she wanted? What she needed for her desire to fully take hold? I had no objections to being Meera's plaything. I would be the luckiest Shade alive.

In all of our conversations, she hadn't mentioned any kind of romantic partner since that first boyfriend she'd had all those years ago, and I couldn't help but wonder if she'd avoided all kinds of romantic relationships since.

It wasn't as though Meera didn't know what she was doing, but she was just hesitant in how she went about it. Like she'd learned the knowledge in a book and was applying it for the first time in the real world.

Not that I had any complaints. Her soft hand felt heavenly around my shaft as she explored, and I groaned as she tightened her grip, squeezing the base where my knot would eventually swell.

"Good?" Meera asked, repeating it, this time a little more intentionally. While part of me was glad for the cover of darkness because it was probably allowing Meera to feel more comfortable, I also wished that she could see me properly. That she could see how every little touch and curious glance made me melt for her.

"Incredible. You're incredible."

"Is it working though?" she breathed, squirming slightly beside me. The scent of her own desire grew more potent with each passing second, and it was intoxicating. "Are you feeding from this?"

If I said no, would she stop? I didn't want that.

I also didn't want to die, as much as this would be a pleasant way to go.

"I don't think so," I admitted. "Maybe it takes a while?"

"That's not the impression I got from the others, though I'm wishing I asked more questions now. Let's try something different."

"It's okay, Meera. We don't have to—"

"Don't finish that sentence, Verner. This is not a hardship for me."

The assertiveness in her tone made my knot throb.

Meera stood, pulling off her heavy trousers, though there was still a thin piece of fabric covering the pussy I'd been doing my best not to fantasize about, because Meera was my friend and that was inappropriate.

"I wish I was more confident," Meera whispered, kneeling again before throwing one leg over my hips, the damp fabric of her panties immediately soaking my cock.

*Fuck.*

"You seem plenty confident right now," I rasped, my claws digging into the hard ground.

"Of course. It's you," she whispered, throwing my words back at me. Meera's hands landed on my chest before she shifted them either side of my head, looking worried that I might have struggled to support her.

"I won't break, Meera. You're safe with me. I'm stronger than I look right at this moment." That wasn't entirely true, but she could lean on me at least.

"Liar," Meera shot back, though there was no heat in it. She rocked her hips teasingly, dragging the material back and forth in a way that felt fucking incredible for me. But more importantly, it seemed to feel fucking incredible for *her*. Her eyes rolled back, teeth sinking into her lower lip, and the power started to flow.

I could only imagine what a rush of power would come through if we were actually fucking.

*Don't imagine that*, I told myself sternly. I'd assured Meera that I'd let her lead this interaction, and I had no intention of going back on my word.

And while I was entirely content to let her lead and go at whatever pace Meera deemed suitable, I was frustrated at how *useless* I was right now. Even if she asked, there was no way I could perform satisfactorily.

"Oh," Meera rasped. "This feels *good*. I didn't... I didn't know it could be like this. I mean, I've seen videos, but I didn't *know...*"

"You're safe with me," I reiterated, as firmly as I could manage while power flowed to me, making me almost dizzy. We'd barely done anything, and yet I was feeding so much faster than I would have from the stores, and I suspected this was only a trickle of what was possible. "You are always safe with me."

"I know."

The words were soft but steady and I watched, enraptured, as she shifted her angle, finding the exact position she wanted. Meera ground her pussy harder against my aching cock for a few more seconds before tipping her head back, pressing her lips together to stifle her moan as she came. It was enchanting to witness. Meera was always so guarded in her expressions, so controlled in her movements.

But in this moment, she was entirely free from every constraint she'd ever put on herself. I wanted to experience it again. And again. I wanted the rest of my life to look like this.

Even with the barrier of her panties, a sudden gush of slick coated my cock, and I shamelessly spilled over my stomach, my knot swelling beneath Meera.

She gasped, lifting up slightly on her knees and looking down, though I doubted she could see anything in the darkness.

"Is that...?"

"That's my knot, yes." I hesitated for a moment. "You can touch if you want to. Not because I'm seeking pleasure or anything. Just if you're... curious."

While I'd offered to assure her that I was fine with her exploring my body, I hadn't *actually* expected Meera to reach between us and circle my knot tentatively with her fingertips. Fortunately, I didn't startle in surprise and ruin the moment for both of us.

"Is the, um, wetness from me?"

I hummed in agreement, wanting to fucking *bathe* in it. I wanted Meera's scent baked into my skin, so everyone knew who I belonged to.

*Don't get carried away, Verner. You have no idea if this means anything to her.*

"I'm so sorry," Meera said with an embarrassed laugh. "That's... I've never done that before. I'm not usually so, um, soaked."

I was going to come again if she kept talking about how wet her pussy was.

"You're producing slick. I've heard that your body produces it in proximity to Shades, so you can accommodate the knot," I rasped.

"I'm not sure any amount of slick could get my body to accommodate this. It's so... firm," she said, gently pressing against it like she was worried she'd hurt me.

"Put your hand on top of mine," I suggested, shifting my grip to carefully cup my knot, keeping my claws out of the way. Meera followed my instruction, moving her hand with mine as I gave my knot a hard squeeze that had my hips lifting slightly. "You don't need to be gentle with it. It's designed to be... squeezed."

I pulled my hand back and Meera immediately took its place,

experimentally massaging my knot with her fingers. My vision whited out from pleasure for a brief moment.

"Harder?"

I made a strangled sound of agreement, and she tightened her grip, massaging my knot like this was something the two of us had done thousands of times before. Even without being able to make out my features, Meera seemed to notice every twitch of my muscles or tiny sound, anything that gave away what felt good.

"This would be a lot sexier if I could see," Meera whispered, echoing my thoughts. "But I feel a lot more confident in the dark."

"Anything you want," I slurred, my hips rocking of their own accord as a tingle started at the base of my spine. "It feels incredible. *You* are incredible."

I really hoped there was no one around because I didn't stand a chance of keeping quiet as I came harder than I ever had in my life, coating Meera's hand in cum. How was this real life? How was this dream of a woman actually touching me?

She pulled her hand away, holding it close to her face to examine it before tentatively sticking out her tongue and licking my cum directly off her palm. My knot pulsated as another small orgasm rattled my bones. Gods. Where had she come from? Would she let me keep her?

"Do you feel, um, fed?" Meera asked, wiping her hand clean on her sweatshirt before resting it lightly on my inner thigh. It felt possessive, though I didn't know if she intended it to be.

"I did feed, thank you. You saved my life."

Meera's blunt nails dug into my skin ever so slightly. "Do you feel *fed*? Tell me the truth, Verner."

"You know I can't lie to you," I replied, pained.

"Tell me what you need, Verner," Meera insisted. "We can go further."

It sounded like she was convincing herself rather than me, and I absolutely wasn't going to take her up on it. If Meera and I ever went any further, it would be because she wanted to more than anything. Because she was willing and desperate and eager for it, and I'd give her everything she wanted.

But we weren't there yet.

"Will you make yourself come for me? It's your arousal that feeds me, not mine."

"That's all? You just want me to get myself off?"

I hesitated. "I think we have be touching somehow for the power to transfer between us. We can just hold hands or something—"

"Can you sit up?"

My upper body rose like I was being pulled by invisible strings, and Meera shyly shifted to sit between my legs, facing away from me. She swallowed thickly before leaning back against me, her soft hair tickling my jaw.

"Could you put your arms around me?" she asked tentatively.

Slowly, so as not to startle her, I banded my arms around her waist. Her full breasts sat heavily on my forearm, and I took a deep, steadying breath to keep my body language relaxed when relaxed was the last thing I felt.

"That's nice," Meera murmured. "But only because it's you. I don't usually like feeling constrained."

I loosened my grip slightly, worried it was too much, and Meera made a faint noise of disapproval. "No, I liked it. Come back."

*Come back.*

*I will. Every time you ask me to.*

# MEERA

## CHAPTER 17

As I draped my legs over Verner's thighs, really putting myself on display, though fortunately there was no one in front of me, I wasn't entirely sure how we'd gotten here but I wasn't upset in the least that this was where we'd ended up.

Well, I *was* upset that Verner had nearly died. I hadn't even considered whether he was at full strength before we'd left for the human realm, and how taxing it would be on him to make the journey.

"I'm sorry I nearly killed you," I breathed, which wasn't the sexiest thing to say while I was circling my clit with my middle finger, but what did I know about being sexy, honestly?

My hand was still faintly sticky from Verner's cum, and the reminder made my pussy *ache*. It wasn't like I never experienced arousal—I definitely did, and I always took care of it myself. But it was never like this. Never this all-encompassing, never this *fierce*. Like if I didn't come, I might actually perish.

"Don't think about that," Verner murmured, squeezing me gently as I arched back against him. "Think about how good you feel right now."

I hummed in agreement, though I was struck with the faint urge to tell him off for being bossy. Whether it was the need for control or just a kink, I wasn't sure. But I wanted to be in charge.

"I do feel very good," I whispered, sliding my finger inside me to drag my wetness up to my clit. The *sound* it made was sexy and appalling all at once. Verner had seemed to think that it was normal, but I was still a little alarmed by this new development in my anatomy. Then I remembered how thick and firm his knot had felt under my hand, and decided not to judge it too hastily.

"I'm desperate to taste you," Verner rasped, his voice low and needy in my ear.

"Next time," I replied breathily, not feeling quite confident enough for that. "Is there going to be a next time?"

"Meera, my love," he whispered, holding me a little closer. "Haven't you realized yet that I adore you? Whenever you want me, I am yours."

I came with a soft cry, biting down on my lower lip to try contain the sound. Touching myself had felt good, but hearing those words had felt so much better. It seemed stupid in hindsight that I hadn't told him how I'd felt about him earlier. That I'd waited until we were in the human realm where he couldn't even reply to me.

"Someone's coming," Verner said suddenly, scrambling to his feet and hauling me up with him. I snatched the clothes I'd shed hastily, and suddenly we were moving as Verner dragged us back through the in-between, into the parked van.

I landed with a thud on the ground, my bare ass hitting the cold floor. While I was glad we hadn't been caught, it was a pretty abrupt end to my orgasm.

Verner hovered, his arms around me as though he was still holding me in his physical embrace, and I burst out laughing, hoping he saw humor in our precarious situation too.

"We didn't think this through at all," I giggled, high off orgasms, half naked, and a sticky mess. It was also a lot colder here, and my sweatshirt was now covered in Shade cum. The way Verner was drifting back and forth made me wonder if he was fretting about it—it was difficult to tell with just the vaguest inclination of body language to go on.

"It's fine. I've got this," I assured him. The van wasn't entirely empty—Harlow had mentioned that she occasionally had to do some long-distance drives for the Hunters, and I dug through a duffel bag and the supplies tucked into the wall storage with a silent apology to her for rifling through her stuff.

Between the bottled water, wet wipes, and a travel-sized pack of tissues, I was able to somewhat get myself cleaned up and dressed, but I was still shivering in my t-shirt and there was no hope for the sweatshirt.

There was a waterproof jacket scrunched up in the bottom of the bag, and I pulled it on reluctantly, tugging at the hem. It was much smaller and tighter than the kind of thing I usually wore, but it did fit.

"We should get this over with," I told Verner shakily. "I don't even know how long we've been parked here. We've probably drawn attention to ourselves already. You're going to have to wait here—there are streetlights outside, and the house will have lights on in every room. Obviously, I'd prefer you go back home because it's safer for you there, but I get the feeling that you're not going to do that."

Verner drifted closer, slowly and intentionally shaking his head. The shadowy hood moved from side to side.

"Didn't think so. Okay, stay here. I'll be back soon."

I carefully let myself out of the van, squeezing through the narrowest gap possible to avoid letting any light in, and locking it behind me.

It was a short walk from where I'd parked to my mother's house, and I was immediately struck by how unchanged the single-family home I'd grown up in looked from the outside. The street lamps illuminated the low chain-link fence out front that had been out of shape when we'd moved in and had clearly never been fixed. The clay-brown paneling that covered the exterior was in need of a good clean, just like it had been on the day I'd been kicked out. From here, the house looked dark and still because—like all good Hunters—Mom had put up blackout blinds so the fact that the house was constantly illuminated on the inside wouldn't attract attention from the neighbors.

Standing out here made me feel like a kid again. A tired kid, with too much responsibility—getting off the school bus each afternoon to somehow do my homework while helping Latika with hers, making her dinner, and getting her ready for bed. And then making sure the house was in perfect order, because I did whatever I could to alleviate my mother's stress in the hopes that maybe it would improve her mood. That maybe she'd come home and be happy to see us for once.

There was no car in the driveway, which used to indicate with absolute certainty that Mom wasn't home, but I wasn't as confident of that now. Latika was grown—maybe she was the one who'd taken the car. Or maybe she didn't live here at all, though I couldn't imagine her moving out before she was married if she was still in Mom's good graces.

Everything was familiar and foreign all at once.

I walked toward the house as though I belonged there in case any of the neighbors were watching, veering left at the last second to make my way around the side of the house. Would there be security cameras now? I kept looking, but as far as I could tell, I couldn't see any.

The window in the laundry had never latched properly, and with a little jiggling, it could be opened from the outside. I'd never brought it up with Mom, because I'd always used it as a way to get in the house after school if I'd forgotten my keys, but I assumed that Latika would have told her at some point since then. Still, it was worth a shot.

My nails bent and protested as I pried away at the window, but it moved exactly the same way I remembered it, coming free with just a little wiggling.

This was definitely too easy. I didn't trust it.

Surely enough, the first real challenge came in the form of actually getting inside the window. I was definitely heavier than I'd been at seventeen, and apparently I'd lost all of my upper-body strength at some point since then too. By the time I'd hefted myself up and climbed awkwardly over the basin, I'd kicked on a tap and knocked over a bottle of fabric softener. There was nothing stealthy about it.

*You're here now,* I told myself sternly. *Too late to turn back.*

The house was silent as I crept out into the hallway, grateful that the ancient carpet disguised my footsteps. The room Latika and I had once shared was at the end of the corridor, and my heart pounded in my chest with each step I took toward it.

"You can't be here."

I startled, spinning around to find my sister staring at me, a hard look on her face. Gone was the baby-faced teenager Latika had been when I'd last seen her. She looked older now. Wiser. More jaded.

We looked more similar now than we'd ever looked as children, though she wore her hair shorter and was far more toned than I'd ever been.

"How are you, Latika?"

Her expression flickered slightly, but it was only the briefest moment of hesitation before she shored herself up again. "Why are you breaking into the house, Meera?"

"I need to collect some things I left behind."

She scoffed. "It's been eight years. Your stuff was thrown out the day after you left."

"I doubt you would have found this."

Latika narrowed her eyes. "It doesn't matter. You have to leave. I'll be nice and let you walk out the door. Mom will be home soon, and she won't be so friendly about it."

I looked at my sister for a long moment, trying to find something in her that I recognized. This had been the worst-case scenario that I'd been preparing myself for. The perfect little Hunter robot who never put a toe out of line because she'd probably been traumatized with stories about my fate.

And even if Mom had never mentioned me at all, which was a distinct possibility, Latika would have felt my absence. She'd been the spirited, rebellious second child to my responsible and obedient eldest daughter once upon a time. Undoubtedly, some of that responsibility had fallen on her shoulders after I'd left.

"Look, I understand that you don't want to see me. I know I shouldn't be here, and that I'm putting you in a difficult position. I wouldn't have risked it if it wasn't important, Latika."

She stared, her throat working hard as she swallowed. My baby sister was in there somewhere, locked away behind protective walls of her own making. *That* was something I recognized.

"Did you go to the shadow realm?" Latika asked quietly. "With the others? No one will tell me the truth. No one talks about you at all."

"Yes, I did."

She grimaced, looking away. "You're ruined then."

I snorted, remembering that I probably still had some Shade cum sticking to my skin despite my best attempts to clean myself up. She had no idea.

"No, Latika. You're ruined if you truly believe that poison. I feel very sorry for you, and I hope you recover from the sickness that has infected your mind."

Her face flushed.

"Do you remember who I told you to avoid before I left?" I asked coolly, some of my affection for my sister being replaced by annoyance. Latika nodded, looking away. "And did you do as I asked?"

She nodded again, shifting her weight uncomfortably from one foot to the other. "Yes."

"Good. I'm sure your teenage years were much more pleasant than mine then. And you didn't have a kid to raise. Aren't you lucky?" I snarked, a little of the bitterness I'd been carrying around creeping out. I turned away, striding purposefully toward the end room and throwing open the door.

It was jarring to see an adult-sized bed in the middle of the room rather than the bunk beds against the wall that we'd shared back then, though it shouldn't have been. After taking a moment to orient myself, I headed for the sliding closet doors, pushing them open and tossing Latika's shoes back into the bedroom behind me to clear the floor.

I could feel Latika standing behind me, but she didn't say anything. Perhaps I'd shocked her into silence.

The ancient carpet came up easily in the corner of the closet, though it probably hadn't been touched since I'd last moved it, and the loose floorboards beneath it were exactly the way I'd left them. It was no coincidence that this hiding spot was here. Randal Jackman had given me very specific instructions on what to do all those years ago.

Carefully, I lifted out the shoebox of documents, tucking it under my arm and covering the hole back up. All I wanted to do now was get out of here—looking through the box would have to wait. What if there had been a leak at some point? There wasn't any guarantee that what I had was even legible at this point.

"What is that?" Latika asked as I moved back out of the closet on my knees before climbing to my feet.

"Nothing you need to worry about."

"I find that hard to believe." She was trying to sound tough, but I could hear the tremor of fear in her voice.

Instinct demanded that I put her mind at ease—to mother her the way I had when we were young. But we were both adults now, and we were standing on two different sides of a battle line that was drawn in blood and betrayal. It wasn't one that could be easily crossed.

I stared at Latika for a long moment, memorizing her features again the way I had the day I'd left all those years ago. Replacing the portrait of her I had in my mind with one that was a little more up-to-date and a little less idealistic.

"I hope I'll see you again someday, little sister. Under different circumstances. Until then… Well, good luck, I suppose. I hope you don't come to regret the choices you've made."

She didn't say anything as I walked past her, out of what had once been our room before heading out the front door into the quiet, dark night.

It was a strange feeling to walk away. To feel like I'd slayed one of my own personal demons, and yet to feel completely hollow inside at the same time, but I didn't allow myself time to reflect on it.

Step one was complete. And that was the easy part.

# VERNER

## CHAPTER 18

G ot it," Meera said, hopping into the front of the contraption I'd been waiting miserably in. Hearing her voice offered some relief, but seeing her would have been far preferable. "I'm going to find us somewhere to stay for the rest of the night and to hide out tomorrow. I'm exhausted, and kind of overwhelmed, and I don't think I'm going to make good decisions right now. I need to think about exactly what I'm going to say to Adela. What if she's changed her number? Oh god, I didn't even think about that..."

It was harder to pay attention to her words when she started driving, and I just did my best to keep up in the safe confines of the darkness she'd created for me. I wasn't entirely confident that she'd find somewhere suitable for us—would I just spend the next day in the back of this vehicle?—but eventually Meera came to a stop and assured me that she'd be back for me shortly.

The short amount of time she was gone felt like hours, but she did eventually return for me, confidently opening the back door of the van.

"I feel pretty certain that you're safe here, though I'm less confident about myself," Meera said cheerfully, ushering me out. "It's probably the dodgiest motel I could have found, but it's dark and it's private."

I moved like the wind, hoping that my body language encouraged Meera to rush too so that we could get inside at least. If that was even an improvement, safety wise. The long building we were parked in front of was eerie and decrepit, and I desperately wanted to whisk Meera away from here.

She led me into a room at the end, having filled Harlow's bag with almost everything she could source from the vehicle.

"I should have packed snacks," Meera mumbled to herself, closing the door behind her and double-checking the lock. For my benefit, all the lights were off, but I suspected Meera didn't need them to know how dismal this room was.

"I'm going to wash up," she said, gesturing at the only other door in the room. "Um, make yourself at home, I guess? This is so grim. How about you go back to the shadow realm and I'll wait here? You'll be a lot more comfortable there. Harlow gave me enough cash that I could stay here for a few nights. Someone can just come back and get me. You know. Later. When everything is said and done."

When *what* is said and done? I asked silently. I was frustrated by my ignorance of the human realm, trying to figure out what it was that Meera was trying to accomplish here. Perhaps that was what we should have been talking about in our brief excursion back to the in-between—though I had been a little distracted at the time.

Then again... we could always go back now? It was quieter than usual after the strange incident with the portals and the new Hunters who'd come through.

I drifted toward Meera subconsciously, and she shot me a look so deliciously challenging that I could have sworn I felt the knot I didn't even have in this form.

"I know that... float. You're floating at me like you're going to sweep me into the in-between, but I'm not going, Verner. I'm going to see this through. I'm the only one who can."

I drifted back, resigned, floating next to the bed.

"Thank you," Meera said gently. "I know this isn't easy for you. And for what it's worth, I still think that you should go home—but I'm selfishly glad you're here."

She disappeared into the washroom, and I heard the sound of rushing water, on top of all the other strange sounds I could pick up around us. It was very loud here. And this room was very awful. Surely, it wouldn't be hard to convince more Hunters to move to the shadow realm if everywhere was like this? I supposed Harlow's home hadn't been too terrible.

After Meera washed up, she re-emerged wearing only a towel, her face a spectacular shade of red. "I forgot I didn't have any clothes to change into. And I should probably save what I have for tomorrow. I did wash my sweatshirt, maybe it'll dry overnight..."

She sighed heavily, grabbing her purse and sitting on the bed, leaning back against the pillows. After a small pause, she pulled out the odd device she called a "phone," and the book I'd seen her regularly writing in all those weeks ago. Opening it to the first page revealed a small white rectangle with some writing on, that looked like it had been attached to the page somehow.

Meera exhaled shakily, tipping her head back to look at me, the phone in her hand. "I think this has been the bravest day of my life. Just... a whole run of brave things in a row. In the spirit of that, I know that we haven't really talked about anything, and we kind of need to—it's a little up in the air right now, but..." She laughed nervously, and I desperately wished I could hold her hand.

"I really like you, Verner. I don't usually like anyone, but it's different with you. The problem is *me*. Whatever this is between us, whatever it turns into, it can never turn into *everything* because I know I can't be that for you. I freeze, and I run, and I clam up. I can't... I can't be what you need me to be."

*We'll see about that.*

There was no denying that Meera did all of those things—I'd seen them firsthand. But I also knew that she came back. And that I could be a steadying presence when her head was feeling stormy.

Most importantly, I didn't think that was so much of a risk going forward anyway. Meera was finding her voice right in front of my eyes. She'd spoken more today than I'd ever heard her speak in one go. She was brave, and assertive, and fully focused on achieving... whatever it was that she was trying to achieve.

Meera wasn't giving herself enough credit.

"Okay." She laughed awkwardly. "Now that we've gotten all that out of the way, I guess I should probably message Adela Cooke, huh? Alright. I've got this. Brave new Meera, taking on the world," she added under her breath.

I startled as the device in her hand lit up, backing a little farther away from the bed, though it wasn't throwing off too much light at least.

"I'm just going to send her a message," Meera muttered to herself. "And ask her to meet tomorrow night. I guess she'll just have to come here," she added with a grimace, glancing at the rather unsavory surroundings.

The moment she finished and set the device down, it buzzed on her thigh and she immediately snatched it back up again.

Meera exhaled shakily. "It's done. She'll be here tomorrow."

It had taken Meera several hours to fall asleep, which was unsurprising. Aside from her general worry about how tomorrow would go, this place was unfamiliar to her and the street outside was incredibly loud.

I hoped my presence offered her at least some comfort. If any human attempted to enter this terrifyingly unsecured place, I would feed on their fear until they were a husk of a person—the king's edict be damned.

Not long after she finally began sleeping peacefully, Meera was tossing and turning beneath the thin sheets.

And I knew she wasn't wearing anything under there, since she'd wanted to keep her clothes as clean as possible for tomorrow.

My throat felt dry, even though I couldn't feel my throat in this form. She'd carefully pulled the towel away once she was already under the sheets, so I hadn't seen anything. But the way she'd looked at me while she'd done it made me think she wouldn't entirely mind if I had.

Rather than settling further into her rest, Meera grew increasingly fidgety over the next few minutes. Her breathing had changed too. And her skin looked different. More flushed.

It was a curse not having my sense of smell to rely on. I felt trapped inside my noncorporeal form in a way that I never had before. Were her dreams distressing her? There had been some mention of a sister, though I'd struggled to make sense of Meera's grumbled words of outrage. Perhaps she was remembering that altercation in her sleep—

No. No, that wasn't what was happening at all.

With the kind of breathy sigh that I remembered all too well from our brief excursion to the in-between, Meera rolled onto her back, the sheet pulling taut across her full breasts, nipples showing through the fabric.

I groaned, a phantom ache forming where my cock should be. I'd never hated this form more. I wanted to be there, in my solid form. Kneeling at her feet and waiting for my goddess to demand the worship she was due.

One day. When Meera realized that we were perfect for one another and that I wasn't going anywhere...

I was going to make her very happy indeed.

She woke up with a start, blinking into the darkness until her gaze settled on me. Tentatively, I moved forward, ghosting my fingers down her cheek.

"Verner," she rasped. "Would it be so inappropriate for me to touch myself right now? It totally is, isn't it? I just... I have these dreams about you."

Dreams? As in, she'd had them before?

"Sometimes it makes it hard to look you in the eye," Meera laughed breathily, sliding her hand beneath the sheet as I drifted closer. I knew that the cover of darkness and the fact that I was able to look but not touch was giving Meera this confidence, but I hoped that she'd remember how safe she felt with me when we were back in the shadow realm together.

I did my best not to be territorial. Not to let those base instincts rule my actions.

But I needed Meera to feel safe and comfortable with me, and to keep dreaming about fucking me until she wanted to do it in real life, because the idea of her doing those things with someone else made me lose my mind.

"I must be ovulating," Meera said with a light laugh that morphed into a soft moan. "Maybe it's a good thing you're not solid right now—I'd probably be demanding you drop those shadows for me."

That sounded perfectly fine to me. Wonderful, actually.

"I'm not going to be able to sleep unless I make myself come. You don't have to look. But if you want to look... I'm okay with it."

Fuck.

I immediately stroked her face, lurching slightly in my enthusiasm. *Yes. Yes, I'm okay with this. Yes, I want to watch.*

Her hand moved a little faster beneath the sheet, thighs spreading apart, and I tentatively ran my hand over hers through the fabric. Asking without words for her to move the sheet away. It was a liberty I shouldn't have taken without asking, but Meera merely shuddered, arching her back slightly.

"You want to see?"

I nodded, exaggerating the movement as much as possible so she couldn't possibly miss my enthusiasm. There was no way of conveying that she didn't have to, that she shouldn't feel any kind of pressure, that I would never push for more than she was willing to give me.

But I didn't think I had to say that with Meera. Surely, she knew by now that nothing mattered to me more than her comfort and happiness.

Meera bit her lower lip, trying to hide a smile. "It's not so scary when it's you."

She kicked off the sheet, revealing her entirely naked body, and in my head, I groaned loud enough that I was certain she could somehow hear it.

I wanted to trace the generous curves of her body with my palms. I wanted to feel the weight of her breasts in my hands, and see if her nipples were sensitive to the faint scratch of my claws. And more than anything, I wanted to bury my face between those thighs with her hands wrapped around my horns, directing my tongue where she wanted it to go.

Well, perhaps not more than anything. While I very much liked the idea of worshiping Meera's body for hours until she was drunk on pleasure, the idea of burying my cock in her was also extremely appealing, if she'd allow it. Would she let me knot her? I'd never done it before, and I never would, unless it was with Meera.

Shamelessly, I moved farther down the bed, positioning myself between her legs as she bent them up, setting her feet flat on the bed.

What a view.

I was merely inches away from her soaked, bare pussy, and yet it felt like miles because I couldn't fucking *touch* her.

There was the subtlest shift in Meera's body language, but suddenly I was certain that she felt more confident. More *sexy*.

I groaned to myself as she sucked her middle finger into her mouth, wetting it before sliding it between her thighs, parting that pretty cunt for me.

"I need this," Meera rasped, immediately honing in on one particular spot and circling her finger teasingly. "I know how selfish I'm being right now..."

*You're not being selfish at all.*

"I'll make it up to you," she whispered, rocking her hips as she moved her finger a little more deliberately. I did my best to memorize the movement, intending to follow the path with my tongue at the first available opportunity. "Or maybe I won't. I'm beginning to think that I'll be a very selfish lover, Verner. I just want you to... just do everything I say, you know? Maybe I have control issues."

I couldn't tell her that I would be more than happy to take orders from her, so instead I shifted up the bed, burying my face against her wet cunt, though none of the arousal stuck to my stupid human-realm form.

Meera gasped in surprise, arching her back, pressing further into me. "Is that your way of saying you wouldn't mind? That's so... hot. The idea of doing this with you in the shadow realm isn't nearly as scary now."

Good. Perfect. That was exactly how I wanted Meera to feel.

"Verner," she whispered after a few moments, digging her heels into the mattress as a shudder ran down the length of her body. Of course she came quietly, her voice as delicate as it was when she was speaking. It was beautiful. I wanted to lean in close and hoard every sound for myself.

I lifted my gaze to Meera's face, where she was staring down at me, shiny fingers still lightly toying with her cunt.

"Maybe one more," she whispered. "Be good, and stay right where you are."

*Yes, my darling. Anything for you.*

# MEERA

## CHAPTER 19

I slept restlessly and woke up feeling hot and sticky and... embarrassed? No, that wasn't quite right. Or maybe it was and there was embarrassment there, but it was also a little more complex than that. I was selfishly glad that Verner wasn't in his corporeal form so we didn't have to talk about what I'd done last night. But I didn't regret that it had happened. A tiny fissure had formed in the wall I'd had up when he'd fed from me in the in-between, but getting myself off in front of him—for no reason other than I wanted to—had been like taking a sledgehammer to it.

There was no going back now. There was no "just friends" after that. The problem was, what *were* we if we weren't just friends? I wasn't built like the other ex-Hunters. I wasn't romantic. I didn't know how to open up and be vulnerable and trust.

Verner deserved everything. All of someone. He had so much to give in return. Could I be that for him when my brain kept fighting me at every turn?

Could I fight back?

I blinked rapidly to clear the sleep from my eyes, startling when I realized Verner wasn't in the room with me. Throwing the sheets off the bed, I sprinted for the bathroom, still naked, just catching myself in time before I turned the lights on.

"There you are," I breathed, clutching my chest. "I'm sorry, I didn't realize how much light would filter through the blinds."

Verner reached out, touching my cheek in a reassuring gesture.

"This is so less than ideal," I murmured, hating that he was stuck in this dark, horrible bathroom. "Is it worth me pointing out again that you can go home? Because you can. This is awful for you."

Verner slowly and deliberately shook his head. After a second's pause, he ran a shadowy finger along my jaw, before dragging it down my neck. And then lower. I shivered at the phantom feel of his touch on my sternum, before his movement came to a stop just above my bellybutton. My usual self-consciousness about my stomach was nowhere to be found, not when I could *feel* how much Verner wanted me.

"I'm going to shower," I mumbled, face heating as I realized how sticky I was between the legs. Even if I wasn't, I'd be showering again, trying not to think about the kinds of sheets I'd been sleeping naked on last night.

There was nowhere for Verner to go, so he hung around as the shower sputtered reluctantly to life and I waited for the water to work its way up to lukewarm. While I couldn't see his eyes—just the hood—it *seemed* like he was watching with interest, probably curious about how things worked in the human realm. This late-eighties motel room definitely wasn't the finest example of new technology.

My stomach complained loudly as I finished washing and drying myself, and I shot Verner a guilty look. "I might have to venture out to get food."

He didn't shake his head, but he didn't nod supportively or touch my face either. It was a necessary evil, and we both knew it.

"I'll be as fast as I can," I promised, heading back into the bedroom to pull on my clothes from yesterday. The sweatshirt still wasn't dry, so I reluctantly put Harlow's tight jacket on top, catching my reflection in the mirror above the small table as I did so.

I looked tired, and my messy bun was more like a bird's nest, but other than that...

Honestly, I looked pretty good. I couldn't remember the last time I looked in a mirror on purpose, but I was certain that the person looking back at me now wasn't the same as the person who'd looked back at me then.

This woman had life in her eyes. She had resolve. Her chin wasn't tucked down, but lifted and proud. She looked like she unapologetically took up space around her like it was hers to take.

She also looked like she'd had several orgasms in the past twenty-four hours, and was intending to have several more.

I liked the woman I saw in my reflection.

I was going to keep her.

"I'll be back as soon as I can," I called to Verner, shoving my feet into my shoes and heading out the door, locking it behind me and making a beeline for the van. I didn't intend on going far, but this area definitely didn't encourage walking. It made me miss the shadow realm even more, where I wandered through peaceful gardens to get wherever I needed to go.

There was a gas station not too far away, and I headed in that direction, intending to fill up the van so I could drive back to Harlow's tonight after my meeting with Adela. I'd stock up on enough gas station snacks to last me the day, and beg Astrid to find a way to reimburse Harlow at some point in the future when Astrid had forgiven me.

*If* Astrid forgave, I corrected uneasily.

If anyone could hold a grudge, it was Astrid. There was no telling how she'd react to what I'd done, and if she'd be able to forgive the fact that I'd gone behind her back.

I headed back to the fueled-up van with a bag of processed snacks that I was certain would make me feel sick later, freezing when I found Latika standing in front of the driver's door with her arms crossed.

Unlike yesterday, she was more determined and less startled. This time, I was the one on the back foot.

"How did you find me?" I asked, glancing around the empty gas station. I wasn't going to find any help here.

"I know this van," Latika replied, narrowing her eyes. "I recognized it when I followed you out last night. The Council would be *very* interested in knowing what kind of company Harlow Miles keeps."

*Shit.*

"I stole it. Harlow doesn't know anything about it. What do you want? Did you not say everything you needed to say yesterday? Are you here to remind me again that I'm ruined?"

Maybe it was my imagination, but I could have sworn she blushed.

"No." Latika cleared her throat. "I should report you. You're on the Council's list."

"I thought they were trying to make peace these days."

"You still have to answer for yourself, Meera. You can't just *leave* the entire realm and swan off with the enemy. There are consequences."

I burst out laughing—I couldn't help myself. "Latika, I don't answer to the Hunters Council. I was banished, remember? They can demand whatever they like, it's got nothing to do with me."

She frowned as though the idea had never occurred to her before. "You can't just ignore the Council, Meera. They're... they're everything."

Finally, *finally*, I saw traces of the twelve-year-old sister I'd left behind. The one who never asked questions, who trusted me implicitly to take care of everything and who assumed that everything in the world was the way it was meant to be.

"What exactly do you think happened to me when I was banished, Latika?"

She fidgeted uneasily. "I don't know. I guess I assumed that you were sent to live with other banished Hunters, and they gave you some kind of menial, crap job in the organization where no one would ever see you, instead of paying for college. Like Kathy," she added dismissively.

Kathy had been an elderly widow, who'd been given a very similar setup to what Latika was describing once her husband had died. No one had even tried to hide their whispers about what a burden to the organization she was. It was probably a similar existence to what those ex-Hunters living in Elverston House had experienced during their time in the Hunters. Not good enough to be considered valuable, but cooperative enough to keep around to do the drudge work that no one else wanted to do.

"That's not what banished means, Latika. Banished means cut off—no financial support, no housing, no contact. Nothing. Being a Hunter is deeply damaging to your sense of empathy, I get that, but please try to envision the person you were at seventeen and try to imagine what that's like. Also, Kathy had given and given and given to the Hunters for her entire life—the way they treated her wasn't acceptable either. Your sense of what's normal—of what constitutes good and bad—is so warped, Latika."

It was the first time I'd really thought of the Hunters as a *cult*, because that's what it was, wasn't it? Latika wasn't just naive, she was brainwashed. She saw the Council as the be all and end all. The hand that giveth and the hand that taketh away.

The little wobbles of doubt that kept sneaking up on me, reminding me that Astrid was going to be mad or that I was going to make life difficult for people, were steadied by Latika's delusions.

Peaceful negotiations weren't going to cut it. We needed a shakeup.

"Report me if you want." I shrugged. "It won't change anything."

"You could come back," Latika whispered. "You could ask them for forgiveness. Isn't that what you want, Meera? Don't you miss me? And Mom?"

"I have always missed you, Latika. And I'm confident that one day, we'll find each other again, and the circumstances will be different. I'm choosing to believe in a future where that's possible. And I miss the idea of having a mother who loved me and nurtured me and wanted what was best for me, but that's not the mother I had. So no, I don't miss her. I don't want anyone's forgiveness. I want them to beg for mine."

I sidestepped her and climbed into the van, setting the bag of snacks on the passenger seat and getting out of there as quickly as I could.

For once, I didn't feel like I was running *from* something, though. I was running *to* something. To vengeance. To justice. To a cleansing by fire, and a new world beyond.

Verner hovered in the darkest corner of the room as night fell, only one light on the nightstand on for Adela's benefit as I waited for her to arrive. Between the nerves and the snacks, I'd been on the verge of throwing up for the past hour.

I stood at the window, obsessively peering out at the parking lot through the blinds, on the lookout for a car that would definitely look too nice to be here.

"It's going to be fine," I repeated under my breath, somewhat for Verner's benefit, but mostly for mine as a sleek, navy vehicle pulled into the lot. "This is fine. No going back now. I'm not worried."

I turned to face Verner, giving him a firm nod that he mirrored back to me, before I headed over to unlock the door, ushering Adela in.

She looked rightfully wary as she peered around the room, her human eyes skipping over Verner entirely. If she got too close to him, she'd definitely be able to feel his presence, though. The hairs on the back of her neck would raise, and she'd be overwhelmed by a general sensation of something being not quite right.

It was a handy tool to have on my side if I needed to make a quick escape.

"So, Meera," Adela began with a tight smile, taking a seat kitty-corner to me at the small table. "You've got a real talent for disappearing."

I opened my mouth, trying to come up with an explanation for my absence before closing it again. On reflection, I probably should have come up with an excuse before she'd gotten here, but it didn't really occur to me that she'd ask.

Adela sighed. "Look, I understand that I probably spooked you. This isn't my first rodeo—I get that you want to just leave this part of your life in the past, but it's still affecting you to this day. Financially, if nothing else. You're paying for his crimes. Imagine how good it's going to feel to get that burden off your shoulders."

"I'm more interested in him finally seeing justice for the things he's done," I admitted.

Adela crooked a smile. "Yeah? Maybe I approached this all wrong. What I should have been saying is imagine how good it'll feel when we nail this fucker to the wall."

I let out a laugh of surprise, some of my nerves abating. "I wasn't ready to hear that then, but I am now. Provided what I have is going to be of any use, I guess."

The shoebox was already sitting there on the table with my notebook of recollections on top, and I slid the whole thing across to Adela. I'm sure there'd be something valuable in there that Adela could use to build her case, but I didn't know if it would be enough to build a *whole* case on. It was several years old at this point—Jackman's operation had probably changed significantly in that time.

Of course, it was too much to ask that Adela merely collect all the things I'd given her and be on her merry way so I could go home. Instead, she leafed through the notebook for a moment before carefully lifting the lid of the nearly decade-old shoebox to examine the documents inside.

I sat there in awkward silence as she held them up to the light, leafing through the stack and occasionally glancing over at me with an unreadable expression on her face.

"How on earth did you get hold of the bank statements?" she murmured.

I shrugged uncomfortably. "I don't want to say I was *entrusted* with a lot of stuff, because that's not quite right. It's more like... he saw me as too small and stupid to be a threat. Sometimes, I'm not sure he saw me as a person at all. Just another object in his collection."

The pitying look Adela shot me made me wish I'd never said any of that. The exhaustion was clearly getting to me if I was spilling my guts to strangers like this. I wanted to go home. *Home* home. Shadow realm home.

"This is a gold mine, Meera."

"Good. I don't mean to be rude, but you have my number and I'd really like to get out of this grimy motel."

"Of course," Adela agreed, putting everything back inside the box with the notebook on top. "I do have your number. Though, I get the feeling you're going to disappear again."

"If you contact this phone, I'll make sure the message gets to me," I assured her, wondering if I could bribe Harlow with fresh vegetables since I had nothing else to barter with. "Good luck with the case."

Adela tapped her nails on the box and smiled. I imagined it was the kind of smile that lawyers who were described as sharks had. "I don't need luck anymore. I've got this."

# MEERA

## CHAPTER 20

I felt jittery and paranoid the entire drive back to Harlow's apartment. I'd used the phone to take pictures of all the evidence, just in case, and the device felt like it weighed several tons in my pocket. What was I even going to do with it? It wasn't going to be usable in the shadow realm.

Could I really ask Harlow to help out with this? Latika had already figured out that the van belonged to Harlow, and I was confident that my half-assed excuse didn't convince her that Harlow wasn't involved.

I drove as slowly as I could without drawing attention to myself, acutely aware that keeping up with the van wasn't easy for Verner.

"Nearly there," I assured him, fretting about how he was holding up. While there were definitely things I needed to discuss with Harlow, I'd already told Verner to walk us right back into the in-between if he was feeling even a little bit low on power. I could figure out how to get a message to Harlow later—after Astrid had ripped me a new one for going behind her back.

To my surprise, Harlow was waiting outside the ground-floor apartment for us when we pulled up, and I wondered if she'd had a tracker on either the van or the phone the entire time. It hadn't even occurred to me to ask, though I couldn't exactly be mad about that, considering all she'd done for us.

"You were gone a whole *twenty-four hours*," she exhaled, shutting the door behind me and locking it while Verner hovered next to me. "What the hell were you even doing?"

"Did anyone come looking for me?"

She shook her head. "They wouldn't come here anyway, would they? It's not like we knew each other. You're basically a stranger who walked into my closet." Harlow pursed her lips, looking thoughtful for a moment. "*The Hunter, the Shade, and the Wardrobe.*"

"Very good," I replied dryly. "Though I'm no longer a Hunter. I'm sorry we were gone longer than you thought. We had a little delay en route."

"To your mom's house?"

"You already know the answer to that."

Harlow blinked owlishly at me. "I mean, sure. I got the general direction. Are you hungry? There's some leftover Margherita pizza in the fridge for you. Want me to heat it up?"

I hesitated, not wanting to linger too long, but also needing to talk to her. Having that conversation over food felt a little less intimidating. "Yes, please."

If nothing else, I'd been living off chips and candy all day, and I was desperate for something with a bit more sustenance. I followed Harlow to the kitchen where she made quick work of reheating a very generous portion of pizza for me, and pouring a glass of apple juice. I took a few moments to freshen up—though I was craving a long hot shower—before taking a seat at the counter.

Verner stayed close, giving my cheek a brief stroke of encouragement when Harlow wasn't looking.

"So?" she prompted, sliding the plate and glass over to me. "How'd the family reunion go?"

"How do you even know that's my mom's house?" I asked curiously. "Do you have access to all their records?"

Maybe it was because Harlow was so young and fun, but I'd obviously underestimated her.

"Yes and no. I mean, they didn't technically *give* me access, but I do *have* access." She shrugged, looking pleased with herself. "They took the whole organization offline after Austin's video, but I'd made copies of everything before then anyway."

"Without the Council knowing?"

"I'm good at what I do. And they're bad at it," Harlow added. "The Council has never been great at keeping up with technology. That's partly why they brought me on board, but they clearly hate relying on my expertise. Maybe I don't give off trustworthy vibes."

"Well, you are a double agent."

She hummed in agreement. "Very true. Maybe I give off backstabbing vibes."

I watched her closely as she ate her own pizza, trying to decide if that was the case. Could *I* trust Harlow? I doubted that Astrid would have anything to do with her if she wasn't at least mostly trustworthy, but Harlow was Astrid's contact, not mine. All I'd done from the moment I'd appeared in her closet was impose on her.

Twisting a little in my seat, I looked at Verner, whose gaze was already trained in my direction. I needed to find my backbone before we headed back to the shadow realm, just in case he was somehow punished for my choices. I needed to be ready to assert myself, to fight for my decisions, and to fight to protect his reputation.

The ex-Hunter cohort of the shadow realm was made up of a sea of big personalities, and letting myself be swept up in the tide of them was no longer an option.

I wiped my hands on a napkin before pulling the phone out of my pocket and setting it down on the counter between Harlow and me. "There are some photos on here of evidence that is pretty damning to the Council. To Randal Jackman in particular. Evidence that I've already given to the feds."

Harlow choked on her pizza, coughing awkwardly for a moment. "To the *feds*? Holy fuck, remind me not to get on your bad side."

Huh. I decided not to object to that. If I could cultivate a reputation for being a fearsome badass, I would happily embrace it.

"Look, I don't know if I'm making the right decision here or not. I want to trust you, Harlow. I want to know that this information will get to where it needs to go if the authorities don't pursue it for whatever reason. And if they *do* pursue it—well, I need a way of staying updated on that from the shadow realm, because I have absolutely no intention of staying here."

"Yeah, of course. Look, I'm no fan of the Council either. I told Astrid that the negotiations were a waste of time, and that I'd be here when she was ready for full anarchy. Which... maybe you beat me to it? What exactly did you get involved in?" Harlow asked, wide-eyed.

I gestured at the phone for her to take a look for herself.

Harlow stared hard at the screen as she flicked through the photos at a rapid pace. "Meera... did you even realize what you were holding on to? It's a few years old, but this... this will raze the Council to the ground. The names on here... Most of these people still serve on the Council. There are even names I recognize from other districts. This... this is a whole restructure waiting to happen."

"Do you think we're ready for that?" I asked, genuinely meaning it. If Astrid's words about Randal Jackman had been right, if getting rid of him put us in a *worse* position, I'd feel awful. I stood by my choice and I knew I'd done the right thing, but it didn't mean the potential consequences weren't terrifying.

Harlow blinked in surprise, dragging her gaze up to mine. "I've never really thought about it. The Council has always seemed so infallible. But if anything will bring them down... well, it's tax evasion, right? They'll subpoena the devil himself if taxes are involved."

I raised my glass of apple juice in toast to that.

"You don't seem very happy though," Harlow hedged. "You've done the hard part. You can celebrate now. Head back to the shadow realm—after you've eaten your pizza, of course—and do your victory lap."

"Let's see what the others have to say first," I muttered. "It wasn't very teamwork-makes-the-dream-work of me to come here on a renegade mission without telling anyone. I suspect they may have some thoughts about that."

Harlow's reaction was somewhat promising though. Her shock was wearing off, and now she was starting to pace the kitchen excitedly, drumming her fingers against the sides of her thighs. "Oh my god, can you imagine? This is going to be insane. I need to have cameras on all of their houses—I need footage of this. Do you think they'll get dragged out of their beds in the middle of the night by the police? I hope it's on the news. Come back from the shadow realm after they get arrested. We'll have a movie night. Popcorn and federal charges."

"I don't know if you'll have time. If the Hunters clean house, you might end up next in line to take charge," I pointed out, only half joking. The existing Council members had been clinging on to their positions for years—the only young person who'd been tapped for leadership in the whole country was Astrid, before she'd turned on them. Clearing out the old guard would leave a power vacuum for a Sebastian-type candidate to swoop into. He wasn't quite as awful as the ones who were there now, I supposed.

Harlow wrinkled her nose. "Fuck that. I don't play nicely with others. Then again, I might have to, because there are a bunch of assholes I don't want anywhere near positions of power who'd be more than willing to jump in."

"You can see why the others might have mixed reactions to what I've done," I sighed. "Better the devil you know, et cetera, et cetera..."

Harlow snorted. "I hope they're not that short-sighted. This is exactly what I've been telling Astrid we needed. A fresh start. A clean slate. Pages and pages of leverage that we can hold over them for the rest of their lives."

She loaded my plate into the dishwasher while I washed my hands in the kitchen, acutely aware that I couldn't put this off any longer.

"I wish I could come back with you," Harlow said wistfully. "I wish I was down with off-grid living and could hack it in the shadow realm full-time. I've been trying to retrain my dopamine responses and be less, you know, chronically online, but it's *so* hard. Do you know what I mean?"

"Not really," I admitted with a sympathetic smile. "Part of avoiding everyone and everything after I was kicked out was *not* going online, which I appreciated even more when I got the shadow realm and didn't miss it. If it helps, one thing Tallulah is really pushing for in the negotiations is for Hunters who want to spend time in the shadow realm being able to move between the two at will. You could work here during the day and get your internet fix, then go to the shadow realm at night. Join us for dinner in the dining hall—"

"Get a shadow daddy boyfriend?" Harlow cut in, eyes wide. "Oh my god, could I do that? I guess I'd have to find someone who was cool with me coming back here during the day. But it wouldn't have to be *every* day. I could live like it was the Middle Ages every so often."

"Absolutely. Why not? And I'm sure you could find someone who was cool with it—every Shade is different. So are all of the relationships between ex-Hunters and Shades."

I could have sworn I could sense Verner silently letting me know that he would *not* be cool with it. That he absolutely wouldn't be fine with me commuting between the human realm and the shadow realm.

Then again, we weren't a couple. Were we?

No, we were friends. Friends who'd kissed and gotten naked together. And who maybe had feelings for each other.

Well, I definitely had feelings for him. But I'd already explained to him that I couldn't be a loving, supportive partner. I didn't know how. Plus, I'd dragged him on a spontaneous, multiday revenge mission in an incredibly dangerous environment for him, when he hadn't even been able to communicate with me.

Verner was a gentleman, and he'd put up with a lot of my shit. But he wasn't an idiot. At some point, he had to put himself first, and I would support that entirely. I wanted him to be happy above anything else. Far above my own happiness. I wanted his life to be beautiful, and meaningful, and easy.

Whatever it took for him to have that, I would do it happily.

Was that... love? Did I *love* him?

"I think it's time to go home," I said awkwardly, looking at his hovering form. Verner immediately cupped my face in agreement.

"That's so fucking cute," Harlow whispered.

It was. If only it was forever.

# VERNER

## CHAPTER 21

**M**y head spun as we entered Harlow's closet again, and I shadow walked Meera back into the darkness. The in-between materialized blessedly fast around us, and I gripped her shoulders tightly as a wave of dizziness came over me. I'd never spent so long in that form, and suddenly my own limbs felt odd and heavy.

"You need to feed," Meera gasped, spinning to face me, her dainty hands gripping my forearms.

*Did I?* That seemed unreasonable. It hadn't been *that* long since I'd last fed from her—I usually went far longer than that without needing to visit the energy stores.

"Verner, you're stumbling. Sit down." I let Meera pull me down to the ground, though she suddenly seemed stronger than she usually did. Or perhaps I was weaker. If we returned to the human realm for any further quests, I was going to ask that we made more frequent trips home. "You need to feed," she repeated more firmly. "I'm going to take care of you."

"You don't have to," I mumbled. "Someone might find us."

They had to have realized we were missing and started properly looking by now. Weak as I was, I might have to kill someone if they saw Meera in a state of undress.

"I'll tell them to go away then. You are more important, Verner."

Meera climbed onto my lap, her arms around my neck helping keep me upright. My hands flexed at her sides, desperate to hold on to her, but not wanting to overstep. When my Meera wanted me to touch her, she would tell me.

"Touch me, Verner," she whispered. My palms immediately landed lightly on the sides of her thighs, wanting the closeness with her more than anything. How far could I go? What exactly did she mean? To my surprise, Meera briefly released her hold on my neck, gripping my wrists and shyly pulling my hands back to cup her ass. My cock throbbed almost painfully.

I'd never been so grateful for my dick before. I'd missed it the past couple of days.

"Someone might come looking for us," I reminded Meera again, worried about the possibility of her being seen in a compromising position. I didn't want to share my Meera. And I suspected she'd hate to be seen that way by anyone too.

"I'll keep my clothes on."

I grunted in acknowledgment of the very sensible compromise, hating that I wouldn't get to see her spread out naked for me again. Not this time, at least.

In the future, most certainly. Meera seemed to be under the impression that she wasn't going to be my mate someday, that she wasn't going to be my wife and the mother of my children. The idea of that person being anyone else was patently absurd.

Meera thought she was too difficult to love, but nothing could be further from the truth. Getting past her defenses had been difficult. Loving her was easy.

She undid the fastenings on our trousers, sliding one hand into her panties, the scent of her desire already perfuming the air around us. After a beat of hesitation, she wrapped the other hand around my aching cock, giving the base of it a squeeze.

Almost immediately, I began feeling better. Feeding from Meera was as addictive as talking to her. As caring about her. As loving her.

"Is it working?" she whispered, staring into my eyes as she circled her clit with her finger. Her grip on my cock was tight and proprietary—she wasn't necessarily doing it to give me pleasure. She was holding my cock because she owned it and we both knew it.

In all ways, Meera's confidence was growing and it was beautiful to witness. Usually, she struggled to maintain eye contact for more than a few seconds, and now she was staring into my soul. She was handling me like she had every right to, because I was hers to handle.

"It's working, my love."

Her cheeks flamed red as she scraped her lower lip with her teeth. I wanted to taste it for myself. I wanted to try our kiss again, now that I knew it was a gesture of intimacy. Whether or not I would be any good at it was still to be determined, but I wanted to try *everything* when it came to her.

"I missed your eyes so much," Meera whispered. "And your smile. And your voice."

"The next time we go into the human realm, you'll be able to hear it," I promised, making her blush all over again. I didn't understand the ins and outs of what had occurred between Meera and the human woman, but I'd gathered enough to know that it wasn't over. That Meera might need to go back someday, and that she was involved in something far bigger than herself. But we weren't going back there unless I could communicate with her, because that had been terrifying.

"If you keep talking sweet to me, I'm going to come," Meera whispered. I couldn't tell if it was a warning or a promise.

"I want you to come, my love."

"And what about what I want?" Meera asked breathily. I groaned, thrusting into her hand. The moments where she fully embraced how sexy and powerful she really was were lethal to my self-control.

"You can have anything you want," I promised her.

"I want to come. Better tell me something nice." She was already moving her hand faster, rocking her hips gently with each movement as my claws dug into her trousers, desperate to get to the skin beneath.

*I'm in love with you.*

As much as I wanted to say that, I managed to hold myself back. Those words probably wouldn't have the impact I wanted. Not yet.

"You are my everything, Meera. You're my light. You're my peace. You're my home. I'm going to be all those things for you too, when you're ready to let me, and not a single moment earlier."

It had been the exact reassurance she needed, and I prided myself on getting it right this time. She came with a soft cry, and the ebbs of power that had been flowing my way turned to a wave before slowing again. No wonder the mated Shades were always having to siphon off their extra energy if this was how much Meera's desire had filled me up with us barely touching one another.

She released me and pulled her hand out of her pants, bashfully wiping her arousal on the leg of her trousers before doing them up and making herself presentable.

"Do I smell like a horny ex-Hunter?" she asked with a shy laugh.

I hummed in agreement, still holding her ass. "You do, yes. It's quite enchanting."

"You say that now. What about when we have to walk out of here and bump into somebody?"

My fingers flexed slightly. Some Shades seemed to like to parade their mates around smelling like sex—the king being one of them. Perhaps I was more possessive than I realized, because I wanted to hoard Meera's desire entirely to myself.

"Mm, I didn't think you'd like that," Meera observed, apparently reading the nuances of my body language. She leaned forward, resting her head on my shoulder and snuggling into my front. It was such an intimate, trusting gesture from such a distrusting woman that I almost wept in gratitude for it. "I'm glad. I'm only like this with you. It's not something I want to... to share with the world."

"You don't have to," I murmured, banding my arms around her back and holding her close.

We both knew that we were putting off the inevitable, lingering in this peaceful moment for as long as we could before we walked out of here and everything changed. Even if our absence had somehow gone unnoticed— impossible for me, since I'd missed one of my shifts—the consequences of Meera's actions would soon make themselves known.

Eventually, there was a shout in the distance. Meera held on to me a little tighter as the sound of footsteps grew louder, seemingly a whole crowd coming to greet us. I didn't even look up. I wanted to stay in this moment for as long as I could.

Hands—human and Shade—pulled her off me, dragging us apart. The voices around us so loud that I didn't have a hope of making out Meera's quiet one, though I could have sworn I heard objection in her tone.

"What were you thinking?" Andrus hissed, his claws digging into my upper arm as he dragged me away. "They'll have your head for this. Did you learn nothing from the idiot duke?"

"He didn't do anything!" Meera shouted as Astrid held her back, surprising all of us with the vehemence in her voice. "Where are you taking him?!"

"Where the fuck have you *been*?" I heard Astrid snap, though her hold on Meera was the embrace of a distressed friend rather than a jailer. It was the only thing that kept my temper in check. "You both just vanished—obviously we need some answers."

Captain Soren moved in front of Meera, blocking my view of her. He softened his voice far more than usual when he spoke to her, though it didn't seem to help. "We'd just like to talk to you both to understand exactly what is going on. To make sure you're safe, and nothing happened against your will—"

"Of course it didn't," Meera snapped. "What are you saying? What are you accusing him of? Verner is the very best Shade in this whole realm—he's honorable, and kind, and wonderful."

I smiled to myself in spite of the dire circumstances, though it didn't last long as Meera was led away. They held me behind, putting some space between the two of us, and I forced my limbs to stay relaxed and my shadows to be still. Showing any sign of frustration or anger now would only make the situation worse.

"It's amazing you didn't die while you were there," Andrus muttered, drawing my attention back to him. "How long were you there? How did you manage to avoid the light?"

"Meera," I replied simply.

Andrus made a sound of disapproval. "I hope you took her as your mate first, or you were playing a fucking dangerous game putting your life in her hands like that."

While many things about our trip to the human realm *had* felt dangerous, that part hadn't. I'd trusted Meera entirely to keep me safe, even under challenging circumstances—like that horrible vehicle.

Andrus leaned in close, sniffing me without any regard for my personal space. "You smell a bit like her. Not the way the other mated pairs smell, though. Always drenched in each other's—"

"Am I going to the Pit?" I interrupted, not needing to hear the end of that sentence.

Andrus made a sound of disagreement. "You're going to the palace for questioning first."

"And Meera?"

"Astrid's instructions were to take her to the healers wing first."

As much as I didn't want to be separated from Meera, I wasn't going to argue with that. She'd barely had a moment to take care of herself over the past few days, and Astrid was assertive enough to ensure that Meera got what she needed.

I exhaled heavily, wondering what my own fate would be. I'd always done everything by the book. I followed the rules. I didn't complain. If I was known for one thing, it was my dependability. That reputation I'd built up over the years had now been thoroughly destroyed.

I didn't regret throwing it away, because Meera was worth it, but it was a slightly unsettling feeling. I was never going to be treated the same way. Life as I'd known it was over.

Worst-case scenario, I may even be facing life in the Pit, or worse. I didn't want to dwell on that, though. I wasn't even sure the idea had occurred to

Meera, and I hoped no one put it in her head.

If I were to be optimistic about it, I could say that perhaps this was the push I needed. The uncertainty with my family situation and my future had been weighing heavily on me for a long time now, and this was an opportunity to address it. To start fresh.

"I'm surprised I'm not receiving the same treatment that the Duke got," I admitted as Andrus led me out of the in-between and through the palace. The stares were excruciating. Every staff member seemed to have found a way to be on the stairs or in the corridors to get a good look at me.

"He's the king's kin, but there was no trust between them," Andrus replied dismissively. "You've loyally guarded the royal wing for years. Of course, you destroyed all that goodwill in one fell swoop, but I imagine it's why you're being brought in for questioning rather than thrown into a cell."

"That's generous of him," I murmured, my mind already back with Meera. Would she fight Astrid on receiving care? The others didn't know Meera, not really. Perhaps they would now that she wasn't holding anything back, that she was *letting* them see the real her, but I worried that the true nature of her stubborn streak would catch them off guard.

Would they be kind to her? I was on unsteady ground as it was. I certainly didn't have enough grace to argue with the captain's mate at this point in time.

I expected Andrus to lead me to the throne room for a formal interrogation, but instead, he took me to a private sitting room in the royal wing of the palace. One I'd only ever guarded from the outside rather than seen the inside of.

It was small but opulent, with heavy velvet drapes covering the walls that gave the space an intimate feel. This was definitely not somewhere that I was meant to be.

"Verner," the king said gravely, gesturing for me to take a seat opposite in one of the stiff-backed chairs. The captain had beaten us up here, and he stood off to the side while King Allerick and Prince Damen sat side by side on a sofa.

Andrus stationed himself at my back as I took my seat, and I couldn't tell if he was guarding me or supporting me. I was beginning to think Andrus was less of an asshole to males than he was to females. It didn't make him less of an asshole in general, but I supposed I understood him a little better now.

"Welcome back," the king said dryly. Damen flashed me his customary grin, but it didn't seem as carefree as it usually did. Recent events appeared to have aged him.

"Thank you, Your Majesty."

Captain Soren shot me an impatient glare, and I sat up a little straighter under the force of his disapproval. I'd always admired the captain's leadership, and an ache was building behind my eyes at the heaviness of letting him down.

"Talk to me," King Allerick sighed, slumping in his seat, his forehead resting on his palm. The guilt I felt at disappointing him—at disappointing anyone—was crushing, but I'd made my choices and now I had to stand by them.

"Meera had something she wished to do in the human realm."

Allerick raised his head to give me a disbelieving look. "You cannot possibly believe that explanation will be sufficient."

"He doesn't," Prince Damen volunteered. "He's clearly protecting Meera. Verner, are you going to tell us anything of value until Meera has given her side of the story?"

"Probably not," I admitted.

The prince laughed, though King Allerick and Captain Soren looked somewhat less amused. "Well, at least you're honest about it."

"We didn't even realize you were gone at first," the captain muttered unhappily. "The ex-Hunters in Elverston House were more than happy to lie to cover up for Meera, and you weren't scheduled for any shifts anyway."

"I hope it hasn't damaged the relationship between the palace and the new residents of Elverston House," I said sincerely. "That's the last thing Meera wants. They feel extremely loyal to her—they understand one another. She knows she put them in a difficult position."

"You're very eager to defend her," the king noted. "Though she isn't your mate."

"No, she's not," I agreed quietly. Whatever they heard in my tone, the three of them decided not to pursue that line of conversation, and I was grateful for it. That was a conversation I needed to have with Meera first.

"I don't know what to do with you, Verner," King Allerick began. "Technically, you didn't do anything wrong. Or rather, we don't know what you did wrong yet since you haven't told us. But Astrid was watching the Hunters carefully and didn't pick up on any signs of interference in the delicate negotiation process, which seemed to be something she was worried about."

I stared back blankly, unable to think of anything to say to that without incriminating myself or Meera. How long would Meera's contact take to act on the information she'd been given? Everything took so long in the human realm. Even just getting from one place to another was an arduous ordeal.

"We don't have any real cause to hold you in the Pit," the king added, the frustration in his voice clear. "Meera has been extremely clear that she never felt coerced in any way. As a high-ranking member of the Guard, you *did* have clearance to go into the human realm, though it was only meant to be for information-gathering purposes and with appropriate permission. Still, that's not enough to arrest you on."

The king gestured for Captain Soren to take over.

"You did abandon your post, though. You know there was never going to be any coming back from that, Verner."

"What are you saying?" I asked, already knowing the answer.

"You have been released from your position in the Guard," the captain replied heavily.

I nodded, my throat tight. Yes, I should have expected that, though I'd done a good job at not thinking about it.

"In addition, we met with your father, who was very disappointed to hear about your recent actions," the king added. "In order to encourage you to be a more responsible citizen of the realm, he has stepped aside. Congratulations, you are now the new Earl of Sunlis."

My stomach dropped to the floor. That position would take me away from the palace on a near-permanent basis—Sunlis was not an estate that ran itself. I didn't even *want* the position, and I was meant to have years before I had to think about it.

"But—"

"It's not the Pit," Andrus cut in, giving me a pointed look.

I fell silent, swallowing thickly. *No, it wasn't.* As far as punishments went, being banished to a grand estate that I had the running of wasn't exactly something I could complain about, though it was a banishment all the same.

"What about Meera?"

The captain gave me a long-suffering look. "You know we're not going to answer that question, Verner. Don't mistake the fact that you're not under arrest for leniency—the ground beneath you is very unsteady at this moment."

I dug my claws into the arms of the chair for a moment before slowly releasing them with a long exhale. There was no world in which I never saw Meera again. It wasn't possible.

After the dust had settled, after the shadows had cleared, all would be well. We would find our way back to one another. I would trust in that.

"Your parents are expecting you," the king added. "You have much to learn about your new role. I assured them you would make your way to Sunlis as soon as you arrived, provided that you were in good health and free of the Pit. As you fit both conditions, you may go there directly. Soren will escort you."

I straightened up as best I could, trying to maintain the last few shreds of my tattered dignity. "Yes, Your Majesty."

# MEERA

## CHAPTER 22

"Where are they taking Verner?" I demanded, wrenching my arm free of Astrid's grip and planting my hands on my hips to glare at her. I wasn't taking one step inside the palace until I knew Verner wasn't being sent away. Tallulah and Ophelia were there too, and while I knew they were trying to offer me support, I felt caged in and outnumbered.

"He's fine," Astrid replied, clearly as annoyed as I was and doing an equally poor job of hiding it. "Are you injured? What do you need?"

"I need the answer to my question."

Astrid huffed dramatically. "He's going to chat to the king about what the two of you have been up to."

"In the Pit?" I pressed.

Astrid narrowed her eyes. "Why would Verner need to be in the Pit, Meera?"

"He doesn't. Obviously. I was just asking."

"Astrid," Tallulah interjected softly, immediately trying to bring the temperature down. "Perhaps this isn't the best venue for this conversation.

Meera, we thought you might need to go to the healers wing—"

"I don't need that. I'm fine. Can't I go to the meeting with the king?"

"No," Astrid replied firmly. "If you don't want to go to the healers wing then we can return to your room—I'll send down to the kitchen for whatever you want. But we are going to talk, Meera. *Without* Verner. You up and left, convinced the Hunters in Elverston House to lie for you, disappeared for over a day, then swanned back in with a massive chip on your shoulder that you never seemed to have before. I mean, come on. You don't think you owe us a fucking explanation?"

Tallulah and Ophelia winced, watching me like they expected me to crumple like tissue paper under the force of Astrid's rage.

But I had plenty of rage of my own. Enough to fuel an argument. Enough to maybe take down an entire organization, if I'd directed it well enough.

"I told you I could replace him myself," I reminded her.

Astrid frowned. "This is about Randal Jackman? I mean, I know you *said* that, but you didn't mean it."

"Astrid," Ophelia chided gently. "Maybe she did."

Tallulah was looking at me like she'd never seen me before, and guilt churned uneasily in my stomach. Not at what I'd done—for the most part, I felt pretty good about that—but at the idea of letting any of them down. I'd misled them. They thought I was a good person. A calm, rational person who always exercised good judgment and didn't make impulsive decisions.

That had never been true. I'd just been pretending that it had been for years.

"Why don't we sit outside?" Ophelia suggested, gesturing to a circular stone table with curved benches around it, surrounded by a manicured flower bed.

I infinitely preferred that idea to being trapped in my room, surrounded by glowering and/or confused faces, so I immediately made my way over, sitting down next to Ophelia while Tallulah and Astrid took the seats opposite.

While it made sense that Verity wasn't here since she no longer lived at court, I desperately wished she was. The two of us had never been the closest out of the group—probably because our personalities were like chalk and cheese. But our backgrounds weren't. If I laid out to the group what I'd done and why, I'd probably find Verity the most understanding out of all of them. Well, except for the new ex-Hunters in Elverston House, but I doubted I'd even have to explain things to them. They would just get it.

The Hunters had a pecking order, and life was not all college scholarships, free housing, and immediate job offers for those at the bottom of it.

"Where's Iris?" I asked.

"The nursery," Ophelia replied. "She's a popular guest there—the babies adore her."

Of course they did—Iris was the sweetest soul in the shadow realm. I should probably spend less time with her, lest I taint her goodness with my anger.

"Enough small talk," Astrid cut in. "Where have you been? What do you mean you were going to replace Randal yourself? Where exactly did you go?"

"I had a meeting." I knew I was being obstinate, but sitting in front of the three of them for an interrogation had put me on the defensive.

She made a strangled noise of disbelief. "With who? And how did you organize it from the shadow realm?"

"With a Criminal Investigation Special Agent from the IRS," I replied, glossing over the how question because I didn't want Harlow to get in trouble for helping me.

The wind itself seemed to stop blowing for a moment. Everyone was silent. Tallulah and Ophelia were slack-jawed and shocked, while Astrid's eyes were narrowed dangerously.

"That's quite the meeting to tee up on short notice," she said flatly.

"From what I gather, she's been investigating Randal Jackman for a while now."

"You didn't think that was pertinent information to mention?" Astrid clipped.

"I had no idea he was on the Council—and definitely no idea that he was leading negotiations from their side. I thought he was just another skeevy guy, just like the other skeevy guys who wield power within the Hunters. When I was young and dumb and afraid of everyone and everything, he'd used that to his advantage. From what I gather now, he was part of something much bigger. Something that a lot of other Councilors might be involved in too."

"What do you mean? What kind of criminal activity are we talking about here?" Ophelia asked nervously.

"Fraud. Tax evasion. There was definitely a business involved—I guess it was a shell company?—and by the sounds of it, other Councilors have gotten on board with it too."

Tallulah exhaled slightly. "Okay. And the IRS know about it now?"

"They'd clearly figured out something was wrong already, and their investigations led them back to me," I corrected. "I still had a lot of the paperwork that I'd kept hidden under a loose floorboard in the closet at my mom's house."

"That's kind of badass," Astrid muttered, leaning back and looking reluctantly impressed. "How come you had that stuff, though?"

I opened my mouth, waiting for my freeze reflex to kick in and silence me, but it never came. Apparently this time, I was ready.

"I'm sure you've all worked out that I'm not from one of the more illustrious Hunter families. Single mom. Immigrants. Barely getting by. We were very dependent on the Council for a lot of things." I cleared my throat uncomfortably, not wanting to cry. I'd never been a crier, and if I was about to start, then I wanted it to be in the comfort of my own room. "Looking back now, I can see that as a parentified teenager with very few friends and an overworked, exhausted mother... I was basically a sitting duck for an older authority figure to swoop in and gain my total trust. He promised me the world—material comforts, help with Latika, less financial pressure on Mom. And he'd give me things too—like a winter jacket, or shoes that didn't have holes in them. Either Mom didn't notice or... I don't know. Maybe she was just happy she didn't have to buy those things for me. This all started when I was a teenager. I just wanted to give you some context for why I let myself get involved in all this."

"You don't have to justify that," Tallulah said quietly. Her voice was gentle, but she was wearing her mama bear expression. "You were a kid, he was an adult. None of the responsibility lies with you."

I nodded awkwardly. "I was a minor, so he used me to run errands and stuff for his business. Collect up documents that he didn't want anyone to see—including his wife. I gave him my social security number. He took out a line of credit in my name—I was still paying it off when I came to the shadow realm. At the time, I thought I'd been helping him, you know? Obviously, I see now it was another tool to control me with."

Everyone was silent as I blew out a shaky breath to steady myself. I could feel myself reaching the upper limits of my bravery when it came to talking about this, and I didn't want to push myself too hard and fall apart completely. I didn't have the luxury of that right now.

"Anyway, that's how I got my hands on the paperwork. I was exiled after he turned on me, and I don't know why he never chased me down and asked me what I did with it. Maybe he just assumed I threw it all away? He never thought particularly highly of my intelligence. I guess even seventeen-year-old me knew that the stuff might come in handy one day, so I stored it in a shoebox under a floorboard, just in case. I didn't have time to grab it when my mom threw me out of the house."

I would have taken shock and looks of faint betrayal over the pity I could now see in their eyes. Seventeen-year-old Meera—eager for validation, and desperate for any kind of love—deserved their pity. Not twenty-five-year-old Meera. Not the person who I was now.

What I wanted—*needed*—now was friendship. Was the love and support of these amazing women who I'd come to care about since I'd moved to the shadow realm. But I also knew that was a tall ask at this exact moment because I was proving not to be the person they always thought I was.

"This, um, certainly changes things," Ophelia said eventually, twisting her wedding ring around her finger absently. "Or it will, if they press charges."

"Isn't the conviction rate, like, ninety percent for the IRS? These guys are fucked," Astrid replied confidently. "The question is when it'll all come out. And you know we can't let Sebastian find out before then, because he'll for sure give them a heads-up—he worships Randal."

Considering how we'd started the conversation, I was surprised that Astrid seemed to have warmed up the fastest. Then again, perhaps I shouldn't have been. I should have known Astrid would respect a vengeance mission. In hindsight, I felt a little silly not telling her about it.

Tallulah nodded uncertainly. "We're going to have to continue the peace talks as normal until it all comes to light. Just act like nothing has changed. But we're in a good position now—we can plan for it, so we have the upper hand when it all falls apart on their end. Though, we could also end up dealing with someone worse. My grandfather has been content to be hands-off in terms of governance since his money talked for him. But if there's a sudden exodus of Councilors... Well, he might deign to lower himself enough to get involved. Honestly, I'm sort of baffled by this whole thing. Why even bother with all this dodgy finance stuff if they had access to Grandfather's money in the first place?"

"As you pointed out, that money came with strings attached," Astrid said, leaning back in her seat and crossing her arms. "Maybe they were working on having their own source of money, separate from the Thibaut family fortune. Isn't there an opportunity here for us to sway the new Council membership in a direction that's more cooperative for us? I'm not saying we should stack the bench, but you know. I'm not *not* saying that."

Astrid was in a good mood, so I opted not to tell her that I'd hijacked her human world contact and already had this exact conversation. It would come out eventually that Harlow had been involved, but surely it could wait. I already had enough damage to control on Jade's behalf, and the other Elverston House Hunters who had covered for me.

"Getting involved in that power struggle could be a slippery slope for us..." Ophelia replied hesitantly. "And as Tallulah said, her grandfather will probably get involved. He's a formidable foe."

I nodded to myself, thinking it over. Sure, we could swoop in and appoint a figurehead, but it wouldn't stick. Lasting, effective change was borne of *belief*. Of people rallying behind someone—or some*ones*—that they truly *believed* in. There were no shortcuts. That depth of feeling couldn't be bought.

"Anyway, that's a conversation for a different day," Ophelia said firmly. "What matters right now is making sure that this conversation stays between us, and Verner's conversation stays with those who are in the room with him right now."

I cleared my throat. "He won't have told them what I've told you. I'm not sure he'd have the vocabulary to explain it even if he tried—there's no IRS in the shadow realm."

"Right, we'll probably need to sit down with the king to lay it all out," Tallulah mused. "What about the other ex-Hunters in the realm, though? It feels a little uncomfortable to hide this from them."

Ophelia exhaled heavily, as the invisible divider between the original ex-Hunters and the new ones grew a little thinner. There was no question that Austin and Verity would be informed, but what about Jade, and Patrick, and the others in Elverston House? Iris was still a little bit of an unknown, but I think we'd all decided to trust her.

And then there was Cora. She'd come over here with Sebastian and her brother—they had been deemed negotiators, but she wasn't. She'd come because she wanted to, and it seemed like she was fitting in well, but her brother's betrayal had changed the way everyone saw her now.

"Sebastian sticks pretty close to Cora when he's in the realm," Astrid pointed out.

There was a general murmur of agreement, though no one seemed wholly comfortable with it. It was difficult to get a read on Cora these days, and it made sense for her to seek out a familiar face in Sebastian. Even if she was fully on our side, it was a big ask to put this secret on her shoulders when she was regularly in his company.

"I'd like to tell Iris myself," I said quietly. "Please."

Ophelia nodded, clearly wanting to ask why but deciding not to.

There was no way that Moriah Nash was coming out of this scandal untouched. If I was going to be the one who sent her parents to prison, the least I could do was tell Iris that myself.

"What about Verner?" I asked. "When can I see him?"

"Let me talk to Allerick," Ophelia said gently. "I'm sure it won't be too long. Just... give things some time to settle down. We'll figure it out."

It was the least comforting answer she could have given me.

# MEERA

## CHAPTER 23

The following week felt like a year. No one would let me see Verner. No one would tell me where he was.

The self-doubt was starting to creep in a little now. Maybe he was avoiding me. Maybe, after speaking to the king and the captain and whoever else, he didn't want to be with the woman who'd ruined his reputation.

And I was almost certain I had. His name was definitely being whispered at court, but he was nowhere to be found. And everyone stopped talking as soon as they saw me coming.

The guilt was eating me alive. If I could see him, I could at least apologize, but I also didn't want to force my presence on him if he hated me now.

Maybe I should write him a note? Then again, I wasn't sure I trusted anyone to deliver it. Ophelia and Astrid had both been cagey when I'd asked questions—possibly because they didn't want to undermine their partners.

I'd spent days trying to get answers out of them, which had conveniently kept me too busy to sit down and have some of the difficult conversations I needed to have with other people. But I wasn't doing that whole avoiding-tricky-topics thing anymore. Today was the day that I put on my big girl pants and went on my apology tour.

Hopefully it would keep me busy enough that I wouldn't spend my time obsessing over Verner and wondering if he even liked me anymore, and if he knew that I *loved* him, and maybe I should have told him that.

The vegetable garden looked even better than when I left it, and I made a note to thank Patrick and ask if I could learn from him. If he wasn't mad at me, that was. I didn't really know how these guys would react to everything, but ultimately, I had put them in a difficult spot with my lie and they had every right to be annoyed about that.

"Meera!" Jade exclaimed, throwing the door open and jogging down the stairs. Had she been watching from the window? I let out a startled sound as she threw her arms around me before belatedly remembering that people didn't usually stand there like a statue when they were being hugged.

God, I was so awkward.

"Hi," I said lamely, patting her on the back. "How are you? Sorry it took me so long to visit—"

"Oh my god, don't apologize." She grabbed my arm, towing me toward the house. "You're, like, a celebrity. Astrid told me what you did."

"Did she?" I asked, surprised.

"Yeah. I'm not meant to tell anyone else yet, which has been killing me. I think she was just feeling me out, trying to decide if I'm trustworthy or not, you know?"

That did sound like Astrid logic.

"Want some tea? I just put the water on to boil. And we can talk privately in the kitchen."

"Sure."

From the front door, it was a straight line down to the kitchen at the back of the house, and meant passing by a lot of the common areas on the ground floor. It was the first time I could really see how different the place looked now—it was busier and brighter. There was more *stuff* everywhere. Clothes lying on couches, and books haphazardly left wherever someone had been sitting to read them. Ten new people had meant a lot more *stuff*—and a busy time for Astrid, sourcing it all—and the house felt more alive than it had in a long time.

It was nice. It still needed a coat of paint and a significant number of repairs, but it felt a lot more homey now.

I missed it here. Sure, Elverston House was a little worn down and needed some love, but so was I. I was connected to this place.

"Here, sit," Jade said, gesturing to the wide ledge by the fireplace where she was boiling the hanging kettle. "So? Have you heard anything from the human realm yet?"

I shook my head. "No. I mean, I guess they have to go through the evidence I gave them and whatever. I don't know how long these things take."

Those were probably the kinds of questions I should have asked Adela at the time, but I hadn't been thinking straight and I'd just wanted to go home.

"It was such a brave thing you did," Jade said, an almost dreamy look on her face as she added the tea leaves to the boiling water to steep.

"I don't know about brave."

Spiteful, yes. Justified, absolutely. Bravery hadn't really come into the equation though.

"What? Of course it was brave. All of us here have fantasized at some point or another about how it would feel to tell a Councilor to go fuck themselves. And you actually did it! And you had the receipts to back it up. You're a hero."

My face heated at the genuine enthusiasm in her voice. She made it sound like I was some kind of crusader for the downtrodden, when in reality I'd been thinking purely of myself.

"I didn't actually tell him to go fuck himself. I didn't see him at all."

Jade pursed her lips. "That's slightly less cool than what I was imagining, I'll admit. But if you get him sent to jail, it'll all be worth it."

I laughed for the first time in the past few days. "That might be true. I'm sorry for leaving you guys in the lurch. I shouldn't have let you cover for me—that wasn't a nice position to put you in."

"What? Oh no, it was fine. We didn't mind. Look, we get it, you know? And sometimes, they just... *don't* get it. They don't understand that sometimes you can't do things by the book, because the book wasn't written for us. Astrid was really trying to talk to me and relate to me, but she was being groomed to join the Council someday. What does she really know about my life?"

The friends I'd had since the beginning weren't elitist snobs who thought less of anyone else. They were great people. And they *were* shaped by their experiences, as we all were.

Ophelia's parents had still paid for her to go to boarding school after she'd been kicked out. Astrid had been shoulder tapped for a future on the Council herself. Tallulah's friends and family had just quietly shuffled her along when she was exiled, and she'd had an income and friends from her college days—paid for by the Hunters Council—to rely on. Austin had been free to pursue his music career, financially supported by his family.

But for those of us at the bottom, we hadn't *benefitted* from the system. We'd been trapped by it. I'd left with nothing. No money, no family, no friends.

No hope.

And yet... we were all here. Jade and the others. Verity. Iris. Myself. We'd found our way here, and now we had the opportunity to build incredible lives for ourselves. We were in a supportive environment where anything was possible.

It was *possible,* but it wouldn't just *happen.*

And the differences that divided us there couldn't just be forgotten, because they formed who we were. But they didn't need to be a barrier between us either.

"She doesn't really know anything about it, but we can tell her," I replied quietly, staring into the fire. "I mean, don't share more than you want to share, of course. But we're all on the same side, aren't we? It's very easy to get caught up in that resentment of how differently our lives played out when we had so much in common, but we also have an amazing opportunity right now to try to balance those scales."

I looked up at Jade while she poured the two cups of tea. "I'm sorry, I don't mean to sound dismissive—"

"You don't. You sound wise. Like you've really put some thought into what life here could look like for us. I haven't done that, honestly. Maybe because I feel like I'm in survival mode all the time."

"It's not easy to think philosophically when your brain is constantly scanning for threats," I agreed, accepting the cup she handed me. "But hopefully you'll start to feel more settled here soon. If there's anything I can do to help, then I want to do it. It's important to me that you feel at home here."

Jade sat down on the other side of the ledge, watching me with a small smile. "You're really easy to talk to. Has anyone ever told you that?"

I paused, my cup halfway to my mouth. "No. Never."

"Oh. Well, they should. You have this really quiet, comforting way of getting people to open up. It's a real gift."

Huh. Not boring. Not glum. Not dull. Quiet and comforting.

I could live with that.

"You seem sad," Iris said, her knitting needles moving at an astonishing rate as she spoke.

"Do I?" I hadn't realized I was being so obvious about it. Then again, I suspected Iris's empathy barometer was more sensitive than most.

She hummed from her seat in the corner while Tilly dozed on the floor. Not for the first time, I admired how perfect Iris's posture was—she looked like she was sitting for a painting at all times. "I know that we've been avoiding the subject, but perhaps now is the time for you to tell me where you went for those few days?"

I sighed heavily. "It probably is."

"Good. You had everyone rather frantic, you know. Damen was my only company and he refused to tell me. He said he didn't want me to worry." She tutted softly. "I might have to tell him off."

I choked slightly on my saliva. "Tell him off?"

"Yes—like how Nana used to tell me off when I was misbehaving. It's unacceptable that he withholds information from me because he's worried I won't be able to handle it. I'm tougher than I seem."

I couldn't imagine Iris telling Prince Damen off. Or anyone off, for that matter. She was like one of the fairytale princesses in the movies my sister used to watch growing up. All soft tones and tinkling laughter. Even her hair looked like spun gold, now the patchy temporary dye had washed out of it.

"I won't argue with that. And you're right—it's wrong of him not to answer your questions honestly. It would be wrong of me not to as well."

Iris nodded. "It would. Now, you tell me where you were and why you're sad. Did you not want to come back?"

"No, no, it's not that," I said hastily. "I definitely wanted to come back. I, um, went to the human realm."

The silence as Iris paused for a moment, her needles stilling, was slightly eerie. After a few seconds, she resumed knitting, though at a much slower pace.

"Why?" she asked eventually, not a trace of judgment in her voice.

"Um. Well... I think I lost my mind a little."

Iris nodded sympathetically. "Did you have an episode? My mother used to have them all the time."

I wasn't sure where to begin with that. Iris was incredibly calm when she talked about her past, but I suspected it was far more traumatic than any of us realized.

There was a high possibility that she'd be thrilled to know her parents were in jail. But there was also a distinct chance that she wouldn't be. Families were complicated.

"Sebastian mentioned some of the Hunters he was working with on the negotiations... I recognized one of the names. It was a guy who'd... taken a particular interest in me." I cleared my throat. "I was only seventeen. I didn't want him, but it didn't matter. When it all came out, no one believed me. I was kicked out, both out of the Hunters and my home."

"So you heard his name, and you wanted vengeance," Iris surmised, looking thoughtful. I hadn't expected her to immediately connect those dots, which I guess meant I was as guilty of underestimating her as everyone else was of underestimating me. "Did you get it?"

"Yes." *And then some.*

"How does it feel?"

No one had asked me that question. I hadn't even asked *myself* that question.

How *did* it feel?

"Kind of good," I said slowly, hyperaware of the fact that I wasn't telling Iris the whole story. That I was leaving out a pretty significant part that impacted her directly. "But kind of hollow at the same time, I suppose. Maybe I thought that revenge on Randal Jackman would be a magic cure to all my problems, but it wasn't—not really. Destroying him didn't erase the damage he's done."

*And I may have created a host of new problems in the process*, I added silently.

Iris hummed. "Do you regret it?'"

"No," I replied instantly, not needing a second to think about it. Yes, it had changed things in a way that I wasn't sure could ever be reversed, and ruining Jackman's life probably wouldn't tangibly improve my own, but I still didn't regret it. I'd returned to the shadow realm feeling more sure of myself and my place here. I was more in control of the ghosts that haunted me, and far more settled in my relationship with Verner—or at least I had been until he'd disappeared.

Perhaps the real revenge was the friends we made along the way?

And I'd leveled the playing field a little on the Hunter side, even if the king and the captain didn't want to admit it yet. The Council may have been the devil we knew, but it was the devil nonetheless. This *could* be a good thing. I was choosing to believe that it was.

We both startled at the sound of a knock on the door, and I quickly moved to open it, finding one of the palace staff standing there.

"You have visitors in the entrance hall. Theon, the Duke of Lindow, and Verity, the Duchess of Lindow." I don't think I imagined the exasperation in the staff member's voice when they spoke. From what I gathered, there were plenty of other dukes and duchesses in the shadow realm, but only Verity and Theon actually insisted on *using* the titles. They really were a match made in heaven.

"Oh, right. Thanks. Iris—do you want to come with me?" I asked guiltily, acutely aware that I still hadn't told her the whole truth about what had happened in the human realm. Then again, maybe now wasn't the time—maybe Moriah Nash would escape from the fallout unscathed, and I would have worried Iris for nothing.

Or I was just a coward. Or both. Maybe my journey to being assertive and confident and speaking my mind wasn't a perfectly linear one.

"No, thank you. I'm expecting a visit from Orabelle soon."

"The king's mother?" I asked, surprised. "I didn't realize you two were close."

Iris laughed. "I'm not sure we are, but she keeps coming back. I think she enjoys my company more than she's willing to admit."

I smiled in spite of myself. "Of course she is. You're incredible company. I'll visit you again later."

"That would be nice, thank you."

To my surprise, Verity and Theon hadn't made use of one of the private drawing rooms at the palace, but were instead waiting in the foyer where everyone could see them, seemingly reveling in the confused looks they were getting.

"There you are!" Verity said, striding over to me in baby pink stilettos that clipped on the stone floor with each step, and pulling me into a hug. "Sorry it's taken me so long to come to the rescue, news travels slowly to Lindow. Or it does when Damen is responsible for delivering it, at least."

"Come to the rescue?" I repeated, having to tip my head back to meet her eye when she was in heels that high.

"Yes, darling. We're off to get your man."

Theon grumbled something incomprehensible from a few feet away, tapping his foot impatiently.

"My... man?"

"Verner—he's your man, no?"

"He's not a *man*, Verity," Theon sighed irritably. "I wish you wouldn't use such deeply offensive terms to describe my fellow Shades."

"Fine, fine. Verner is your *Shade*, isn't he? Ugh, it just doesn't have the same ring to it."

"I... Um. Well, I don't know," I admitted. "I thought he was. But I don't know where he is, and I haven't heard from him. And I kind of told him that I couldn't be the sort of partner he needed—"

"What on earth did you say that for? Why couldn't you? Oh my god, Meera, you two have been giving each other puppy dog eyes almost since we arrived in the shadow realm. He is *obsessed* with you. You're more low-key, so I don't know what the hell is going through your head most of the time, but I feel like the obsession was pretty mutual."

"It was. It is."

"Then why the hesitation?" She threw her hands up in exasperation. "Hunt that man—sorry, honey. That *Shade*—down and wife him up. Shake that bare neck in his face and make it happen, boo."

I laughed at the visual, having forgotten how absurd Verity could be, and she grinned smugly.

"Yeah? Is that a yes? Are we going?" she pressed, nudging my shoulder. "Do you want to change first?"

I hadn't wanted to, but now I did. I guessed I could put in a little more effort. My t-shirt had a tea stain on the hem from breakfast.

"Okay. Yeah, okay. And yes, I'll change. But I don't even know where he is."

"I do," she replied, crossing her arms and giving me a self-satisfied grin.

"Actually, *I* do," her husband corrected.

Verity rolled her eyes. "What's yours is mine, babycakes—including all the gossip in your brain. Wait here while we get ready. We'll be back in a minute."

Theon slunk over to the wall, obediently leaning against it with his arms crossed. They were an unconventional couple, but there was no denying that it worked.

We'd only made it around the first corner toward my room when we came face-to-face with the Bishop sisters, and Ophelia's bodyguard, Levana. Only Astrid looked somewhat pleased to see me—which was weird in itself, since *pleased* wasn't an expression Astrid usually wore.

"Hey, rebel," she said with a catlike grin. "Started any revolutions today?"

"No, but it's still early," I replied, giving her a wry smile. Ophelia relaxed slightly, though I could tell that the tension of the situation was still bothering her. Levana looked ready to string me up with some shadow magic, and I remembered Verner mentioning that they were old friends. Shoot, maybe I shouldn't be taking advice from Verity. Maybe this whole idea was idiotic.

"We were just dropping Orabelle with Iris," Ophelia said with a tentative smile. "Iris mentioned she'd seen you."

"Yes. I, um, didn't get a chance to talk to her about everything yet." I cleared my throat, glancing at Levana before returning my gaze to Ophelia.

"Is no one going to say hi to me? Am I just invisible now?" Verity complained with a dramatic sigh. "This is what I get for moving away from the palace. You all just forget about me."

It was the perfect distraction—Ophelia immediately felt bad and fell over herself to make Verity feel welcome.

"I'll just go change," I mumbled quietly, ducking around them and heading down to my room. I wasn't surprised that Astrid followed behind me, slipping in as I shut the door.

She waited in silence, averting her eyes as I changed into a somewhat presentable-looking sundress and brushing my hair.

"Are you going to track him down?"

"Who?"

She shot me a disbelieving look. "Come on, now. I'm not an idiot. I noticed it weeks ago, and even if I hadn't, he left begging me to keep you safe."

He'd done that?

"So, what is this about? Are you warning me not to go?"

"No. I mean, would it help if I did? Apparently, you're far more impulsive than any of us realized," she added dryly.

My face heated. "Those were special circumstances."

"Bullshit. You look ready to march into battle right now." She sighed. "Listen, I feel bad for the way this has all unfolded. You could have communicated with me, but I could have definitely been more patient. More willing to hear what you were trying to tell me—I realize now how hard that conversation must have been for you. And the Verner thing... Honestly, Soren is pretty salty about it. It's a big deal in the Guard to abandon your post. He really let Soren down."

I swallowed thickly. "I understand. I don't know if it would help at all to point out to Soren that it was entirely my fault. I *asked* Verner to take me to the human realm."

"He could have said no," Astrid pointed out.

"Could Soren have said no to you?"

Astrid reeled back, though the gesture was subtle because it was her. "It's that serious between you guys?"

"It is for me. And I don't know if I can give him what he's looking for, but for Verner, I'd try."

Verity threw the door open, marching in with a brilliant smile on her face. "Don't you fucking steal my thunder, Astrid Bishop. I see that look on your face—your resolve is crumbling. But, alas, it is too late. For *I* will be the one to bring this knight in shining armor to the beleaguered prince in the palace so she can free him with true love's kiss."

Astrid wrinkled her nose. "Yeah, that's all you. I don't want to do that."

"Beleaguered prince?" I repeated, fiddling with my hair as if it would magically look full-bodied and not frizzy for the first time in its life.

"You'll see," Verity replied airily. "Let's go, madame knight. Your prince awaits."

# VERNER

## CHAPTER 24

The chamber was my least favorite room at Sunlis. The walls, floor, and the large rectangular table that dominated the space were all made of the same black marble, and the room was built underground—it meant to function as a safe place for strategizing in the event of an attack.

While there was an abundance of silver orbs to keep the place safe from shadow walking, it still felt incredibly oppressive, and I'd barely left this room for the past week. Talks had gone on all day and well into the night, every night, as I tried to convince my father to renounce his abdication, and he tried to convince me to merely live my life exactly the way he did and never complain about it.

"We've been too lenient on you," Mother sighed, not for the first time. Not only were my parents here, but an assortment of relatives from both sides of the family, all buzzing around like insects, pushing their own interests. Osric had made sure he was here, of course. While my father and I sat at opposite heads of the table, Osric was around halfway down, his claws touching lightly where he clasped his hands over his stomach, looking like nothing could have amused him more than these discussions. My uncle stood supportively behind his son, one hand resting on Osric's shoulder.

It was clear what they wanted. They were hoping that Father wouldn't back down, in which case I'd be forced to step aside also, and then the position would be Osric's.

And there had been many moments over the past few days where that had seemed pretty tempting. I could walk away and finally be free to live my life on my own terms.

But now I had Meera to consider.

What kind of future could I offer her if I gave up my inheritance now? I owned no property of my own for us to live in. While I could probably afford to purchase something, it wouldn't be anywhere near as grand as Sunlis, and would have no staff. Meera deserved the best. She'd suffered enough—I wanted her life to be nothing but comfortable from here on out.

I wanted her to have every meal prepared by a chef to her liking, and for the bed to be made for her each morning with the fabrics she chose. I wanted Meera to spend her days in complete and utter relaxation, only choosing to indulge in activities that brought her joy, like gardening, and helping deliver babies.

As far as hobbies went, I could think of more relaxing options, but I would support her in all her endeavors.

Except, the pressure to do that *now* would be too much for either of us. Meera wasn't even entirely confident that she wanted to be in a relationship with me yet. I definitely didn't feel equipped to run the estate. If my father would give us just a few more years to get accustomed to it all, that would be more than sufficient.

I'd already been fired from my job. How else was I going to provide for my love?

"All this objection is because of the Hunter," Father said, more forcefully than I'd expected him to. Perhaps something in my expression indicated that Meera was on my mind. "Give her up, Verner. Hasn't she done enough damage?"

"I will not give Meera up. I will never give her up."

His fist hit the table with a thud, making everyone else in the room startle. I surveyed him coolly, disappointed that he'd displayed such a loss of control. Despite our differences, I'd always admired him—he was my father, after all, and a dignified figure of authority in both the local community and the shadow realm as a whole. Perhaps this was the first time I'd ever really looked at him, not as the Earl of Sunlis, but just as a Shade. As a male. As a peer.

And now, technically, a subordinate. Perhaps I should stop objecting. I could take up the seat, be miserable for a few years while I got the lay of the land, and hope that I didn't run the estate into the ground. In the meantime, Meera could come and visit to her heart's content until she felt comfortable enough to move in.

*That might never happen*, I remembered uneasily. Meera wouldn't want to leave her garden. She'd struggle to move away from her friends.

And Sunlis would probably be hostile to her, at least for a while. The staff here were loyal to my parents, and if they didn't like her, the employees wouldn't either.

"It seems we're at an impasse," I said mildly. "Or rather, you are. You can't stop me from taking Meera as my wife and mate, and I assure you that I intend to do both. All that's left to decide is whether you are going to accept that fact, and accept us into your lives accordingly."

I was being high-handed—making assumptions about Meera's wishes that I had no idea about. But this wasn't the venue to show any sign of weakness. I had to make a choice and stand by it.

"I cannot fathom why you're being so stubborn about this," Mother muttered. "You've never been stubborn before. Your obedience has always been much remarked on by everyone."

"There's never been anything I cared enough to fight for until now," I countered. "I'll fight for Meera. I will *always* fight for Meera."

"That's the problem, don't you see?" Mother hissed, glancing around in embarrassment at our audience. "You should be looking for quiet, appropriate civility in a relationship. Or no relationship at all—your father and I are hardly the norm. Simply produce Sunlis's heir and be done with it. No need for all this... heated emotion. You're wanting to uproot the natural order of things, Verner."

"Yes, cousin," Osric agreed, sticking out his chest. Perhaps it was the abundance of self-importance that made him puff out that way. "Maintaining the honorable traditions of Sunlis is essential to our future success."

I wished I could roll my eyes the way Meera could. The action perfectly captured a sense of disdain.

"I understand I'm not the perfect heir the way Elisaria was—"

"Don't you *dare* speak her name," Father hissed, slamming his hands down on the table and raising slightly from his seat. "Not in *my* house—"

"*My* house," I interjected firmly. "Is it not? You stood aside. I am the Earl of Sunlis now. And my first act will be having my sister's name restored to the records."

"You wouldn't dare," he rumbled.

"I assure you, I would. I have been trying to work with you, to negotiate with you, to come to a solution that suits everyone involved. I see now that my efforts were futile. If you aren't with me, you're against me, and I'll use all this newfound authority you have so kindly gifted me to deal with you accordingly."

I surveyed all the spectators in the room, letting them know that the message wasn't exclusively for my father.

It didn't feel particularly natural for me to speak in such a way, but I had been letting far too much disrespect for me and my future mate slide. I needed to channel some of Meera's quiet fierceness and make things happen.

"You're ruining everything!" Mother wailed, collapsing onto her forearms on the table. Before I could respond to that, the door to the chamber flew open, and Theon, Duke of Lindow, marched in like he owned the estate.

"I would say I'm sorry to interrupt," he began in a bored voice. "But my duchess asked me to do it, so I'm not sorry."

The duchess in question sauntered in behind him, all gracefulness and mischief.

And followed by a faintly terrified-looking Meera.

# MEERA

## CHAPTER 25

Verner's family home was like something out of a storybook.

The architecture in this part of the realm was nothing like the palace. Sunlis was more like a collection of towers, connected by covered walkways that were open on either side—probably because of the suffocating heat. Every corridor was lined with lush foliage, and I wondered what it would look like when it was entirely colorful, rather than just shades of gray with the odd hint of green like it was now.

I'd never been to East Asia, but the polished timber, extended eaves above the open-sided walkways, and ornate carvings reminded me of that region of the human realm.

"It's actually obscene how hot it is here," Verity panted, peeling off her fishnet arm warmers as though that was the key to cooling off.

Theon grunted in agreement, marching ahead. I didn't know him well enough to know whether he was in a worse mood than usual or not, but I hazarded a guess that he didn't like being away from Lindow. From what Verity had said, his home was a real sanctuary for him.

"Do you know where we're going?" I whispered. I had no idea why I was bothering to be quiet—Theon had already barged past a staff member in the entryway, and Verity was loudly exclaiming over everything that she'd spotted of interest. I was pretty sure Theon had agreed to build her a whole Sunlis-inspired wing at Lindow at this point.

"I've been here before," Theon clipped. "Back when I was the Crown Prince, I toured many family estates."

We headed down winding stairs to ground level where the trees towered above us, before going along a corridor and heading down yet again, this time beneath the surface. This area felt a little more slick, a little less tuned in with nature. But it was cooler, which was nice. I'd only been here ten minutes, and I was already sweating.

The humidity in this part of the realm was *oppressive*. I felt the energy draining out of me with each passing second.

We came to a tall set of grand black double doors, and Theon threw them open like he was walking into his own house. I heard the voices from within the room go quiet, and I took a steadying breath before I followed after Verity, hoping I looked—and smelled—less scared than I felt.

"Meera?" Verner stood immediately from his spot at the head of the table on the far side of the room for me, looking at me as though he'd seen a ghost. "You're here."

"Yes. Why is that?" the Shade at the opposite end of the table snapped, glaring at me. He looked too much like Verner to be anything other than his father.

Apparently, I'd already made a poor impression with the in-laws.

I should have planned what I was going to say. I should have written something down—something romantic, and understanding, and reassuring. Shoot, what was I *doing* here? I wanted Verner, but I didn't know how to convince him that I was worth the hassle.

Seeing his house had me even more unsure—what on earth would he want *me* for? Verner was *rich* rich, and I brought nothing to the table except human-realm vegetables that he didn't even like.

Damn it. I hadn't thought this through.

"Hey, big guy," Verity said, slinging an arm over my shoulders and looking at Verner. "This is all you. Meera has done the scary part—don't let her down now."

"Verity," I chided softly, not wanting to put Verner on the spot.

"Stop telling me off, he knows I'm right."

"I do know that," Verner agreed, straightening up and surveying the room. "Will you stand with me, Meera? I've missed you terribly, and I want nothing more than to hold you right now."

"I've missed you too," I whispered, feeling the eyes of the room follow me as I walked down the length of the table on my own, coming to stand in front of Verner. He pulled me into his embrace immediately, shrouding me in shadows that mostly hid me from the rest of the room.

"I can't believe you're here," he murmured for my ears only. "It never occurred to me that you'd seek me out. This mess is my problem to deal with, I suppose. Not yours. You shouldn't be dragged into this."

I tipped my head back so I could see his face, narrowing my eyes at him. "Verner, whatever mess you're in is because of me. I dragged you into an entirely different *realm* to deal with my problems. If anyone would have told me where you were, I would have come sooner—you never left me alone, even when it put you at risk. Why would I leave you? We're a team, you and I."

I didn't like speaking in front of people, it usually gave me heart palpitations. But with Verner holding me, staring into my eyes as though they held the answers to all of his questions, I felt invincible.

"Are we, Meera?" he asked softly. "Are you ready for that?"

"Yes." Heat crawled up the back of my neck. I hated that Verner even had to ask, but I'd been so wishy-washy about it, and he'd been more than patient with me. "We're more than that."

"I've been trying not to rush you, my love. I know this is a lot for you to process, and I want you to know that you're always safe with me. That your heart is always safe with me. But I've been in love with you for so long that I can't even remember a time before I felt any other way. If you need more time for your feelings to develop—"

"I don't." Hearing how he felt gave me the security I needed to give *him* the words that had been floating around my head since we were in the human realm. Except, how could mere *words* be enough? How could I capture the depth of what I felt for Verner in a way that would make him truly feel it?

Nothing was adequate. But I was done flailing in silence, forever fighting to articulate myself and giving up when it got hard.

"You're the love of my life," I said simply.

Because maybe the words didn't have to be perfect. They just had to be true.

Verner exhaled as though the weight of the world had been lifted from his shoulders, pulling me in tightly against him. "Thank the goddesses for that."

I moved my hands up to his chest so I could rub soothing circles into his skin with my thumbs. "Did you ever doubt it?"

"Perhaps a little." He squeezed my waist reassuringly. "I didn't doubt that we'd be together—that seemed certain. But that you'd love me the way I love you? That didn't seem possible. And if you ever did, I thought I'd have to wait years."

I was shaking my head before he'd even finished speaking. "Even when I was convincing myself that I could never be in a relationship, that I wouldn't know how, that I wouldn't be good at it, I always thought... but if I did, it would be you. You'd be my first and only choice."

Verner pulled me into him again, pressing a firm kiss on the top of my head. I wanted to do a lot more than forehead kisses. I wanted to solidify our union, ideally with a mating bite, but the fact that we were surrounded by his entire family was keeping my libido—and hopefully my scent—in check.

"I will *not* tolerate this!" Verner's father said, slamming his hand down on the table hard enough to make me jump. "You will ruin this house. The family name. Our legacy. Verner, how can you be so selfish?"

Verner sighed heavily, tucking me into his side as he turned to face his parents. His shadows wrapped around me like a comforting blanket, and I wanted to wear them every minute of every day.

"I see now what a waste of time these talks have been. It was foolish of me not to see it earlier—there is simply no middle ground where we can meet. You want me to give up Meera, and I will not. There's no halfway."

I didn't mean to cling to Verner like a koala bear, but just hearing the fact that they'd been telling him to give me up had me wanting to wrap myself around him and never let go.

"What is it that you're proposing then, *my lord*?" his father asked with a pointed sneer.

I sucked in a quiet breath. Verner had already inherited his family seat? When and how had that happened?

Verner hummed thoughtfully, gently cupping my cheek and pulling my gaze up to his. The claw of his thumb drifted lightly over my skin as he pushed my sweaty hair back off my face, and I dreaded to think what I looked like right now.

"I wanted all of this to be ours," he said quietly. "You deserve the best, Meera. You deserve a life of luxury, and I wanted to be the one to give that to you. But I also don't think they'll ever accept us here. Is the luxury worth it if we don't have happiness?"

I blinked up at him, baffled at his line of thinking. "Of course it isn't. And I don't *want* a life of luxury—I want to work. I want to be busy, and to feel like I'm contributing. I want my garden." I hesitated for a moment, clearing my throat. "Verner, this is a beautiful home, but I don't even think I'd survive in this climate. It's so *hot* here."

Clearly, I'd been gone from the mother country too long. I'd adapted to Denver's semiarid climate.

"You don't want to live here?" Verner repeated, sounding suddenly hopeful.

"I mean, not to sound ungrateful or anything—it's beautiful. But I don't think I could be happy here, away from court and Elverston House and the garden."

*And surrounded by your hostile family,* I added silently. That part probably went without saying.

I'd never had the desire that Austin, Verity, and Tallulah all seemed to have to get away from the palace. I had no desire to lead, but I liked being in the thick of things, even if it was just to observe them from the outskirts. Would they let us stay there, though? Verner had been fired because of me—I had no idea what his current relationship with the king or the captain looked like. Surely, they wouldn't kick us out?

"You're not welcome in the palace," a female Shade snapped. Perhaps his mother? "Unless you are staying in the family apartments as the Earl of Sunlis."

"He *is* the Earl of Sunlis, for Godwin stepped aside," Theon drawled, sounding desperately bored with the proceedings. "How fortunate for you all that Verner seems to care about accommodating you all rather than simply telling you the way things will be now that he is in charge."

"Some of us are more tyrannical than others, honey," Verity said cheerfully before turning to face us. "If tensions are high at the palace, then you guys should come stay with us for a bit—we've got heaps of room at Lindow. I'm sure the king will get over his temper tantrum eventually, and then you can move back there if you still want to."

Theon made a sound of annoyance, and Verity narrowed his eyes at him. "I know you're not objecting, pookie. We have literally hundreds of rooms. Even if they live there forever, it wouldn't be a problem for us. I hope you do—I'd love the company."

"We *use* those rooms," Theon objected.

Verity raised an eyebrow. "You can use me in any of the other rooms, darling."

Verner patted me firmly on the back as I choked on my own laugh. Living with the two of them would certainly be an experience. It was a generous offer, and I was grateful for it.

"What do you think?" I asked Verner. "How do you feel about a fresh start?"

"I think it's just what we need, my love."

# VERNER

## CHAPTER 26

Sunlis was in uproar when I left. Technically, I hadn't relinquished my position yet—I would need to go in front of the monarch for that—but they all knew that it was my intention. Perhaps I wouldn't rush it, though. The estate wouldn't fall apart without me actively managing it for a little while, and I wasn't in the mood to be as cognizant of my parents' feelings as I usually was.

They'd gotten themselves into this mess by trying to force me into the role early in the first place.

I followed Theon and his mate, my arm around Meera's shoulders, as we made our way down to the entry room near the front of the property, having settled on returning to Lindow with them for the time being.

A small part of me—the part that didn't like to disappoint anyone—felt guilty that I was essentially leaving my family to eat themselves alive. But that was their decision to make, it wasn't as though I hadn't tried to handle the situation in a dignified and orderly fashion.

"Are you okay?" Meera whispered, looking up at me. The trust in her eyes was an astounding thing. Had she ever looked at me like that before? So openly? So honestly? Things had shifted so much between us in just the past hour, that it made me feel foolish for not telling her I loved her earlier.

*Of course*, she'd needed to hear it—even if she hadn't been ready to say it back yet. Meera wasn't used to being loved, but she would be. I'd make sure of it.

"I'm wonderful, my love. What about you? Are you sure you don't want to go back to the palace? Even if I'm not welcome, there's no reason you should feel pushed out—"

"I'm not going anywhere you're not," Meera replied stubbornly. I squeezed her a little tighter into my side as we entered the in-between. I didn't think I'd ever be able to walk through here now without remembering what Meera and I had done in the darkness. Her scent sweetened slightly, and I wondered if she was thinking the same thing.

With a jolt, I realized my jaw was beginning to ache, and I ran my tongue over my teeth, finding them slightly sharper than usual.

I wanted to bite Meera. I wanted it more than anything.

*Slow down. Talk about this rationally. Bring the subject up in a light-hearted way so you don't terrify her. There's no rush.*

"I want to bite you."

Damn it.

Meera's scent bloomed. "Good."

Good?

"Is that... do you want that?" I asked, not daring to hope.

"Could you *please* talk about that when you're alone?" Theon groused. "The scent is quite distracting. Look, we're here. We'll show you to your rooms, and see you whenever you resurface."

Verity laughed while Meera hid her face against my arm.

"Get it, girl," Verity called over her shoulder. "We'll leave some dinner outside your door for you later—we can do the whole welcome feast thing tomorrow."

That sounded like an excellent notion to me, but Meera seemed embarrassed so I kept my agreement to myself.

Lindow used to be the main royal residence, and while it wasn't as grand as the current palace, it was far larger than Sunlis. I barely paid attention while Verity led us up the stairs and down corridors to a suite of rooms in the opposite wing to where they stayed.

"Fortunately, I'd just got these all done up because I was hoping to start having guests," Verity said proudly, throwing the door open and gesturing for us to enter. "Honestly, I'm just going to leave you guys to it. I'll see you whenever you come up for air. Kay, bye!"

Meera turned as red as one of the vegetables she grew in her garden while Verity closed the door behind her, laughing merrily down the corridor.

"We don't have to do a single thing you don't want to do," I assured Meera, making sure not to crowd her. There appeared to be a living room, washroom, and two separate bedrooms in this suite—it was a very generous amount of space. I idly wondered what kind of grand guests it had housed in the past back when this had been the royal residence.

Meera walked straight past me, heading for the larger bedroom without saying a word. I hesitated in the living room, wondering whether or not I was meant to follow.

"Come here, Verner."

I almost fell over my own feet in my haste to get to her. Meera stood next to the edge of the bed, looking radiant in her blue dress, hands clasped in front of her.

"Can we try something?" she asked.

I almost laughed at the absurdity of the question—as if I would deny her anything. "Of course."

In this more confined space, the scent of Meera's perfume grew truly intoxicating.

"Lie on the bed," Meera commanded. "Please," she added as an afterthought.

"You don't have to say please to me," I assured her, hastening to follow orders.

"Drop your shadows."

I gladly released my hold on them, exposing my naked body for her perusal. Her scent sweetened, and I could have sworn I could taste a phantom trace of her slick on my tongue, though I'd never actually tried it before.

"Does it bother you that I boss you around?" Meera asked softly, pulling her hair over one shoulder. I wasn't sure if the move had been subconscious or not, but it had the effect of exposing the smooth skin of her neck.

"Not at all. It's very attractive to me."

She hummed, running her soft fingertips down my arm before pulling her touch away. "Lie on top of your hands for me?"

I groaned as I complied, feeling utterly at her mercy. My cock stood out obscenely, already shiny with silvery precum. I *ached* for Meera.

"The very first dream I had about you, it was just like this..." Meera climbed up on the bed next to me, kicking off her shoes and rearranging her dress so the fabric fanned out around her.

"And what did you do with me once you had me at your mercy?"

She laughed lightly. "Nothing. I kept trying to... to *envision* you—" She paused, tracing my cock with her fingers. "—but I couldn't make it look right in my mind. It was distracting. The reality is so much better."

"What will you do with me now?"

Meera hummed. "That's a good question. A large part of me wants to take my time."

She wrapped her fingers around the base of my shaft, squeezing where my knot was barely beginning to swell. My hips shifted of their own accord, thrusting desperately into her grip, and Meera immediately stopped, giving me a warning look that sent more precum flowing from the tip of my cock.

I had no idea what I expected her to do next, but it definitely wasn't lean over me and *lick* it.

"Meera!" I gasped, fighting not to come immediately.

"Good?" she asked. "Make sure you tell me if you don't like anything—I don't actually know what I'm doing."

"Whatever it is, keep doing it."

She grinned, shifting her position slightly before angling herself over my cock again. This time, she sucked the head of it into her mouth, and I could have sworn I briefly died before coming back to life again. What *was* that? No one had ever done that to me before.

With Meera's blunt teeth, there was absolutely no fear as she lowered her head, taking more of my shaft down her throat. I held myself as still as I could, not wanting to startle her in any way.

"Meera," I rasped. "Give me your throat, my love. Let me claim you, please."

She pulled her head away, leaving my cock shiny from more than just precum. "All in good time. I'm so wet—are you sure this slick thing is normal?"

"Very sure. Will you let me taste you now?"

"Do you want to?" she asked skeptically.

"I might die if I don't." I was worried that it would take more convincing, but apparently Meera was content with that answer. She pulled her dress over her head, revealing her undergarments and glorious bare skin. I wanted to lick every inch of it.

She seemed to watch me for a moment, her confidence growing in whatever she saw in my expression. With more deliberate seductiveness, she unclipped the contraption that contained her breasts, before sliding down the small scrap of fabric that covered her pussy.

How necessary were those items? I was very much in favor of scrapping them completely.

"Will you come up here, my love? I want to feel you pressing down on my horns as you ride my tongue."

"Now who's being bossy, hm?" Meera asked, crawling up my body. "But I'll allow it because that sounds like a very fun time. Are you sure I won't crush you?"

"I'm hoping you do," I replied, enamored with the idea of those thick thighs wrapped around my face.

She was a curious dichotomy, my Meera. She clearly wanted to be in control, but she was also inexperienced and shy. I couldn't wait to see how her confidence would develop over the course of our lives.

Perhaps, my sweet, gentle love would pin me down by my throat one day while she rode my cock, taking all that she wanted from me? What a beautiful future to look forward to.

For now, I was more than content to be patient as she experimentally swung her leg over my face, gently holding on to my horns and hovering slightly above me. Did Meera not realize how long my tongue was?

Perhaps I'd give her a demonstration.

I helped myself to a generous swipe of her slick, groaning at how sweet the taste was. How many times a day would she deign to feed me this? I would never get enough.

"Verner!" Meera gasped, lifting up on her knees slightly. "Your tongue is..." She swallowed thickly before lowering herself back down. "Do that again."

"Gladly. You can hold my horns tighter. As tight as you can, that's it..." Fuck, it felt like a direct line to my cock.

I set to work licking her sweet cunt as thoroughly as I could with my hands still constrained under my body, thrusting the air occasionally as Meera adjusted her grip on my horns. It took me a moment to figure out exactly which spot gave her pleasure, but once I had it, I devoted all of my attention to massaging her clit as slick ran down my chin.

She was my very own goddess. I would worship her until the end of my days.

"Oh, I'm going to come," Meera whispered, seemingly surprised by the fact. She ground down a little harder on my tongue, yanking my horns with the perfect level of roughness, and I had to fight back my own orgasm as Meera's began. I did my best to catch as much of her nectar on my tongue as I could, but my lower face and throat were glistening with it.

I hoped she ordered me not to wash it off.

"Oh my..." Meera breathed, climbing off me on shaky legs. "Oh! I've made such a mess of you."

She wiped my chin, and I practically panted, hoping she was massaging it deeper into my skin.

"You like that, hm?" She tilted her head to the side, swiping up some of the slick in one hand and dragging it down my throat to my chest, coating me in her. "Oh yes. You definitely like that."

"I want to knot you, my love. Please. I'll do anything."

"I like when you beg," Meera said sweetly, climbing over my hips and rubbing her perfect cunt up and down my cock.

"Can I use my hands?"

She hummed thoughtfully. "Not yet."

I made a slightly pained sound as she reached between us, lining up my cock with her entrance and sinking down slowly, her eyes going from sultry to wide in an instant. "It's bigger than I thought."

"You can take it, my love. My Meera. You're meant for me."

Meera bit her lip, rocking back slowly. "I'm going to do my best. What about your knot, though?"

"You don't have to take it right now. We can try another day," I assured her. "There's no rush."

Her body relaxed slightly at that, and she braced her hands on my chest as she worked her way down my shaft, her breasts swaying with each movement. I was glad she didn't expect me to speak, because I doubted I could get the words out. The feeling of her warm, wet cunt clasping my cock was...

I was desperate with the need to bite her. To claim this perfect woman as my own. I'd never felt so possessive in my life.

"Will you..." I hesitated. "Will you do that thing again? Where you pressed your lips to mine?"

Meera looked at me in surprise. "When I kissed you?"

"Yes. It's not something Shades do. I didn't expect it then. If I had... well, things would have gone differently."

She let out a breathy laugh, still rolling her hips, taking me deeper. "Oh my god, you didn't know what I was doing. Now I feel ridiculous—yes, of course. I'll kiss you whenever you want."

Meera leaned in, softly molding her pillowy lips to my firm ones. I did my best to follow her lead, not entirely sure that I was doing it right, but her tongue swiped teasingly at my mouth and I was a goner.

"What is that?" I groaned against her. "That felt nice."

"Give me your tongue," she demanded, immediately playing with it with her own. Here I was thinking this was a gesture of *sweetness*. What we were doing was filthy. I enjoyed it thoroughly.

"Oh, that feels so *good*," Meera moaned breathily as she reached the hilt, tipping her head back. "I feel so full. Okay, you can use your hands now. Fuck me like you mean it."

I didn't need telling twice. I sat up instantly, grabbing Meera's ass to bounce her on my cock. She grabbed my shoulders to stabilize herself, throwing her head back and teasing me with her throat.

"Will you let me lick your pussy again after I come?" I rasped, licking the shell of her ear. "I've been fantasizing about it since you played with your cunt in front of my face in the human realm."

"You want to? Even if you…"

"Even then," I assured her.

"Will you feed your cum into my mouth?" she asked innocently.

I couldn't hold back. I came with a loud groan, careful to keep my hands on her ass loose so she could move off my knot as it began to swell. But my attention was elsewhere. I dipped my head, my horns immediately tangling in her hair as I sunk my teeth into the junction between Meera's neck and shoulder.

"Oh, fuck," Meera cried, tightening around me, her nails digging into my shoulders. Instead of rising off me like I expected, she lowered herself down, holding on tightly as my knot began to swell.

Carefully, I extracted my teeth from her skin. "We don't have to—" I began.

"No, it feels good. I want to. Fuck," she mumbled, surprising me with her filthy mouth when she was usually so polite. "It feels *really* good, like it's rubbing against, ohhh..."

I couldn't help but smile as her eyes rolled back, the knot locking into place as her pussy milked every drop of cum from my body.

Meera slumped against me, resting her head on my shoulder, and I bundled her tightly into my arms, a noise rumbling out of my chest that made us both startle.

"What was that?" she asked, smiling up at me, her scent bright with happiness.

"I think... I think it might have been my purr." I cleared my throat, slightly embarrassed. "I'd heard of it, but I've never experienced it for myself."

"Why now do you think?"

I considered the question, my hands drifting down to idly cup her ass. "I don't think I could let myself be truly happy until I knew you loved me. Until I knew you were really mine. You seem too good to be true, Meera."

She spluttered, "I could say the same about you."

"Good. Is that not the way it should be? That we both feel as though we've won?"

"That's exactly the way it should be," Meera agreed, her eyes rolling back as I shifted slightly, setting off another chain of orgasms.

*Mine.* She was mine.

No matter what happened, we could handle it. So long as we had each other.

# MEERA

## CHAPTER 27

No one sought us out for the next couple of days, so I guessed Verity and Theon had taken care of any questions anyone at the palace had about our whereabouts.

I was never going to be able to look any of them in the eye again.

"Verity brought you these clothes?" Verner asked, holding up the yellow t-shirt I'd laid out on the bed to put on. "This is my favorite color on you."

"It's cute that you have a favorite color on me," I said, blushing as though he hadn't been eating me out from behind an hour ago. Everything I'd wanted to try, he was more than game for. The power was going straight to my head.

"I'm nearly ready," I said, grabbing the t-shirt and pulling it on before knotting it on one side so the waist of my jeans was visible, and tying up my hair to show off my pretty bite mark.

Verner's shadows rippled, his gaze fixated on my neck. If we didn't leave this instant, we were going to end up in bed for another two days.

"Behave," I said sternly. "You're so jittery, Verner. You need to siphon."

He laughed. "Not a problem I've ever had before, but yes. And I need to talk to the king. To formally relinquish my title."

"How are you feeling about that?"

"Fine," Verner said, looking completely unbothered. "It wasn't as though the idea had never occurred to me before—I'd never wanted the role. Back then, I thought I'd just remain in the Guard forever, but I'll find something else to do."

Guilt churned uneasily in my stomach, and Verner immediately crossed the room, lifting me into his arms. "Don't you dare feel bad about that, Meera."

"You lost your job because of me!"

"And I would do so again, happily. Come on, let's go."

I squeaked as he carried me out of the room like I weighed nothing, grabbing his horns reflexively to steady myself.

Verner stopped instantly, blowing out a hot puff of breath at my throat, right above my mating mark. "Unless you've changed your mind about going to the palace today?"

I released his horns reluctantly, shifting my hands to his shoulders. "No. But let's not stay too long. I have plans for you later."

"That sounds like an excellent notion, my love."

The king hummed, lounging back in his seat as he surveyed the two of us. It was just him and Captain Soren for this conversation, and I wished Ophelia were here, but apparently she was busy with her queenly responsibilities.

"You two being mated makes it easier in a way," the king said slowly. "We're probably being slow to adapt to all the changes around here, but I think everyone was struggling with what to make of the situation. Now that you're a couple... well, it all makes sense, doesn't it?" He shrugged. "I would do anything for Ophelia."

"Yes," Verner agreed. "There was never any chance of me denying Meera anything."

I was blushing so hard I'd probably turned purple. Maybe I should have sat this meeting out. I had plenty of people I wanted to talk to while I was here. I could have done that instead.

But I hadn't wanted Verner to face this alone, in case the king was difficult about it.

"You have made some very loyal friends at Elverston House," the king said, switching his focus to me.

I nodded mutely. I'd only managed to quickly thank Jade in passing before I'd disappeared again, and I intended to go there next.

"The most recent crop of ex-Hunters have different needs and expectations to the group you came in with," King Allerick said, watching me carefully. "My wife's attempts to get to know them and make them feel welcome have been... not enthusiastically received, perhaps."

I winced. "Ophelia is nothing like the Hunters that hurt them, but her family is from that class. They may be projecting a little on her and the others, but I'm sure it'll get better in time. Those wounds are still quite fresh."

"But they like you," the king pointed out. "And I assume you like their company—you still seem happy to spend time at Elverston House. Or am I wrong about that?"

"No, you're not wrong." I glanced at Verner, squeezing his hand a little tighter. Where was this conversation going? I couldn't tell if I was in trouble or not.

King Allerick sighed heavily. "I suspect we didn't handle this well. Any of this. As Ophelia mentioned to me, this situation illuminated some blind spots we weren't aware we had, and I apologize that the two of you bore the brunt of that mishandling."

"That's okay," I said awkwardly, because I didn't have the first clue how to accept an apology—let alone one from royalty.

The king grimaced. "It's not really. Regardless, I hope I can make amends going forward. Much like the palace, there are apartments behind Elverston House, built into the lower level. They were originally for staff, and have been long since closed up. Ophelia and I have talked about renovating one for the two of you."

"But Shades aren't allowed there," Verner pointed out, as confused I was.

"A rule that was established because we thought it was in the ex-Hunters' best interest," the captain interjected. "But having talked to the ex-Hunters at Elverston House, it's become clear that there has been too much separation. For those who want to start building relationships outside of the group and getting comfortable around Shades, there hasn't been an easy avenue for them to do that. Walking into a dining hall full of Shades at dinnertime is not a simple ask."

"I'm aware," I said, perhaps a little more wryly than I'd intended.

The king smiled, though it always looked slightly sarcastic when he did it. "Ophelia spoke to all of them, and they were quite adamant that they wanted a Shade point of contact. Someone that they could trust to help them get acquainted with the shadow realm. They were quite adamant, too, that it should be Verner."

"Me?" he repeated. "I've never spoken to them."

"They indicated as much," the king replied. "But they seemed to feel as though they knew you from watching your interactions with Meera from a distance. And, of course, they already like and trust Meera, so the fact that you're now mated is only an advantage."

Verner cleared his throat. "But do *you* entrust me with such a position? I know I damaged your opinion of me with my actions."

I was gripping his hand so tightly, my fingers were beginning to ache. Whatever it took to make up for the damage I'd done to Verner's reputation, I'd do it. He didn't seem to mind the fallout, but I did. He hadn't deserved that.

"There's no denying you put us in a difficult position," Captain Soren began. "But part of the reason why it was so difficult for me to accept that was because you had always been one of the most honorable and reliable members of the Guard. You've demonstrated on multiple occasions that you can review your opinions and change them accordingly when presented with new information. You're calm, rational, and not ruled by your ego the way so many who get to your level of success within the Guard become. Prove to me that I'm not making a mistake by trusting you again, Verner."

"Yes, Captain," he replied instantly, inclining his head in respect.

The king nodded once, looking at me again. "Does this role sound like something you'd be interested in, Meera? It would be both of you. You both need to be happy with it."

It sounded like a dream to me. Live in Elverston House, but in a private area with our own space. Work with the new arrivals to help them feel more comfortable here—I was planning on doing that anyway. And the best part would be working alongside Verner each day, and having others recognize his goodness and kindness the way I did.

"It sounds perfect to me," I admitted. "We'd be... intermediaries of sorts?"

"That would be part of it," King Allerick replied. "Though, Ophelia described the role more like the parental figures she had when she was sent away for her education."

"Dorm parents?" I suggested with a light laugh before glancing at Verner. "How do you feel about having kids?" I teased.

"Positively. Though, ten ex-Hunters is certainly a unique trial run," he replied dryly, squeezing my hand back.

Huh. The topic of children hadn't actually come up before now—to be honest, we'd been a little distracted—and I was suddenly very aware of the fact that I wasn't using any kind of birth control. It had never even occurred to me, since I hadn't needed it in the past.

That was definitely a conversation for later.

"If the residents of Elverston House are happy, and Verner is happy, then yes. Absolutely. I would love that."

"As would I," Verner replied.

"Good, then it is agreed. Perhaps you could go there now and speak with them, Meera? If they are content to proceed, then we will need to make plans to renovate an apartment—it will require Shades being on the property, but in a way that causes as little disruption as possible. Verner, that would be a good opportunity for you to supervise the work and build relationships with the ex-Hunters who live there."

He nodded in agreement.

"What about the house itself?" I asked, forcing myself to be brave and use my voice when I thought it was important. "Elverston House is falling apart. It needs repairs too. If they're comfortable to have Shades on the premises—in the house—is getting it fixed up a possibility?"

"Yes, of course," the king agreed. "I hadn't realized it was that bad. Whatever you need, we will make that happen."

It was the start of a brand new era.

# VERNER

## EPILOGUE

**A FEW WEEKS LATER**

Jade is coming up the path," Meera said quietly from her spot by the window in our new apartment where she was shucking peas into a large bowl.

"Shall I leave?" I asked, already standing up to go. It was well established by now that sometimes these visits were for "girl talk," which I was very much not supposed to be part of.

"Wait and see if she says the code word first," Meera laughed, setting aside the vegetables to open the door.

"You guys need to come with me right now," Jade panted, slumping against the door frame. "Harlow is here."

Meera spilled the bowl of peas in her haste to stand up, but I didn't even think she noticed. We immediately followed Jade down the path that led to our small home, and through the newly cleared walkway around the side of Elverston House to the front of the building where Meera's gardens were.

"Where is she?" I asked, taking one step for Meera and Jade's every three.

"By the portal," Jade replied, out of breath. "She just got here. I came straight to get you. Obviously, there's a crowd there now."

"Sebastian?" Meera asked.

"Yep, he's there too. Big day for him, finding out the big secret," Jade chuckled. She was friendly, albeit slightly terrifying. For the most part, Patrick was the one I spent time with. He'd become a true friend to me—more than even the Shade friends I'd had, who'd distanced themselves at the first hint of a scandal. My parents had been silent since I'd given up my position and Osric had taken over, but I suspected it wouldn't last forever. They were too opinionated to stay quiet for long.

Harlow was bouncing on the balls of her feet when we arrived, standing uncomfortably in front of the portal with an audience of Shades and ex-Hunters around her. Fortunately, Astrid had stationed herself next to her as a bodyguard, which probably somewhat helped with the nerves, but it was still a lot of unfamiliar faces to be surrounded by.

"There you are!" Harlow said, perking up at the sight of Meera. "How've you been? I see you've got yourself a mate. Good for you. Was this your silent buddy when you came to visit? Nice to finally meet you."

"Yes, this is Verner," Meera replied distractedly, grabbing my hand and pulling me in close. "Are you okay? Has something happened?"

"I'm just here to report on some arrests," she said cheerfully. "Randal Jackman, Moriah Nash, Giles Nash, Bradley Gilmour, Vivyan Woodham, Tatyana Sherburn." She paused for a moment. "Oh! And Eddie Harrison. A clean sweep, baby. The charges are all slightly different—lots of variations of conspiracy and fraud, though."

"What?" Sebastian rasped, clutching his chest. "What do you mean? Oh my god, I need to get back to the human realm. What is going on?"

"Might be an idea," Astrid agreed, always happy to see the back of him.

"I need to talk to Iris," Meera said, giving me a panicked look. She'd been hoping that Iris's parents weren't involved so that this conversation wouldn't have to happen, but luck hadn't been on our side in that particular case.

"A lot of conversations need to be had," Ophelia said faintly. "This changes everything."

Harlow looked around awkwardly, rocking back and forth on the balls of her feet. "Is it cool if I go? It's just that I was kind of in the middle of a raid—not a real-life one, I mean on my computer—but I wanted to share the news with you guys, so..."

"You can go," Astrid said, clapping her on the shoulder. "I appreciate you keeping us updated. I'll head over in a few hours to see what's going on, okay?"

"I'll break out the pickles. See you in a bit."

"Wow," Meera breathed, leaning heavily against my side. "It really happened."

"You really did it," I corrected quietly.

She bit down on her lip to hide her smile. "I really did."

"Come here."

I nearly stumbled over my feet, knowing exactly what that soft, husky tone meant. My mate had needs, and I was going to fulfill them if it was the last thing I did.

She was sitting in the enormous armchair in the corner of the apartment, her chin propped up on her hand, watching me with faint interest while I'd put away the supplies I'd gotten from the market.

"Where do you want me, my love?"

She spread her legs wide, patting the space between them for me to sit in front of her.

I was panting before I even sat down, my shadows disappearing of their own accord and my cock hard.

"You know where I want you."

I did. I leaned back, angling my body to one side so I didn't crush her, but moving close enough that she could reach around to grab my cock. She was so much smaller than me, but she'd learned exactly how to position me to make me feel vulnerable and her powerful.

"You're so good," Meera whispered in my ear before dragging her teeth along my shoulder, already pumping the base of my cock just the way I liked to stimulate my knot.

"My love, you know I don't last like this," I groaned, thrusting up into her hand instantly.

"You'll last for me."

"I won't. Meera, I won't. You're too good at that—" I sucked in a breath at the perfect twisting gesture she did with her wrist. She knew how helpless I was against that.

"Don't come yet, Verner," she chided. "I have to sit on your face still."

The base of my cock was aching, my knot already desperate to expand. Nothing was sexier to me than the confidence she'd gained in the past few weeks.

She tutted as I rocked my hips, losing the thin hold I had on my self-control.

"Don't be impatient. You'll get what you need."

"You say that, and yet I haven't tasted your cunt in hours," I grumbled. "*That* is something I need."

"You're right. How cruel of me." She released my cock, tapping my thigh to get me to move forward so she could climb out. I watched as she came around to stand in front of me, lifting her dress to reveal that she wasn't wearing anything underneath it, and her thighs were already glistening with slick.

"Come here," I growled, hooking my forearms beneath her inner thighs and lifting her clear off the ground so she could drape her legs over my shoulders. She grabbed my horns for balance, not fretting and fussing about whether or not she was too heavy for me like she had the first time I'd tried that move.

"I've needed this all day," I said, my voice muffled as I pressed a kiss to her pussy.

"You're getting it now. Less talking, more making me come. No making you come, though. Behave yourself."

I let out a hiss of pleasure as she massaged my horns, the little tease. But it was easy to follow instructions when the instructions were to make her come.

Meera wriggled and squirmed as I roughly tongue fucked her pussy, gripping her ass tightly to hold her in place. The texture of my tongue drove her wild, and I made sure to grind it against her clit just the way she liked, not wasting any time wringing that orgasm out of her. It was difficult to take my time with her when she was climbing all over me like this. It made me want to bury my knot in her instantly.

"Verner!" she gasped, leaning back as she came. I immediately lifted her down, sitting her directly onto my cock while her walls squeezed around me.

"Cheeky," she laughed breathily, rocking her hips a few times before lifting off me and turning around.

I groaned at the view as she braced her hands on my knees, lowering herself onto my dick while shooting me a cocky look over her shoulder.

"I couldn't resist," I said unapologetically, holding her hips and helping her move. This *angle*. Fuck. "My love…"

"Don't you tell me you can't last. You'll last until I say you do."

Meera leaned back against me, bracing her feet on the edge of the chair, grabbing my forearms to steady herself. From over her shoulder, I watched her perfect breasts bounce with each thrust, though my favorite sight was the faint outline of my bite on her neck. I could stare at that all day.

Could I die of too much pleasure? If Meera wasn't constantly filling me with healing power, then it seemed highly possible.

"Right there," Meera gasped, her nails digging into my wrists. I kept doing exactly what I was doing, whispering words of praise in her ear until she came with a hoarse cry, her walls tightening around me until I couldn't do anything but follow. Meera gasped as my knot swelled, locking into place, and I rested my hand on her lower abdomen so I could feel the bulge under my palm.

"It's so good. How is it always so good?" she panted, pushing her sticky hair off her forehead and lolling back against my shoulder.

"Because it's us, my love. It will always be this good."

# THANK YOU

Thank you, reader! I can't believe there's only one book to go in the Shades of Sin series. These characters have been living in my head for close to three years now, and it's been such a joy bringing them to life on paper and sharing them with you. I'm so grateful to everyone who has read and supported this series, I couldn't do what I do without you <3

I squeezed in a trip to Edinburgh for RARE while working on this book, but it was the day I spent visiting my family in Singapore on the way back that gave me a lot of inspo. If you think the fictional "ojurac" cake sounds tasty, then definitely see if you can track down some nonya kueh in real life and give it a try!

Steph at Rawls Reads and Marcelle at Books Checked were the dream team behind this one, thank you both so much for being so amazing (and for your patience!)

I'd also like to thank my PA, Nikki, my friends, and give a special shoutout to my awesome Ream subscribers.

Colette R. xx

P.S. To keep up with the latest news and releases, join my Facebook Reader Group or subscribe to my newsletter.

# ABOUTTHE AUTHOR

Colette Rhodes is a paranormal romance author from New Zealand. She loves to write about love in all its forms, and adores imperfect heroes and heroines who find perfection in each other. You'll often find her trying to justify her degree by including ancient history and mythological influences in her work.

If she's not writing, then you're almost certain to find her reading—ideally with a cup of tea in hand and a scented candle burning to match the mood.

Keep up with Colette here:

coletterhodes.com

@coletterhodes_author

# ALSO BY COLETTE

**SHADES OF SIN:**

Luxuria

Superbia

Gula

Avaritia

Invidia

Ira

Acedia

**STATE OF GRACE:**

Run Riot

Silver Bullet

Wild Game

Dare Not

Saving Grace

**ON THE SHELF:**

Scheme

Excess

**THREE BEARS DUET:**

Gilded Mess

Golden Chaos

**LITTLE RED DUET:**

Scarlet Disaster

Seeing Red


**KNOTTY BY NATURE:**

(WhyChoose omegaverse with T.S. Snow)

Allure Part 1

Allure Part 2


**EMPATH FOUND:**

Empath Found: The Complete Trilogy


**DEADLY DRAGONS:**

The (Not) Cursed Dragon

The (Not) Satisfied Dragon


**STANDALONE:**

Dead of Spring (MF - Hades & Persephone retelling)

Colette Rhodes
ROMANCE AUTHOR